## Something st... to happen...

D0390367

Taylor reached out a... ...ir palms flat against the window glass to support herself. That was when it happened.

The ocean disappeared, and in its place were flames. Taylor could even smell the smoke, seeping through the seams of the closed sash. A figure in white crawled toward the window where she was standing now.

"Mama! Mama!" Taylor cried.

She screamed as her palms were yanked from the glass, where they had cleaved so tightly, she felt as if they might be fusing to the pane.

She stared down at the palms of her hands and could hardly believe what she saw. Though they appeared to be normal, Taylor felt the flesh of her palms seared as if deeply burned.

## ABOUT THE AUTHOR

This is Alice Orr's fifth Intrigue novel. It is set in Key West where Alice and her husband have spent a number of romantic vacations. She has written the heat of that tropical romance into this book and invites you to enjoy it as much as she did.

In addition to her writing life, Alice is a literary agent, wife and mother and lives in New York City. She also lectures nationally on writing and publishing. You can write to her at Alice Orr Agency, Inc., 305 Madison Avenue, New York, N.Y. 10165. Alice would love to hear from you.

## Books by Alice Orr

### HARLEQUIN INTRIGUE

56—SABOTAGE
169—PAST SINS
216—COLD SUMMER
266—CAMP FEAR

Don't miss any of our special offers. Write to us at the following address for information on our newest releases.

Harlequin Reader Service
U.S.: 3010 Walden Ave., P.O. Box 1325, Buffalo, NY 14269
Canadian: P.O. Box 609, Fort Erie, Ont. L2A 5X3

# Key West Heat

## Alice Orr

## *Harlequin Books*

TORONTO • NEW YORK • LONDON
AMSTERDAM • PARIS • SYDNEY • HAMBURG
STOCKHOLM • ATHENS • TOKYO • MILAN
MADRID • WARSAW • BUDAPEST • AUCKLAND

If you purchased this book without a cover you should be aware
that this book is stolen property. It was reported as "unsold and
destroyed" to the publisher, and neither the author nor the
publisher has received any payment for this "stripped book."

To my husband, Jonathan—
always my romantic hero
To my map artist—
Ed Vesneske, who is also my dear son
To my editor—
Julianne Moore, a true jewel

ISBN 0-373-22324-2

KEY WEST HEAT

Copyright © 1995 by Alice Orr

All rights reserved. Except for use in any review, the reproduction or
utilization of this work in whole or in part in any form by any electronic,
mechanical or other means, now known or hereafter invented, including
xerography, photocopying and recording, or in any information storage
or retrieval system, is forbidden without the written permission of the
publisher, Harlequin Enterprises Limited, 225 Duncan Mill Road,
Don Mills, Ontario, Canada M3B 3K9.

All characters in this book have no existence outside the imagination of
the author and have no relation whatsoever to anyone bearing the same
name or names. They are not even distantly inspired by any individual
known or unknown to the author, and all incidents are pure invention.

This edition published by arrangement with Harlequin Enterprises B.V.

® and TM are trademarks of the publisher. Trademarks indicated with
® are registered in the United States Patent and Trademark Office, the
Canadian Trade Marks Office and in other countries.

Printed in U.S.A.

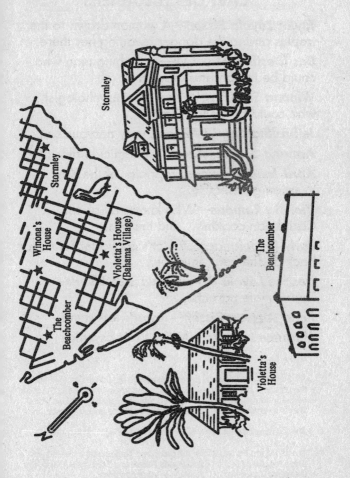

Stormley

Winona's House

Stormley

Violetta's House
(Bahama Village)

The Beachcomber

The Beachcomber

Violetta's House

# CAST OF CHARACTERS

**Taylor Loyola Bissett**—A woman drawn to the tropics and to the danger awaiting her there.

**Des (Destiny) Maxwell**—A dashing man who could be the greatest danger of all.

**Winona Starling**—A Key West psychologist who could be Taylor's savior.

**Jethro Starling**—Winona's very nervous son.

**Armand Santos**—Key West homicide detective.

**April Jane Cooney**—Proprietor of the Key Westian guesthouse.

**Violetta Ramone**—Who knows all about Caribbean cooking...and the past.

**Early Rhinelander**—Taylor's confidant for as far back as she can remember.

**Desiree Loyola & Paul Lawrence Bissett**—Taylor's late parents.

**Pearl & Netta Bissett**—Taylor's late aunts.

**Madame Leopold**—A Key West psychic.

# Prologue

Des smelled it before he saw it. He was not quite fourteen, but he knew right off what it was: the thing you smell a few blocks away or on the breeze and hope won't come close enough to smart your eyes and chafe your throat. The heavy, old-wood scent of it was almost pleasant at first, like bonfires or leaves burning. But there weren't that many falling leaves in Key West, except those ripped from branches by a blasting hurricane. And there was nothing pleasant about the way this made him feel. He held his breath, as if doing that could make the danger on the wind go away by magic, like when a little kid closes his eyes and thinks that makes him invisible. Pretty soon, Des had to breathe again, and the smoke smell was still there.

The wind was blowing hard. Tonight's gale hadn't been upgraded to hurricane from tropical storm yet, but Des guessed it was on the way there. He'd been feeling funny all day. That happens when there's a wild drop on the barometer. He'd taken it in stride the way any real conch would, conchs being native Key Westers. He was even a little bit excited, like when a big adventure is about to hit and you don't know how it's going to turn out. He liked that in the movies, but he knew there was a big difference between the screen and life. In real life, adventures could mess you up bad. Still, the lurking storm and rising wind had his heart beating fast all day—till now.

What made his heart beat fast now was fear.

He knew where the smoke smell was coming from. For a moment, he did nothing, not because he was scared, even though he was. He just couldn't believe what was happening. The worst time ever to have a fire is in a high wind. Everybody knows that. The flames blow up twice as fast in a storm, and there was no rain yet. And the smell of smoke was coming from the place he loved best in all the world.

Thinking that got Des started running. In the few seconds of his hesitation, flames had broken through the roof at the back of the tall Victorian perched at the edge of the sea, with so much water so nearby, yet too far away to be of help now. By the time Des reached the veranda steps he could hear the fire, cracking and popping and racing through the long, narrow rooms.

Miss Desiree always left the windows open, especially where they looked out onto the water. That meant the sea wind would be howling inside, feeding the hungry fire and helping it grow. Des caught his breath with a gasp of horror that sucked in more smoke and made him choke. Her room was back there too, where the sea view was best, the loveliest room he had ever been in.

He knew by heart where to find the front staircase, even with his eyes already tearing nearly blind. He took the wide steps two at a time. It occurred to him that the thick, rose-colored carpet would turn into an instant river of fire when the flames reached this part of the house. The only way out after that would be the roof. The back stairwell was sure to be an inferno by now. Des hurried faster against the smoke that wanted to stop his lungs. He would do what had to be done when the time came. He would get her out no matter what. He whispered that promise to himself and to her. Praying he could keep it scared him more even than the smoke and flames.

Then there was a sound, faint against the crack and whoosh of the fire, but Des heard it anyway. Until that moment, he had forgotten there was anyone besides Miss Desiree in the house. Now he remembered the little girl was in here, too. That had to be her crying. It was more a child's sound than a grown woman's, so it had to be the little girl. He hesitated another instant. Miss Desiree was along the balustrade in the other direction and all the way to the rear of the house, if she hadn't already gotten herself out. The girl was down the hall to the right from where he now stood and definitely still inside this house that was being rapidly consumed by flame.

He knew he couldn't wait to decide. The fire was gaining ground too fast for that. He ran down the hall toward the crying sound. All the doors along the hallway were closed. Maybe she had heard that you shouldn't open a door in a fire. Even a kid her age might know that. Then, he got to the door with the crying behind it and knew the real reason she hadn't come out. The door was locked, and there was no key in the hole. The child's cries were more strangled now, rasping with smoke like Des's throat. He croaked a reassurance that he would get her out even though he wasn't sure how.

"Under the rug," the child rasped from the other side of the door. "I think she put the key under the rug."

Des dropped to his knees and pawed at the hallway carpet. The electric lights had gone out. Probably the system had been burned out by the fire. It was too dark to see, and his streaming eyes were useless anyway. Des fought down his terror as he prayed to find a bump under the rough wool nap. When his fingers touched it he almost cried out with joy and relief. He fished the key out and lunged at the door, feeling for the keyhole. The key took two turns to catch, and Des thought he might go crazy from being so scared in the meantime.

Then the door was open, and the little girl had leapt into his arms.

"Keep low," he said. "There's not so much smoke near the floor."

If that was true, Des couldn't tell. The smoke was pretty thick everywhere by now. They stumbled and crawled toward the staircase. They had just reached the top of the stairs when, with a roar and a crash, the flames broke through into the hallway at the opposite end from where they had just been. Des saw orange and blue lick up the delicately flowered wallpaper. Then a line of fire shot toward them down the center of the hallway ceiling, like a flaming arrow in a cowboy movie.

The child's high-pitched scream was right next to his ear, and he wanted to tell her to shut up. Instead, he grabbed her arm and pulled her down the stairs, bumping her from one step to another, knowing that if he lost his grip on her she would fall. He also knew that if he didn't drag her this rough way they could lose their race against the flames and be caught in the river of burning carpet he had imagined on his way up these same stairs.

Suddenly, he remembered what his mission had been when he first ran into this house. He had come to save the mother, not the child. He had not thought for even a second that he could lose his own life in the attempt. He had only cared about Miss Desiree. He glanced back toward the stairway and the balustrade to the left toward her room. Flames rimmed the opening to the hallway in that direction. In less than a moment they would spread into a wall of fire across the only way he might possibly reach her.

Des continued his plunge down the stairs with the child in tow. He couldn't afford to hesitate for a second, even though what he was doing could cost the life of the person he loved more than anyone or anything in the world.

She would want you to save her baby, a voice inside him said. She always called the little girl her baby. He knew the voice was speaking truth, whether he wanted to hear it or not.

They had reached the heavy front door. In a flash of premonition, Des saw the etched glass cracking from the heat of the fire and the pale veneer curling into charred blackness. Though none of that had happened yet, he knew it would, and very soon.

Des shoved the door open and dragged himself and the child onto the veranda. Wind was whipping the lime trees that bordered the brick walk from the house to the road. Miss Desiree took such pride in those lime trees. She would hate to see them wracked and bent by the storm, even though she would know they were plenty strong enough to survive.

Des dropped the child's arm, and she fell onto the bricks. He didn't pick her up. The child was safe now. He knew that the mother, unlike her trees, would not survive this night. He heard the sirens in the same moment he came to understand that there was no use running back inside. He would only turn to charring blackness along with the white-painted woodwork and the chintz-covered chairs and all the rest of the bright, beautiful things she loved. She wouldn't want that to happen to him.

"Desiree," he whispered because his throat was too raw to scream. Her name was so like his own, Desiree and

Destiny, that people said they should have been mother and son. But they weren't. She was only the closest thing he'd had to a mother since his own mom died before he was old enough to know her.

Des reached down and grabbed the child's arm again and began dragging her along the brick path, getting her away from the house as a second-story window exploded too close above them. He could only move in a crouch now. He was weak from gasping for breath. He felt the hard brick through the soles of his sneakers and then the softer sod as he pulled himself and his burden onto the lawn just inside the gate and the tall fence. He fell to the grass and buried his face in it, surprised that he could smell the greenness through the smoke that filled the wide yard and sooted the flower beds.

Des heard the trucks and the shouts of the men as they dragged heavy hoses down the path to shoot a futile stream of water at the blazing hulk that was already too far gone to save.

It was too late. Too late for her house. Too late for her. Too late for Des, and for the one bright shiny part of his lonely life.

He wrapped his arms around the child who lay sobbing at his side. He needed somebody to hang on to, even this kid he'd always been a little jealous of. She sobbed against him as his eyes continued to stream, not only from the smoke and fire this time, but also from tears he wasn't ashamed to cry.

# Chapter One

*Twenty-Four Years Later*

She should have come here long ago. Taylor Loyola Bissett knew that the minute she stepped from the cab. She was out of her element, as her Great-Aunt Pearl would have put it, but that was exactly what Taylor wanted to be. "Stay where you know the territory and the territory knows you," her aunt said over and over, like a chant. "That way you will always be in tune." Taylor could feel herself out of tune with this place already, and that both frightened and thrilled her.

Her immediate impulse, conditioned by years of Aunt Pearl, was to get back in the cab and escape. But Taylor never did anything on impulse, at least not before today. Besides, all the way from the Key West Airport she had been less than at ease with the driver of this outlandish pink taxi who looked like he'd just crawled off skid row. She'd prefer not to drive any further with him, not even back to the airport. She couldn't leave the Keys yet anyway, anymore than she had been able to resist coming in the first place. There was something to be settled for her on this island. She'd been haunted by that feeling for weeks now. She had to find out what it was all about.

Maybe then she could put the past, what little she could recall of it, to rest at last.

Taylor climbed out of the cab, dragging her belongings with her. She should have had the driver help with her bags, but he hadn't offered and she hadn't asked. She did stupidly independent things like that sometimes. Her hair was heavy on her neck from the humidity, and tendrils clung to the dampness of her cheeks. By the time she lugged this load up the steps to the guest-house porch, she'd be drenched with perspiration, and the Key Westian looked too small to have a bellboy. She stopped to catch her breath and also to try to get a handle on her apprehension.

Everything bad that ever happened to the Bissett family had happened on this island, starting with the day her father, Paul Lawrence Bissett, met Desiree Loyola. He was a young naval officer, fresh from a small town in northern New York State and green as the valley of the St. Lawrence River for which he had been named. She was a pale-eyed beauty who captured the young naval officer without so much as a shot over his bow. He married her and gave her Stormley, a tall, stately house by the sea, as a wedding gift. His maiden aunts did not approve. Netta moved to the Keys to watch out for Paul and his interests, but not even that was enough to prevent disaster. Within a few years, he had deserted both country and family, and his beautiful wife was dead, consumed by the inferno that some said was her deserved end.

After that, Taylor had been taken back to northern New York to be raised by her great-aunt, Pearl Bissett. Netta Bissett remained in Key West. Pearl had passed away two years previously, and now Netta was gone too. During Pearl's final illness, she had instructed Taylor to sell off all Bissett holdings on Key West, especially Stormley, after Netta died. Taylor worked full-time managing the Bissett family's considerable north-country interests. Still, lawyers and realtors could have handled the Key West details. That had been Aunt Pearl's plan. Taylor wouldn't even have to show up here, where nothing but bad fortune had ever befallen her and those she cared about.

Taylor would have been content to go along with it—except for the dreams. They began a few months before Pearl died. They came in the hour before dawn and were filled with creatures made of tangled green foliage and smoke. Sometimes Taylor was embraced by these creatures. Other times they pursued her. She awoke with her heart pounding from both terror and fascination, and with the certainty that these images had something to do with this Isle of Bones where she was born.

"Leave well enough alone," Aunt Pearl would have said were she still alive. "Don't ask for trouble."

But the dreams felt to Taylor as if she already had trouble. Not even her long, soothing talks with Early Rhinelander could erase those shadows from her mind. Early, the dear family friend who had brought her north from the Keys as a toddler with Pearl, had stayed in New York and become Taylor's most trusted confidant. Unfortunately, even Early couldn't resolve this restlessness in Taylor's spirit. She'd known somehow that only returning to her birthplace could accomplish that. So, here she was, damp and uncomfortable in her too-heavy clothing, standing on the low curbstone of the Key Westian Guest House on Amelia Street.

It was after ten at night. She had taken the last commuter flight from Tampa on the mainland. She wasn't even sure there would be anybody around to check her in at this hour. She should have mentioned the time she'd be arriving when she made the reservation. She didn't ordinarily neglect details like that, but her whirlwind decision and departure had been anything but ordinary for her. It occurred to Taylor that there might be a price to be paid for that hastiness.

What looked like a single lamp burned behind the lace curtains of the guest-house door. Maybe she should go up there and see if anybody was available to help carry her bags. She was about to do that when she noticed something peculiar down the block, back along the way the cab had driven.

The streetlights were far apart and shadowed by the thick greenery of tropical trees. The moon was also barely visible through the veil of foliage. Taylor could feel the dark blue of the sky more than she could see it. Still, she was sure she had seen a car being driven slowly along the opposite curb with its headlights off. That car had stopped a few houses from where she stood, and was still there. She couldn't make out who was inside the car from this distance in the near darkness. Why had the car been driven without headlights? Why did the driver just sit there now, without getting out?

Maybe a pair of lovers were lingering for a last kiss in the tropical night. The car appeared to be dark in color, but Taylor couldn't really tell. The shadows here might make anything look dark. Taylor remembered the pink cab. Hadn't she noticed the cabdriver watching her a bit too attentively in his rearview mirror? She strained to make out the contours of the car down the street. Had the cab looked like that? She usually noticed such things. Tonight she had not, another example of not being quite herself in this place.

Maybe the lovers didn't want the neighbors to see them drive up and start kissing in the car, so they turned the headlights off. That scenario was preferable to imagining she was being stalked by a cabdriver. Taylor shook her head in wonder that she was even taking time to contemplate such theories about the simple presence of a parked car. The heat, which her north-country metabolism found so difficult to assimilate in mid-February, must be addling her brain. She bent down to pick up the bigger of her bags in one hand, then balanced it by slinging the smaller duffel over her opposite shoulder along with her purse. She straightened up slowly and was about to turn toward the guesthouse when she saw that the car had begun to move.

It crept along even more slowly than when she had first noticed it coming down the street. For a moment, she wasn't entirely certain the car was moving at all. Then she saw that the gap had widened between the body of the vehicle and the curb. The car was creeping in her direction with its headlights still off, like a dark, crawling hulk in the night. Taylor shuddered, causing the strap of the carryall to slide down her arm, shifting the balance she had so carefully adjusted and pulling her precariously to one side.

Taylor tried to hunch the strap back upward. Rough fabric chafed her neck as her jacket was pulled askew. She could feel her clothes sticking to her everywhere. She longed to drop the bags right here and make a beeline for what she hoped would be the air-conditioned lobby of the guesthouse. But what if that was exactly what the driver of the car wanted her to do? What if he was after her luggage? She'd heard about thieves who prey on tourists in resort areas.

The car was close enough now for Taylor to see it more clearly. It was either dark green or navy blue. She recognized now why she hadn't been able to see inside and still could not. The windows were tinted and opaque from the outside looking in. The wide, blank eye of the windshield made a sinister image as the car continued its slow, steady advance.

This was definitely not the pink taxicab she had taken from the airport. This car was not only darker in color, it was also of much more recent vintage. Its sleek surface glistened like brand-new in the occasional patch of streetlight. Taylor's common sense told her that this was not the kind of vehicle likely to be owned by a petty luggage thief. She held tight to her bags anyway and staggered toward the guest-house steps. Meanwhile, her overheated brain registered the fact that the car was picking up speed.

She struggled through the opening in the white picket fence that surrounded the guesthouse. Her suitcase bounced clumsily as she thumped it upward from step to step. She looked over her shoulder to see the car almost at the curb where she had been standing only a moment ago. Her heart jumped, and her right shin bumped sharply against the edge of the top step, almost sending her sprawling across the porch floor. Taylor lunged onto the porch just as the light behind the lace curtain glowed suddenly brighter, and the door opened.

"What's goin' on out here?" drawled an amused female voice. "You're makin' enough noise to wake 'em up all the way over at City Cemetery."

"I'm sorry," Taylor gasped as she struggled toward the door, "but I have to get inside."

"Slow down, honey," the woman in the doorway said. She touched Taylor's arm. "Heaven's sake, you've worked yourself up to a mighty sweat."

Taylor pressed forward, but the tall woman's strong grip restrained her.

"What's eatin' you, girl?"

"That car," Taylor blurted out, jerking her head toward the street.

"What car might you be referrin' to?"

Taylor spun around, half expecting to see the dark hulk with its blind, black windows crash through the white pickets and mount the porch steps after her. What she did see made her let the carryall and purse drop to the floor on one side of her and the suitcase plop down on the other. The street appeared even more shadowed in contrast with this lighted porch. The opposite side was lined with frame houses set close to the sidewalk. She could just make out the clusters of bougainvillea tumbling everywhere, from the balconies and along fence tops. But there was no dark car in sight.

Taylor hurried to the edge of the porch and peered down the street in the direction the car had been headed. The roadway was empty, except for a few parked vehicles along the nearer curb. Could the dark car have slipped into hiding among those vehicles? Taylor moved down a step, as if she were about to run to the street and check the parked cars. She hesitated. Did she really want to do that? Her heart was still pounding from the fright her stumbling flight had given her.

"Wait up, hon." The tall woman was beginning to sound concerned. She crossed the porch to Taylor. "Where are you dashing off to?"

"There was a car...." Taylor gestured down the street.

"I didn't see any car. I didn't hear one, either."

Taylor dropped her arm to her side. Now that she thought about it, she hadn't heard the car herself. Maybe she couldn't have heard anything above the thumping of her heart. Or, maybe the car's engine had purred too smoothly to be noticeable. But would that still have been the case after it picked up speed?

"You just flew in from up north. Right?" the woman asked.

"What?" Taylor looked up at her. "Yes, that's right. I flew from New York State."

"Well, that explains it." She took Taylor by the arm and urged her back toward the door. "You snowbirds sometimes get a little rattled when you first wing it down here to the tropics."

"Snowbirds?" Taylor bent to pick up her bags, but the tall woman beat her to it.

"I'll get those," she said. "Paradise can be disorienting, you know, especially at first."

Taylor glanced back toward the street one more time before stepping through the doorway. "I'm not so sure about this being paradise," she muttered.

"I didn't catch that."

"It's not important."

"Whatever you say, hon." The woman set Taylor's bags down in front of a high registration desk that looked as if it must be a valuable antique—oak, aged to a reddish grain, topped with a slab of white marble veined by rose-colored streaks. The woman walked behind it and extended her hand across the marble. "My name is April Jane Cooney. I run this place."

April Jane was tall, all right. Taylor hadn't imagined that part at least. However, she was beginning to question her perceptions about the dark car. Maybe April Jane was right. The drastic transition from driving through a northern New York blizzard this morning to stepping into this land of exotica tonight might be enough to distort anybody's perceptions.

"Now, let's get you checked in so you can settle yourself down and take a nice, long bath. That'll have you a hundred percent again in a jiffy. There's even some stuff in your room that makes heaps of bath bubbles. Look in the cupboard under the bathroom sink. Or maybe you like showers best. Lots of New Yorkers don't like to take the time for a bath."

"I'm not from New York *City*. I'm from rural New York *State*," Taylor said, feeling she was being put on the defensive. "There's a big difference."

"I suppose there is," April Jane said, turning the leather-bound register toward Taylor. "Sign here. We do it the old-fashioned way at the Key Westian."

Taylor managed a thin smile. She did want to get to her room. Whether she would shower or bathe once she got there wasn't important to her right now. She did *not* want to hear anymore about how uptight snowbirds are or what a paradise this place was supposed to be. She was even beginning to resent the golden-brown tan above the curve of April Jane's peasant-style blouse. Her hair was streaked with blond as further evidence of how much time she clocked in the tropical sun. Suddenly, Taylor was more aware than she wanted to be of her own hair clinging to her neck, the damp wrinkles staining her jacket, the perspiration trickling between her breasts. Suddenly, she wished she could will herself back to this morning's frigid blizzard. She would be comfortable there, where the chill made her feel sharp and alert the way she liked to be. Aunt Pearl's warnings about what happened when you strayed too far from home echoed in Taylor's brain as she scrawled her name in the register. She dropped the pen and grabbed her bags from the floor.

"Let me help you with those, hon," April Jane drawled.

"I'll get them myself," Taylor said a little too harshly.

"Suit yourself." April Jane sounded amused again. "Second floor."

Taylor hoisted the bags as best she could and struggled toward the stairs. She knew what a pathetic, bedraggled sight she must be right now, but she didn't care. She told herself that if she could just be alone, she'd be able to sort everything out. She'd know what she was or was not seeing. She would be able to tell the difference between a harmless illusion and real danger. And, there would be no more overwhelming urges to run back home like a frightened child. She chose not to remind herself that it had been an overwhelming urge that had brought her here in the first place.

IT WAS LESS THAN AN HOUR later when Taylor wandered out onto the terrace of her second-floor room two blocks off Duval Street. She had taken a shower after all and put on a sleeveless cotton dress. The night air rested on her bare arms, warm and slightly moist and unbelievably warm. The fronds of a tall coconut palm brushed the terrace railing. The scent of night flowers surrounded her, as soft and shimmering as the silver light from the haloed moon or as a whisper of romantic memory. She understood how someone might be so seduced by this place that they could never leave. April Jane might be right. This could possibly be paradise after all. Taylor walked back inside where a circling ceiling fan had cooled the room to a pleasant evening temperature. The shower had revived her from her previously overheated state. What couldn't be so easily cooled was the reason for her visit to the Keys. She had come here with a burning need to find out why this place haunted her so, and she had very few clues to go on—except for three names.

She had already unpacked the leather portfolio and slipped it between the bed and the nightstand. It contained a copy of Aunt Netta's will and descriptions of the three heirs she had mentioned in addition to Taylor. There were two relatively small and perfectly understandable bequests, one to Violetta Ramone who had cooked for Netta and kept house at Stormley, where Netta had lived after it was rebuilt, and another to Netta's longtime friend Winona Starling. The third bequest was larger and more mysterious. Netta had left it to a man with the unlikely name of Destiny Maxwell and the enigmatic instruction "he will know what it is for."

The description of Mr. Maxwell was not so mysterious, but it was definitely troubling. He was in his late thirties, a lot younger than Aunt Netta had been. Yet, he had apparently been her frequent companion both socially and privately. He owned and operated a Key West saloon called the Beachcomber on lower Duval Street. Had he been Aunt Netta's young lover? Was that what she meant by his knowing what the bequest would be for? Taylor wasn't really bothered by that possibility. Aunt Netta had been free to spend her time with whomever she chose and to leave her money to them if she wished. Taylor respected that, though she didn't like to think that her aunt might have been taken advantage of by an opportunist.

What Taylor was more curious about, however, was if Netta might have confided in Mr. Maxwell. Had she told him things about the Bissett family and its history in Key West? If so, Taylor wanted to know those things, along with whatever Violetta Ramone and Winona Starling might have to tell. It was too late at night to go calling on either of them right now, but a Key West saloon was sure to be open at this hour.

Taylor picked up her small handbag and the room key on her way to the door. She took a few steps toward the front stairway then thought better of it. She had a feeling that, despite April Jane's casual manner, she kept a close watch over things around here and would be far too interested in the reason for Taylor's going out alone so late. She used the back stairs to avoid that interest. The back door had a release bar across it. That meant it could be opened from the inside only. Taylor would have to take the front entrance back in. She could see herself tiptoeing barefoot up the stairs like a teenager out past curfew. The thought made her smile, but that smile disappeared as soon as she stepped outside and the door clicked shut behind her.

The back door did not open onto a street or a well-lit path as she'd thought it would. Instead, a pattern of flat stones led from the stoop through an overhang of foliage with no visible light along the way. Taylor moved cautiously down the steps to the stone walk and the entrance to the overgrown pathway. She could see that the foliage actually arched over the path for some distance to the street beyond. The light from the opposite entrance was just bright enough to reveal that much. There must be a wood or wire trellis structure that kept the greenery from filling in the opening altogether.

A shudder ran through her. She had been suddenly reminded of her dreams. There was a tunnel much like this in one of them, made up of long, undulating fronds that reached out to grab her as she ran through. She still trembled at the remembered sense of great danger lurking among those wild, grasping, green things. Taylor's experience with the dark car had made her skittish already. She would have preferred not to be reminded of her nightmares right now. She told herself that there was no person lying in wait along this passageway or she would be able to make out their shape even in the dim light. She couldn't be accosted from the side because of the trellis and the thickness of the shrubbery.

But what about non-persons? Wasn't this the tropics, after all? Weren't snakes and other creepy-crawly things common to this part of the world? She took a deep breath against that possibility. Another deep breath and Taylor was into the tunnel, which smelled faintly of leaf mold. She hurried but would not allow herself to run. Her heart tripped at the sound of her own footsteps and the attention they might arouse among whatever beings lurked within the green wall that surrounded her.

"Stay where you know the territory and the territory knows you." Aunt Pearl's words rang in Taylor's head as haunting accompaniment to her hurried steps. She could almost feel Aunt Pearl keeping pace and whispering, "I told you so. I told you so. I told you so."

Taylor didn't take a full breath again until she was out of the passage. She didn't slow her pace until she was standing beneath a street lamp where she was forced to stop for a moment to get her bearings. She had studied a Key West street map on the way down here in the plane. She knew precisely where the guesthouse was located in relation to the place she was now headed. Her exit through the backyards had taken her one block closer to her destination. She took a few more deep breaths to slow the tripping of her heart then set out along the cracked pavement toward Duval Street.

Small, modest houses lined the block on both sides. She was alone on the street—no people, no vehicles parked in possible ambush, no leafy nightmare creatures in evidence. Duval Street was famous for its noisy nightlife, but all was quiet here. She had deliberately chosen an address near the center of things but still at some distance from the hubbub of Mallory Square, with its sunset worshippers and late-night revels. Her guesthouse was only a few blocks from the southernmost point on the island, which the brochures all bragged of as also being the southernmost point in the entire United States. *Almost not in the same country with the rest of us,* Taylor thought, and wasn't sure how she felt about that. She was reminded yet again of being out of her element.

The tropical air caught in her heavy hair. She could feel it there like a gossamer web among the strands. She raked her fingers through it and felt the coolness of that web and the fullness of the waves made suddenly untamable by this place. She pulled the strap of her handbag from her shoulder and began fishing inside for a wide-toothed comb that might bring the honey-colored mass under control. She was still poking around in her purse when she felt a movement behind her.

"What's an angel like you doin' out here on her own?"

He must have come out of one of the shop doorways that bordered the street. She was on Duval now. The shops were all closed along here, and there was no one else on the street, at least not near enough to be of help if she needed it. He was tall and very thin. His clothes hung loosely on him. His shirt was open several buttons at the neck, and his pants fit more like pajamas than trousers. She thought he might be wearing sandals from the sound of his shuffling along the pavement, but she couldn't see his feet in the shadowy night.

She began walking fast away from him, down Duval Street toward the bright neon and the sound of music ahead. She could see that the lighted shop fronts were closer on the opposite side. She would cross the street when she got there, maybe step inside one of the open boutiques till she was sure she wasn't being followed any longer. She could hear him, still laughing softly behind her. She glanced back over her shoulder.

"Fluff out your wings and fly away, angel," he said. "There ain't no heaven hereabouts."

## Chapter Two

"Desiree," he breathed.

Des Maxwell was behind the false mirror over the Beachcomber's long, teakwood bar. This observation post had been here when he bought the place. He'd thought about getting rid of it. He didn't like keeping tabs on people when they didn't know he was doing it. Instead, he told everybody who worked for him that from back here he had a clear view of everything, including the cash register. He figured that would keep most of them honest. There's no such thing as being too careful in the bar business.

You can't be too careful about a lot of things. Like letting yourself get blindsided the way he just did when she walked in and sat down. Of course, he knew she wasn't Desiree. He'd seen Taylor Bissett's photograph at Netta's house, and Desiree had been dead almost twenty-four years now. That was just about time enough for him to get used to how much she had meant to him and how much of his life had died with her—like the only chance he'd ever had of anything even close to a family. Now, as he stared through the one-way glass at the woman who was the vision of her mother, he knew there hadn't been time enough to get over his loss after all.

Des had half expected the daughter to show up here someday. Then again, he'd half expected her not to. Either way, she'd caught him by surprise tonight. It had never occurred to him that in real life she would look almost identical to her mother. Not even the photograph had convinced him of that. Nothing could have convinced him that anybody could look so much like Desiree. Nobody ever had. He pressed closer to the glass. The hair, especially, was as he remembered, and the skin he knew would be moist and cool in the night air, the way Desiree was cool while being warm and caring at the same time. He couldn't tell if Desiree's daughter might be warm and caring too. She was certainly beautiful. She was also subdued and aloof in that white dress, at least a world away from the halter tops and jeans cut off high enough to show some back cheek along the bar. She didn't flash her body around that way any more than her mother would have done.

Still, there was something different about her, some way she wasn't Desiree. Des couldn't put his finger on it. He felt he needed to know what that difference was. He had to set her apart from Desiree, especially considering what a lot of people suspected about that night twenty-four years ago, and the fire. Taylor was only a kid then, younger than he was by several years. Even if what they said about her and the fire was true, she couldn't have really understood what she was doing. Knowing that hadn't kept him from wishing a thousand times that he'd done what he first meant to do that night and saved the mother instead of the child.

That regret rose in him now. Suddenly, he felt the need, stronger than ever, to set them apart from each other in his mind, these two women who would have looked like sisters, were they standing side by side. He knew he would be able to tell from the eyes. Unfortunately, Taylor Bissett was halfway across the room, and the mirror glass on the other side of here could stand a polish to clear up the view. He would have to go down there for a closer look.

Des headed for the steps that led to a side door at the end of the bar. He glanced one more time through the back of the mirror. "Damn," he cursed as he saw a lanky man walk up behind Taylor with a smile on his face that said he intended to get to know her very well, very fast. Des quickened his pace toward the door.

WHEN TAYLOR FELT someone at her shoulder, she thought it might be the person she had come here to find. She looked up to see a dark-haired man of wiry build, attractive in a rawboned sort of way. He leaned over and flashed her a quick smile that told her he was just a stranger trying to pick her up, after all.

"I bet you won't believe this, but I know you," he said, starting out with the most clichéd of pickup lines.

"I beg your pardon. I don't think I know *you*."

"It was when you were a kid," he said. "May I?" He gestured at the chair next to hers and sat down in it before she could say whether she wanted him to or not. His movements were abrupt, like a darting animal's, so much so that there was no time to react.

Taylor hesitated. Was this a new twist on an old line? "Are you trying to say you knew me when I was a child here in Key West?"

"That's right. I did."

Taylor almost laughed at him. She had left here as barely more than an infant, and she hadn't been back since. How could he possibly recognize her now as an adult?

"That was so long ago. You probably don't remember," he said. "Your aunt used to bring you to my mother's house almost every day. I'd sneak around corners to get a look at you. You were almost as pretty then as you are now."

"Thank you for the compliment. But you're right, I don't remember you. What did you say your name was?"

"Oh, sorry. I was so surprised to see you I forgot my manners. I'm Jethro."

He took her hand and shook it briefly. His grip was firm, but darting like the rest of him.

"Was it my Aunt Netta who brought me to your house when I was small?"

"That's right. That was her name. But you weren't so small. I could already tell you were going to be tall like you are now."

Taylor was again tempted to laugh. She had seen pictures of herself at three years old. She had been average size then, maybe even a bit small for her age. Her first growth spurt hadn't happened till a couple of years later, at least. She was about to throw this guy some lines of her own, of the brush-off variety, when she noticed a man coming through a doorway at the end of the bar that extended the length of the room. He stopped for a moment to say something to the bartender. Taylor was looking at him with such concentration that, when he turned, he caught her staring. The directness of his gaze connected them, one to another, across the room with a flash of electric intimacy that almost made Taylor look away. She felt suddenly apprehensive, but she held his stare despite the flutter in her chest that was her heart picking up speed.

He was powerfully angular, almost too imposing for the low-ceilinged barroom. The lines of his face might have been chiseled from the rich-grained wood of the beams supporting that ceiling. His cheekbones were high and resolute, like the ridge of collarbone below his square, dimpled chin. He seemed out of place somehow in this smoky barroom, as if he was meant to be out-of-doors, among trees and landscapes as rugged as himself.

He began walking across the room. He was headed, in as straight a line as possible, directly toward her. She had guessed who he was the moment she saw him. He walked as if he owned the place, and that meant he had to be Destiny Maxwell. She felt that ownership reach out toward her the way it sometimes did with very strong-minded men. She steeled herself against its strength. She wasn't about to be dominated, especially not by this particular man, no matter how strong-minded he might be. If this was to be a test of wills, she was determined to come out the winner.

Still, she couldn't deny how attractive he was. She had seen it in the photographs in her portfolio, but those had only been pictures. The man in the flesh was even better-looking, almost disturbingly so. She would have preferred that not to be the case, but Taylor wasn't accustomed to lying to herself. She had to admit, if only in private silence, that even the way he walked was somehow unsettling to her. He moved fast across the room without appearing to hurry at all, as if he wanted to make it clear that he wasn't the kind of man who hurried for anybody. He might put on a little speed when his priorities required it, but he didn't hurry. That would mean behaving as if something really mattered to him. Taylor guessed that this man didn't like things to matter to him, or to let anybody know they did.

Des Maxwell might possibly be the handsomest man she had ever seen. He might also be the coolest and the most detached, and that coolness and detachment intrigued her. It also made her increasingly uneasy with every step he took because, the closer he got, the more striking he looked. As he approached she noticed more details about him, such as that he was quite tall, six feet or more. She couldn't tell exactly from this angle. His hair was bronze and gold, much like April Jane Cooney's. His deep, copper tan made Taylor aware of her own snowbird-pale skin.

Taylor felt a sudden shift of perspective, as if she had turned abruptly at an angle to see something not visible in her former line of vision. However, she hadn't moved a muscle. She knew what was happening. She had experienced it before. The barroom scene disappeared for her for an instant and was replaced by something much more disturbing. She could see her body stretched out full length and naked. His nude body lay atop hers. Their skin touched, almost blended, but remained mysteriously different, like night from day.

Then the image was gone, as suddenly as it had materialized, and she was watching him stride toward her once again. Unfortunately, as with other such experiences, the shadow of the vision remained, along with its aura of strong sensuality. Taylor struggled to erase that sensation from her consciousness. She reminded herself that she'd always been put off by men who were what she thought of as too handsome. Vanity usually came along with such physical gifts, and arrogance. The way this particular man moved led her to suspect a generous portion of both.

Still, Taylor had to concede that the very sight of him had shaken her. Or, could it be just the vision she was reacting to? She hadn't gotten over being startled when this kind of thing happened. She doubted she ever would.

The experience made her feel unprotected, as if her usual defenses had toppled and she was left completely vulnerable. She definitely didn't want to feel that way now, in front of Des Maxwell. She stifled the impulse to swallow hard against the rapid beating of her heart.

"Well, Jethro," the tall man said when he reached the table. "You usually don't prowl your way in here till the weekend."

She wouldn't go so far as to say there was a sneer in his voice, but it came very close to that. Meanwhile, though he was talking to Jethro, Destiny Maxwell was staring at her. His green eyes didn't waver an instant from their study of her face. She felt their imposition so keenly that she was tempted to slap him for his rudeness, or maybe to dispel the shock his close-up gaze seemed to be causing to her system. She could actually feel her stomach tightening into a knot under his scrutiny. The vision of herself naked under him had already unnerved her. His stare couldn't help but add to her uneasiness. She felt the warmth of a blush rise unbidden beneath the white cotton of her dress. The thought that he deserved a slap grew stronger, as if he might, in some deliberately insolent manner, be forcing this blush upon her, all the while enjoying her embarrassment.

"You two know each other. Right?" Jethro asked, glancing from one icy stare to the other.

"Not really," Taylor said.

"I'm afraid you're wrong about that. I'm Des Maxwell, and you are Taylor Bissett, which means I've known you almost all your life."

Maxwell sounded so aloof he might not have been there at all, as if his words had been spoken with no connection to the rest of him. Taylor found that aloofness as provoking as his rude gaze and his calculated movements. Besides, she was getting tired of being declared an old acquaintance by men she had no memory of ever meeting.

"I beg your pardon, sir," she said. "I do not know you."

The waitress walked up behind Maxwell with a frothy white drink on her tray. "He ordered you a piña colada," she said with a nod toward Maxwell in response to Taylor's inquiring glance.

Taylor caught the flash of adoration in the young woman's eyes as she looked up at her boss. Unfortunately, Taylor couldn't help understanding that look. In addition to the attractions she had already noted, his hair fell winsomely across his forehead, and a thatch of sun-blond curls peeked through the open neck of his shirt in disturbing contrast with his tanned skin. He was positively spilling over with masculine charm, and she was keenly aware of the danger in that. She told herself she was determined to avoid such danger and that it was the power of this determination which made her hand tremble as she reached into her purse for her wallet.

"The drink is on the house," he said and took hold of her wrist before she could pull out her money.

His fingers were warm against the thin skin above her pulse. She felt that pulse quicken as if it might begin at any moment to pump visibly beneath his touch. She pulled her hand away from him before that self-betrayal could happen.

"I prefer to pay my own way," she said, handing a bill to the waitress, who had watched this exchange with considerable interest.

"Suit yourself," Maxwell said with a shrug.

"Say, you two, what's all this sparring about anyway?" Jethro darted halfway up from his seat and yanked the chair opposite Taylor's away from the table. "Why don't you sit down and take a load off, Des?"

"What do you say, Ms. Bissett? Should I take a load off, as Jethro puts it, or take a walk?"

Taylor stared straight back at him. She forced herself to be just as cool as he was. "Suit yourself."

"In that case, I accept your invitation, Jethro," Maxwell said, sitting. "How've you been, anyway?"

"I've been super, Des." Jethro looked bewildered, as if he might be surprised by Maxwell's acknowledging him at all.

"And how's Winona?"

"Oh, Ma's always tip-top."

"That's when she isn't *over* the top," Maxwell said almost under his breath.

"Wait a minute," Taylor interrupted at the sound of the less than common female name. "Is your mother Winona Starling?"

"She sure is," Jethro said enthusiastically. "That's who your aunt used to bring you to see when you were a kid, like I told you."

"I remember that," Maxwell said.

"Well, I don't remember any of it."

Taylor felt her annoyance deflate suddenly. Too many people seemed to know more about her life than she did. Meanwhile, Maxwell was watching her. He appeared more thoughtful than arrogant this time.

"What exactly do you remember?" he asked.

His green-eyed gaze had turned unexpectedly warm as honey, or at least it felt startlingly that way to her.

"I remember almost nothing," she said.

"Loss of memory can come in handy sometimes."

The warmth had vanished from his eyes and his voice, as if she might have imagined them there, like one of her visions. Taylor had been about to lower her barriers against him long enough to ask what he might know of her early childhood here in Key West. His renewed coolness put a stop to that.

"Are you accusing me of lying about what I do or do not remember?"

"I'm not accusing you of anything. I was only making an observation."

"You really don't remember anything about being a kid here?" Jethro chimed in.

Taylor didn't answer him. The fascination in Jethro's voice and the quizzical way he was looking at her made her feel like a specimen in a jar. Des Maxwell's smart-aleck detachment had revived the urge to slap him, hard and fast, straight across his sneering face. Taylor wished she had stayed in her room at the guesthouse and taken a bubble bath as April Jane Cooney advised.

Taylor pushed her chair back from the table and stood. "I have to be going."

Maxwell took a moment to let his smile appear, so slow and wide that she could tell it was insincere. "Don't let me chase you away."

Taylor picked up her purse instead of doing what she really wanted to do with her hand to his arrogant smirk.

"I never let anyone chase me anywhere," she said.

Despite that declaration, Taylor walked fast to the open doorway and out into the street. "Calm down," she said, then glanced around to see if anybody had noticed her talking to herself. Two young men in T-shirts with beer bottles in their hands turned from lounging against the building to look her up and down in impudent appraisal. She avoided their eyes and would have begun walking back toward Amelia Street, when a recollection of the shuffling bum and his sly laugh kept her riveted

where she stood, uncertain for the moment what to do
next.

Emotion burned her cheeks. She had kept herself in
check through all that had happened these past weeks, so
soon after the death of Aunt Netta, Taylor's last real remaining family. Her sense of loss, the trip down here, her
scare outside the guesthouse earlier this evening—each
pressure had piled upon the others. She had been closer
to her saturation point than she realized when she walked
into Maxwell's bar. Then she saw him, with his brazen
attitude, as if he couldn't care less about any of it. That
was the last straw. Tears trembled on Taylor's lashes. She
didn't want anybody to see her wipe them away or know
how upset she was. She wouldn't give Des Maxwell that
satisfaction, even if he didn't know about it. She willed
the tears to dry where they stood and vowed there would
be no more.

"Are you all right?"

Taylor whirled around. She half hoped to find Maxwell standing there, so she could deliver the slap she'd
resisted giving him in the bar. Instead, it was Jethro
Starling.

"You looked so upset when you left. I thought I
should come after you." He seemed pretty agitated himself, with his eyes wide open in a startled expression.

"Thanks," Taylor said, after a deep breath.

"One reason Des gets to people is that they know they
can't get to him."

Taylor was surprised to hear such a sober assessment
from someone so high-strung he could hardly stand still
on the pavement.

"I noticed that."

"Look. Why don't you let me give you a ride home?
It's late for you to be out here on your own."

Taylor hesitated, and that made him fidget more than ever.

"I wouldn't hurt you or anything like that. I could get you a cab if you don't want to drive with me."

Taylor glanced up and down the street. It was late. She didn't see any taxis, but she could call one as Jethro said. She remembered the creepy guy in the pink cab from the airport, almost as scary as the shuffling bum had been. Her instincts told her Jethro was harmless. Besides, Aunt Netta had known his family.

"I'd like a ride, thank you," she said.

"Great. My car's right over there." He pointed to a red Corvette at the opposite curb.

As they walked across the street, Taylor caught sight of a dark sedan parked farther down the block. She stopped short, but then she saw that the windshield was transparent, not black glass. She continued walking.

"Maxwell really did get to you, didn't he?" Jethro said as he opened the car door for her.

She didn't feel like explaining about the sedan. "Maybe," she said. "Does he ever get to you?"

"As long as I've got my good luck going for me, nothing bothers me."

Taylor couldn't help smiling as he slammed her car door and hurried around to get in the driver's side. She would have guessed that there was hardly anything that *didn't* bother Jethro. He flipped the car into gear and made a U-turn in the middle of the block, causing a pickup truck to screech to a halt in the opposite lane. The truck honked noisily, and Jethro honked back before taking off southward on Duval Street.

"How did you know my guesthouse was in this direction?" Taylor asked.

"Guesthouse? I thought you'd be staying at your family's place by the shore."

"No. I have a room not far from here on Amelia Street." Aunt Netta might have been able to live with the ghosts of Stormley, but Taylor wasn't. "Your family must have known mine pretty well."

"Just about everybody knows my mother."

"That reminds me," Taylor said, thinking of the question she'd had earlier, before her encounter with Des Maxwell knocked it out of her mind. "Exactly how old was I when you last saw me?"

"I'd say you were about six or seven."

Taylor needed a moment to take that in. "I don't see how that could be possible. I left Key West when I was three years old, and I haven't been back since."

"Oh, no. That's not right. You were six or seven like I said. I remember you used to bring your library book with you sometimes. Three-year-olds don't read library books. You were old enough to be in school last time I saw you."

"Maybe you have me mixed up with somebody else," Taylor said.

"It was you, all right. I wouldn't get that mixed up. I had kind of a crush on you." He smiled over at her. He looked embarrassed. "I used to watch you especially."

Taylor didn't feel entirely comfortable with Jethro's infatuation story, whether or not he might be correct in his memory of her as the object of those affections. She was even less comfortable when he took a sudden right turn off Duval Street.

"Where are you going?" she asked. "I told you my guesthouse was off Duval." She slid her hand onto the door handle and got ready for a fast escape.

"Amelia Street is one-way. I can't turn onto it from Duval."

"Oh, I see."

Taylor relaxed some, but she kept her grip on the door handle. At the end of the block the headlights picked out white letters on a telephone pole. Vertically they read Whitehead Street. Jethro made another turn, to the left this time. It was definitely darker here, with far fewer people around than back on Duval. If Jethro Starling intended to do her harm, she was giving him every opportunity. She could hardly believe she had climbed into a car with a stranger, and a strange-acting stranger at that. She was about to make her move and shove open the door when the car slowed. The pole marker on the corner ahead said Amelia Street, and Jethro was signaling to make a left turn.

Taylor was about to breathe a sigh of relief when she heard sirens. A whirling light reflected in the sports car's rearview mirror. She turned to see two police cars behind them. Jethro steered to the side of the road. The police cars sped past and around the corner onto Amelia and the block where she was staying. She was surprised by that. This had seemed like such a quiet street, not at all the kind of place she would expect screaming sirens.

Then, Taylor remembered the dark sedan and the certainty that it was stalking her down that same quiet block. A wave of apprehension swept over her even before she saw that the police had stopped in front of the Key Westian and were already headed toward the porch. Jethro turned the Corvette onto the same block and slowed to a stop near the corner.

"Which house are you staying at?" he asked.

Taylor didn't answer right away.

She lowered the car window to get a clearer view. She didn't like what she saw. Two policemen had stationed themselves on either side of the guest-house door, and their guns were drawn.

# Chapter Three

Des turned out the headlights of his Jeep and coasted to a stop within sight of the scene. Following Jethro's flashy car had been easy. Des hadn't really decided to follow them. It just happened. She'd marched out of the place, twitching her hips in that white dress. Was she aware that he could see the outline of her body through the fine material? Had she planned to use her charms to get what she wanted out of him, whatever that might be? Then she saw him and lost control for some reason and went running off before she could put her plan in motion. Was that what happened all those years ago? Did she lose control back then too? That's what everybody said at the time.

Des let out a deep sigh. For almost as long as he could remember, he'd been pushing the past as far out of his mind as he could get it, especially his memories of that night. The air heavy with smoke, the running, choking, eyes raw and red, his heart screaming with the pain of being left alone again. He had been the beachcomber boy. Desiree had been the lovely lady from the beautiful house who walked the beach alone. He made her laugh sometimes. She gave him a pair of jeans without holes in them and boots made of real leather. She had given him books, too, and helped him learn to read as well as the kids who didn't have to cut school to do odd jobs for money to live on.

Most important, she taught him things about himself he never knew, such as that he was smart and had courage and could do anything he wanted if he put his mind to it. His Uncle Murph might have done those things himself after Des's mother died when he was only a baby, but Uncle Murph was generally too drunk to do much of anything but mumble and pass out. Desiree taught Des there was another way to be. It was the most significant lesson of his life. But what had he done for her in return? What if she had known that in the end he would leave her in a burning house to die? He knew the answer. She would say, "Thank you for saving my baby," with the smile that had always made his heart feel full.

Tonight Desiree's baby had walked back into his life, and he was trying his best not to care. For the most part, Des had kept himself from caring much about anything after the night of the Stormley fire. Now, he could feel the forces of hurt and memory threatening that resolve, and Taylor Bissett was to blame. Why had she come back here, anyway? What was she after? Anger flared. Des gripped the steering wheel hard, as if to choke the life out of that rage so he could return to the safety of coolness again. He didn't want any of this to be happening. He wanted to go back to the Beachcomber and joke with the customers and the barmaids as he did every other night. Old tragedies, a beautiful woman with a screwed-up past—he didn't need any of it.

Unfortunately, at this moment he couldn't seem to stop wondering whether he would ever get to see Taylor Bissett smile. He forced his temper back under control. His guess was that she wouldn't be smiling right now. She was too far away for him to make out her face, but he was sure about that all the same. Des had seen the cop cars streak past the Corvette and careen around the corner. He'd pulled over to let them pass. When the 'Vette turned down the same street as the police cars, he thought Jethro might just be rubbernecking, trying to get a peek at the excitement. He was fool enough to do something like that. Maybe she was a thrill-seeker too.

Des saw the car door open on the passenger side of the Corvette. The police were all out of the two cars now. Two officers were on the path leading to the porch, but off to the side, probably to remain out of range of the front door. Two other officers had assumed break-in positions flanking that door. Des returned his attention to the sports car. Taylor was getting out of her side as Jethro's door flew open and he jumped out, too. He ran around to her side and appeared to be trying to prevent her from exiting the car.

Through the open window of the Jeep, Des heard the police on the porch shout that they were coming in. He heard the thud of the door being kicked open. Des remembered that his field glasses were in the glove compartment. He pulled them out and peered through the eyepiece. A few adjustments brought the front of the guesthouse into focus. He flashed past the police officers on the walk. Something caught his attention, and he flashed back. There was excitement here, all right. Those cops had pistols in their hands.

Des refocused the glasses to direct his gaze back down the street to the Corvette. Taylor was out of the car now and trying to get to the sidewalk, but Jethro was blocking her way. Her back was to Des. She had managed to move onto the sidewalk, and that put her near a streetlight. She turned to say something to Jethro, and Des saw

her face. Her expression was intense. She seemed to be
explaining something to Jethro or trying to convince him
of something. Des was beginning to doubt that her interest in this situation was limited to idle curiosity over
some exciting police action. She looked as if she might be
more personally involved than that.

Des saw one of the policemen approach Jethro and
Taylor. The magnifying lens showed the policeman talking to them, and her answering. The conversation continued for a few moments, during which she grew
increasingly agitated. Jethro was merely listening to the
exchange. One of the two cops who had entered the
guesthouse came out on the porch and called the other
officers to him.

Taylor watched the cop walk away. She had one hand
clamped over her mouth, as if to hold back a scream or
a sob. Jethro was looking very nervous. He moved toward her and gestured as if he might take her by the
shoulders, perhaps to comfort her. Instead, he dropped
his arms and began to drum his fingers against the sides
of his thighs. Meanwhile, she had started walking slowly
toward the guesthouse. Her back was toward Des again,
but he could see the tension in her shoulders.

One of the officers had gone down the walk at the side
of the guesthouse toward the back of the building. The
other officer stationed outside had returned to his patrol
car and was speaking into the two-way radio. She climbed
the steps, getting close enough to look through the front
door into the foyer before one of the policemen from inside came out and backed her off. Des thought he saw her
stagger against the cop, but the glasses still didn't give a
good view of her face.

The policeman moved her away from the door and let
her sit down on the top step. She put her head in her

hands, and could have been crying. Des couldn't tell. Jethro had kept his distance. Now the policeman beckoned him toward the porch. Jethro hesitated, then shrugged and trudged forward. Des stayed out of sight in the Jeep, despite his sudden impulse to help Taylor. He'd given in to that same impulse twenty-some years ago and lived to regret it. Besides, he wasn't quite ready to become part of the scene he'd been watching through his field glasses, especially not before he knew exactly what was going on.

He continued watching. Eventually, an ambulance arrived, then the medical examiner's car. A while later, a stretcher was carried out of the house. The figure on the stretcher was encased in a black bag, completely covered from head to toe.

Des sighed and lowered the field glasses to the passenger seat of the Jeep. "What is it about you, Taylor Bissett?" he asked out loud. "Whenever you're around, people have a habit of dying."

APRIL JANE COONEY had been robbed and murdered. According to one of the uniformed officers who knew her, she never kept much currency in the cashbox. She was too savvy for that. Her assailant had taken whatever little there was, anyway. The metal box had been pried open and left near the body. April Jane must have put up a fight. What was left of the lamp from the registration desk lay in pieces on the floor near the opposite wall. The lamp's base was shattered, as if it had been thrown very hard. A small dent at about head height on the white wall supported that theory.

One of the policemen had taken Taylor into a sitting room off the guest-house entryway. He had left the lace-curtained double glass doors ajar, so she could hear them discussing what might have happened to April Jane. Taylor heard the words and even put them together into sentences in her mind. Still, they weren't entirely understandable to her. She guessed that she wasn't letting herself fully comprehend what she was hearing, because then she would have to believe it. She would have to absorb the very scary fact that a woman she had spoken with less than two hours ago was now on her way to the city morgue, the victim of a senseless, violent crime.

What if Taylor had been here when the thief came in? She felt guilty thinking such a self-centered thought, but she couldn't help it. What if her uneasiness about walking the trellis path behind the guesthouse had actually been some instinct telling her there was a would-be murderer lurking in the shrubbery? She shuddered at the thought and wished someone would turn off the ceiling fan. The sitting room had turned suddenly chilly.

Taylor had overheard the police saying there was only one guest in the house when the attack happened, an older man on the third floor in the back. He had stayed in tonight and taken a pill to help him sleep off a sunburn. He hadn't heard a thing. The other guests were out on the town, like most Key West tourists at this time of night. Consequently, there were no witnesses. A neighbor across the street had heard glass shattering and saw the vestibule light go out suddenly. She didn't see anybody run out of the house, but she suspected something might be wrong and called the police. By the time they arrived, April Jane was dead. Her killer had fled, probably out the back way. The police had already begun canvassing the neighborhood, both on Amelia Street and one block north on Virginia Street, to find out if anyone had seen anything.

Taylor had heard Jethro's voice out in the entryway shortly after the policeman brought her into this room. Her knees had gone weak, and she had asked to sit down. She couldn't make out what Jethro was saying. Then she didn't hear him anymore. Next, she heard a policeman talking to a guest who had returned to the Key Westian and was demanding to know what had happened here. The policeman said that everyone would have to be questioned. He added that the guest-house residents would not be allowed to sleep here tonight because it was a major crime scene and had to be sealed off to all but official visitors.

Taylor was suddenly very tired. A series of adrenaline charges had kept her nerves tingling, through her arrival on this exotic island, her near escape from being run down and her unsettling encounter with Des Maxwell. This most recent jolt—the discovery of a dead body in her hotel—had sapped her final reserves of even that nervous energy. Now, all she wanted was to sleep. The police weren't about to let her go to her room and lie down there. They might think it bizarre of her to curl up here on this settee, but she was too tired to care much what they thought. She was almost too tired to care where in the devil she might sleep tonight.

"Miss Bissett is a personal acquaintance of mine, and I would like to talk with her."

The voice from the entryway had obviously been raised for emphasis. That was why Taylor could hear the words so clearly. But it wasn't the loudness or even the demanding tone, that cut through her head-nodding stupor and snapped her to full attention. She had met very few people on Key West in her few hours here. Yet, she was certain she knew the owner of that deep, resonating voice. One glance at the opening between the double doors confirmed this certainty.

Taylor had no idea why Des Maxwell was here. Nonetheless, the sight of his brown, muscled arm flexing impatiently as he backed the policeman gradually toward the half-open doorway, told Taylor that she was no longer stranded and alone. A wave of relief swept over her, as deep as it was probably irrational. Taylor reminded herself that Des Maxwell was not a likely candidate for friend in need where she was concerned. Still, he was a familiar face in what felt at the moment like very alien territory. She couldn't help being grateful to him for that.

There was something else about that face besides familiarity, something that struck her with a blow that took her breath away. It had happened when she had first laid eyes on him earlier in the Beachcomber barroom. It happened again now, with even greater force because he didn't know she was looking at him and she didn't have to be so careful to hide her reaction. She tried to tell herself she was only tired, otherwise his handsomeness wouldn't have this effect on her. Still, she couldn't keep the thought from crossing her mind that the word "manly" had been invented with someone like Des Maxwell in mind. Meanwhile, Des and the officer had walked out of the foyer and through the lace-curtained doors into the sitting room. The two of them appeared to know each other.

"Come on, Tony," Des was saying. "What do you think I'm going to do? Abscond with your prisoner?"

"She's not in custody, Des, and you know it. We're just keeping her here to talk to Detective Santos. He's on his way."

"Does he have to talk to her tonight? Can't it wait till the morning?"

"She may have been the last one to see April Jane alive. Santos will want to question her about that." Tony glanced over at Taylor on the settee. "There's something else too," he added, barely loud enough for her to hear.

"What's that?" Des asked, also glancing at Taylor then looking away.

She didn't like the way they were talking about her instead of *to* her. She was even less pleased when Tony leaned toward Des and said something in a whisper. Des's expression remained as unreadable as usual, except for a slight tightening around the eyes.

"Wait just a moment here," Taylor said, rousing herself from the settee and mustering as much indignation as she could manage in her state of near exhaustion. "If you have something to say that relates to me, I want to hear it."

Des gave her a cautionary look with "Keep quiet and let me take care of things" written all over it. That made Taylor even more indignant. Suddenly, she didn't want anybody taking care of things for her, not even this man whose brawny body tempted her to do just that—at least until she wasn't feeling quite so tired and out of sync with everything.

"I appreciate your concern, Mr. Maxwell," she said, "but I am perfectly capable of handling this myself."

"I thought you said she was a friend of yours," the officer said to Des. "How come she calls you by your last name if you're such great friends?"

"We're recent acquaintances," Taylor said before Des could answer.

She was determined to speak for herself in every way. "Please tell me what you were whispering about with Mr. Maxwell."

"That's confidential police information."

"If it's so confidential, why were you sharing it with Mr. Maxwell? Is he a member of the police force?" Taylor levelled a steady gaze at the officer. "You can answer that question for me, or for my attorney."

"I think I can help you out with that one, Miss..." The man who had stepped through the doorway consulted a notepad before going on. "Miss Bissett," he said. "You are Taylor Bissett, aren't you?"

"Yes, I am."

He was medium height and sallow-complected. Taylor noticed a slight muscle tic in his left cheek. Even without that added clue, his manner told her that he took his job very seriously. In laid-back Key West, he was anything but laid-back.

"I'm Detective Santos. I'll be taking charge of this investigation. What are you doing here, Maxwell?" Santos shot a dark-eyed, suspicious gaze at Des. "How do you know Miss Bissett?"

"She's Netta Bissett's niece."

"Oh, yes," Santos said with a nod. "Your friend with the big house in Casa Marina."

Taylor thought she might have heard a hint of sarcasm in the way he said "friend." Or maybe she was imagining that. Either way, Taylor didn't like the tone of the discussion or that her aunt was its subject.

"If you have questions that have to do with me or my family, I must insist that you address them to me."

"I see."

Santos looked her over, no doubt taking in her rumpled dress and unruly hair and probably doubting that she was as capable of taking charge as she claimed. Taylor smoothed her skirt and stood very straight. She wasn't about to be intimidated by this officious man. Des Maxwell was another story. He was looking at her too, and she felt his gaze as if it had fingers to reach out and touch her. Those fingers travelled over her, but not at all in the same way Santos had looked at her. There was nothing in the line of duty about Des's eyes. She warmed to the tropical intensity of their touch, from the skin on down into the center of her where she suddenly felt desperately in need of warming.

"Since you are speaking on your own behalf," Santos said, with unmistakable sarcasm this time, "maybe you can tell me why the perpetrator appears to have been in your room when the victim encountered him."

"In my room?"

"You're in . . . " Santos again consulted his notepad. "Second floor, front left?"

"That's right."

"According to my officers, there are no signs of disturbance in any of the other rooms, but it looks like there was quite a disturbance in yours."

"I don't know why that would be."

Taylor was confused. Why would a thief single out her room? She hadn't brought any valuables with her to Key West. This time, she was relieved when Des intervened.

"Isn't Miss Bissett's room off the veranda?" he asked. "Maybe the guy climbed in that way. April Jane could have heard him and gone up to investigate. The struggle might have started up there and ended up down here when April Jane ran down to call the cops."

"Interesting theory," Santos said with something like a sneer. "Did you think that up all by yourself, or do you have an inside source of information I should know about?''

"I was making the point that the guy could just have happened to come in through Taylor's room."

"Maybe."

Santos was looking Taylor over again. She might have been unsettled by that, but her attention seemed to be stuck on the way her name sounded when Des spoke it and how that sound spread over her like heat, the same way the touch of his gaze had done. Once again, she told herself that such thoughts were only the effects of exhaustion on her overtaxed mind. Unfortunately, she wasn't as sure that was true as she would have preferred to be.

"What makes you think there was a struggle?" Santos was asking Des. "I only said there were signs of a disturbance."

"I assumed you were talking about the same kind of thing as out there." Des gestured toward the entryway with its shattered lamp and general disarray. "That looks like the scene of a struggle to me. Besides, I knew April Jane. She would have put up a fight, and she was strong enough to give the guy a pretty hard time."

Taylor had to agree. April Jane hadn't come across as a woman who would sit still for being pushed around, or for letting somebody rob the place, either.

"What about you, Miss Bissett?" Santos asked. "Do you think the perpetrator just happened to be in your room when the victim found him and decided to give him a hard time, like Des says?"

Hearing April Jane repeatedly referred to as a victim brought the body bag and the city morgue to Taylor's mind once more. She swallowed the lump of sudden grief in her throat.

She hadn't known April Jane Cooney personally, but the woman had to have deserved something better than to be a live human being one minute and a victim the next. The true horror of what had happened here tonight was beginning to impress itself upon Taylor. She was seized by a terror that felt familiar somehow. Why familiar? She had experienced very little violence in her life. Yet, this deep-down fear had been with her before. It had been with her in her dreams.

"Miss Bissett, is there some reason you don't want to answer my question?" Santos was studying her with continued interest.

"What was the question again?"

"Do you think that the perpetrator just happened to be in your room?"

"I can't think of any other explanation." Actually, she couldn't think much of anything right now. "Detective Santos, would it be possible to continue this in the morning? I've had an exhausting day."

"Murder can do that to you." Santos was at it with the sarcasm again. "By the way, do you have somewhere else to stay? This place will have to be closed down, at least for the next few nights."

Taylor searched for an answer. She didn't really know anybody here in the Keys. She didn't know the hotels either. And, she didn't want to stay at Stormley. She wasn't ready for that yet.

"You can come to my place," Des said.

Santos glanced back and forth between them with obvious interest. For the moment, Taylor couldn't think what to say, especially since the suggestion had tripped loose that flutter in her heart she'd felt earlier.

"There's a room at the Beachcomber over the café," Des said. "It's quite comfortable and very private."

He'd emphasized the privacy part. Taylor wondered if his offer might be her only recourse. She thought of asking Santos if he had any recommendations. She was wavering between taking a chance that he'd offer her a cot in the local jail and taking a chance on Des's invitation when a flurry of motion turned everyone's attention toward the door.

The woman who had swept in was dressed all in white, from her turbanned head to her slippered feet. Her clothes appeared to swirl around her—a loose tunic top, full-legged trousers and a kind of shawl or train draped over her shoulder—all in soft, mobile fabrics. Her skin was light by Key West standards, but brightened by dramatic makeup, as were her very round eyes, which were almost as dark as Detective Santos's.

"My dear child," she exclaimed as she advanced on Taylor with open arms.

Santos stepped into the path of this swirling, white onslaught. "Mrs. Starling," he said. "I believe we've met."

"Of course," she replied. "I have met everyone on this island."

Jethro appeared in the doorway, confirming Taylor's guess that this woman was Winona Starling.

"May I ask what you're doing here?" Santos inquired.

"I have come to the rescue of this beleaguered young woman," Winona pronounced. "It is what my dear friend Netta would have wished."

Taylor had spent entirely too much of her life being hovered over and protected and rescued. She had vowed that wasn't going to happen anymore, but right now that vow felt less crucial than usual. She did her best to ignore the twinge of regret that it wouldn't be Des Maxwell's brown, muscled wing under which she would find shelter from what was left of this harrowing night.

## Chapter Four

Folds of dark trees, rolling and rippling, soft as velvet on her body. Sliding over her, along her skin, clinging to the roundness of her breasts, catching on the hard points of her nipples. Fingers of leaves, satin-smooth, slipping between her thighs, whispering there till a moan rose in her throat and her body rose to meet the lover.

In the background, like a rising wind, another moan, repeated in rhythm, first too faintly to be understood, then louder, *Danger. Danger. Danger.* Something spoke in her mind for a breath of a moment of her having heard that warning rhythm before. But that thought was being rapidly swallowed by sensations so intense that there was no possibility of thought left. The warning rhythm remained, but only as an echo now, far off at the edge of her beyond the sensations. At the center of her there was no longer room for anything other than the lover.

The leaves had suddenly turned to flesh. They were his fingers now, opening her wide and wider while she drew deep breaths, as deep as the probe of his touch. He moved astride her and plunged inside. She arched to meet him with a cry of triumph and pleading. They rode one another, desperate and groaning. The power of their thrusting slapped the bed against the wall to punctuate their passion—*thump, thump, thump*—drowning out even the faint remaining echo of the danger warning...

*Thump, thump, thump.*

Knock, knock, knock.

The sound was transforming yet again, to become different but the same. Taylor knew the ache deep inside her was real, but the man had melted away in the light that greeted her fluttering eyelids. He had been a dream. She could barely stand to discover that, the ache of missing him was so strong and torturing. The velvet leaves and folding trees retreated as well. Only the sound remained.

Knock, knock, knock.

Taylor's mind began to understand where she was—in a guest bedroom of the Starling house. Yet, part of her longed to stay, if even for only a moment more, in the place of undulating leaves and plunging passion. The cool of the air conditioner chilled the damp places on her body and banished the warm satin that had stroked her skin only an instant ago. Still, the mood of it was with her. She had been making love with a man of power and lust. She even knew who that man was. It had been a long time since she'd made love in real life. Because of that, she had turned herself off till she seemed not to care much anymore.

One night in the tropics, and she was being tormented by erotic dreams of—

The knocking was more insistent now. Taylor's gradually clearing mind followed the cadence of it to the wide doors, and through them onto what she guessed must be another veranda. There had been a veranda off her room at the guesthouse, but she wasn't there now. The colors were different in this room—creamy-golden walls and doorways, rich floral patterns in the bedding and on the floors. A stained-glass skylight echoed those patterns in its design, refracting the morning light into pools of color along the walls. Winona Starling was obviously a woman of sensuous tastes. The thought nudged the longing ache to sharpness again. Taylor sat up straight from the rumpled pillows, intending that rapid movement to dispel the last vestiges of the dream as she calmed her still-ragged breath toward its normal pace. At this new angle, she could make out the figure behind the slanted slats of the wooden blinds at the veranda doors. She almost fell back onto the pillows in surprise.

"Oh, no," she gasped, though something inside her was saying quite the opposite.

It was the man from her dream. There was no mistaking Des Maxwell's silhouette. She knew instantly who he was. She didn't know why he was here. She would have to answer his knock to find out. It was also the only way to keep him from waking the rest of the house. But maybe that would be best. Then Jethro or someone would send Des away. Meanwhile, the warning rhythm from her dream had returned. Its chant of *danger, danger, danger* droned beneath her thoughts. Still, as her head cleared she knew she didn't really want a scene involving the entire household. She'd had enough of scenes last night. She eased out of bed and tiptoed to the veranda door.

"What are you doing here?" she whispered through the space between the blind and doorframe.

"I can't hear you," Des said, more loudly than she would have preferred.

She suspected he wasn't telling the truth. After all, she could hear *him*. Why wouldn't he be able to hear her? She also suspected he wasn't going to go away without seeing her face-to-face. Maybe she would have a better chance of getting rid of him that way. She unlocked the door but kept her body behind the closed blinds that covered the glass. She was very aware that her nipples were still visibly aroused beneath the oversize, white T-shirt that Winona had taken for Taylor, along with a change of clothes, from the guesthouse. She definitely didn't want him to see that. Just considering the possibility made her nipples harder still.

Taylor edged the door open a crack and was greeted by the soft, warm scent of the Key West morning. The sun was up, and already brighter than on the sunniest of northern New York days. She was tempted to throw the door wide and be embraced by the fragrance of jasmine and frangipani from Winona's garden arbor. Taylor had longed for the exhilaration of pure freedom much of her life. In this first instant of her first tropical morning, she felt the proximity of that freedom sweep over her. Then, Des Maxwell stepped across her line of vision through the crack in the doorway, and the sensation disappeared.

"I apologize for waking you up," he said.

She put her finger to her lips to shush him into speaking more quietly. The sun might be up and bright, but the hour was early. Roosters crowed at the dawn somewhere in the distance. Before she could ask him what he wanted, he went on, but in a whisper this time.

"I didn't want you to miss your first morning here. I thought you might sleep through it." He hesitated a moment, as if just now realizing he might have judged the situation wrong. "And I thought you might want to get your stuff out of the guesthouse, at least anything you don't want the cops pawing through."

Taylor had been about to scold him for disturbing her so early after yesterday being such a grueling day for her, but what he was saying made sense. Besides, she agreed with him. She wouldn't be able to go back to sleep, anyway. The warning of danger from her dream tried to intervene upon that thought but she pushed it aside.

"I would like to get my things," she said.

"You might also like to eat something. I have croissants in my car. There's a place over on Duval that makes them fresh. They're the best this side of New Orleans."

The mention of food reminded Taylor of how long it had been since she'd eaten last. Late yesterday afternoon on the plane, which felt like very long ago indeed. The rumbling in her stomach agreed. She was definitely hungry. Still, she hesitated as another recollection of her dream returned, the memory of another kind of hunger. She might have fantasized about Maxwell in the most intimate of ways, but she didn't really know him. This early morning visit smacked somewhat of the bizarre. She did have serious questions about his relationship with Netta. It occurred to Taylor that he might be trying to work the same spell on her that had charmed her aging aunt. Taylor's still-damp body might be more vulnerable to those charms than her will to resist was strong. Perhaps it would be wise to keep a safe distance from Des Maxwell, at least until she felt more her usual in-control self than she did at this moment. She didn't know what to do, which way to choose—another uncharacteristic state for her to be in.

"We could go to the Key Westian," he was saying, "then drive up to the beach for a little breakfast."

"Wait a minute." Something had suddenly occurred to her. "Didn't the police say they were sealing the guesthouse?"

"We can get past that."

Taylor hesitated.

"Aren't you curious to see whether the guy who killed April Jane might have had some special reason to be in your room, after all?'' Des asked. ''The cops suggested that could be the case. Remember?''

Taylor did remember that, and she was definitely curious about it.

''I figured we'd be smart to go there early, before anybody's around,'' Des said. ''Less chance of being stopped that way.''

Taylor nodded. He was right, or maybe she merely couldn't think of a good argument this early in the morning. The soft air from the veranda had cooled her body from the frenzy of her dream. More practical considerations were supplanting her qualms about being alone with Des Maxwell. She could surely govern her emotions as successfully with him as she always had with other men. She ignored the danger warning yet again.

''I'll get dressed and be with you in a few minutes,'' she said.

''You can come out this way,'' he said, indicating the end of the veranda. ''There are stairs around the corner of the house and a path to the street. I'm parked out there in the red Jeep.''

She might have known he'd have a car like that. Where she came from, mostly oversexed adolescents drove Jeeps, especially red ones.

DES HAD the T-top on the Jeep. All of a sudden, he wasn't sure that had been the right choice. Maybe it would be too breezy for her in the open air. He thought of her full, wavy hair, how it had haloed her face last night in curling strands against her long, white neck. Her hair had been wilder a few moments ago. Even through the narrow door opening he could see how tossed and tousled she was. The memory of that wildness, along with the bright flush of her cheeks from sleep, flashed through

him now with an intensity that sped straight to his groin.
He'd felt the same stab of lust on the veranda, at the first
glimpse of her misty blue eyes, so sultry in their sleepy
softness. He'd had to hold himself back from shoving
through the door and grabbing her. He couldn't remember ever having the urge to put his hands on a woman
come over him so strong. Still, she didn't strike him as the
kind of woman you grabbed.

But what kind of woman was she? Des smiled at the
question and at himself. Obviously, she had to be the
kind of woman who could get him out of bed at dawn
and off to the Croissanterie before anybody was around
but the bird-watchers. The buttery aroma from the
pasteboard box on the back seat enticed him, but Taylor
Bissett had been the real enticement. For what felt like
the hundredth time this morning, Des asked himself what
was going on with him, anyway. He didn't run after
women. He didn't have to. They generally came after
him. He didn't kid himself that they thought of him as
some kind of stud. He figured his general lack of interest turned them on. Sandra had told him that. He'd
married her thinking she could break through the wall
he'd had around him for so long. They'd grown to be
friends but nothing more. The deep parts of him remained untouched, no matter how much he'd wished
them not only touched but overwhelmed.

Sandra said once that he reminded her of a conch shell,
spiny hard outside with secret folds inside where he kept
his heart tucked into the place nobody could reach. Sandra had a poetic nature and said things like that sometimes. When they finally called it quits, she claimed she
had no regrets, except maybe for the time he'd taken out
of the middle of her life. Des regretted that, too. He never
wanted to hurt her. He had only hoped to make himself

feel something intensely and, eventually, to find the loving family he had never known. Well, he felt something intense right now, though he couldn't yet put words to what exactly it might be.

"More than lust. Less than love." Had that been a line from one of Sandra's poems?

Taylor emerged from the pathway between clumps of flowering shrubbery, and all thinking of anything but her and the way she looked vanished from Des's mind. He would have liked to call to her to stand still for a moment, framed by the colorful blossoms. She was pale by contrast, but hardly pallid. Her features were more vivid to him than the reddest petals. She walked into the sunlight that touched her winter-white skin and made it luminous. Her shoulders were bare except for the straps of her tank top. He would have to make sure she put on sunblock or a jacket as protection from the mounting sun. He would rather put his arms around her and shield her with himself, but sunblock would probably have to do.

She had walked almost close enough for him to make out the misty blue of her eyes. Then, she pulled a pair of dark-tinted sunglasses from the pocket of her long, full skirt and put them on. "Don't do that!" he wanted to cry out. Instead, he said, "You're very tropical this morning. I'd have thought you'd need to do some shopping before you got to look so Key West."

"We have summer where I come from," she said with a less-than-summery smile.

*Damn!* he swore at himself. That had been the wrong thing to say. He had managed to put his foot in his mouth with his first step.

Speaking of feet, as she climbed into the Jeep he saw that she was wearing sandals made of leather straps. Her toes were clearly visible, including their pink-coral nails. She polishes her toenails! he thought. The discovery caught in his throat and almost made him groan. She seemed so proper, and painted toenails had always struck him as very sensual. They hid under a woman's shoes and stockings, like a slightly racy secret. They made him wonder what other secrets there might be beneath her breezy clothes. He particularly wondered about the parts that might be tinted as pink and coral as her toes.

"There's sunblock in the glove compartment. I think you might need it," he said, wishing he could say much more, while also telling himself to keep cool. Keeping cool had always been his modus operandi, after all.

"I brought my own lotion," she said, tapping the small shoulder bag she was carrying. "As I said, we have summer where I come from, and sun too."

*Not sun like this,* he wanted to say but didn't. He could already sense she liked to do things for herself. Desiree had been that way, too.

The thought dropped like a stone to Des's gut. Had he inadvertently stumbled upon the key to what was really going on here this morning? Could he be transferring his adolescent admiration of the mother to her daughter? That might explain why she'd gotten under his skin so fast. He'd better slow down and take some time to check out his own feelings, especially since he was not accustomed to letting himself know he had any. A retreat into the conch shell appeared to be definitely in order, at least until he had sorted things out.

Meanwhile, Taylor had been examining the houses, mostly white but in a mix of sizes and architectural styles, as they drove up Elizabeth Street. "What lovely homes," she said. "I had no idea Key West was so beautiful."

"You don't remember very much of it, do you?"

"No, I don't."

"You were old enough to remember when you left here."

"That's what you and Jethro have been telling me."

She gripped her purse in one hand and nervously twiddled the strap with the other. Des could see how uneasy this subject made her. He couldn't resist the urge to find out more about that and about the mystery of her past.

"How come you never came back here to the Keys?"

"Key West was always described to me as somewhere I wouldn't want to be. Terrible things happened to my family here. Besides that, my aunt told me it was a trashy place, a honky-tonk town full of drunks and nothing more."

"Your aunt was wrong."

"You really love it here, don't you?" She turned to look at him. He wished he could see the expression in her eyes behind her dark glasses.

"This is the closest I'll probably ever come to heaven. I'm sure of that," he said, thinking that having her around might bring heaven closer still. "Of course, you have to get off lower Duval Street if you don't like the honky-tonk your aunt told you about. She was right about that much. That part of town is bars and booze and wall-to-wall tourists, especially after dark."

"That's where the Beachcomber is."

"Right."

"So, you must like honky-tonks."

"I like my place and the people who come in there. I own the café next door too."

They turned onto Truman Avenue, heading west. He picked up speed a little, and the breeze lifted her honey-colored hair from her milky shoulders. Des was glad he'd left the T-top on the Jeep after all.

"Are you telling me that your Aunt Netta discouraged you from coming, even for a visit? She loved it here."

Taylor appeared to be studying him from behind her dark glasses. "Maybe Aunt Netta did love it here. She just didn't love the idea of *me* here."

"How come your aunts cared so much about that in the first place?"

Taylor looked away again, out of the window on her side of the car. "They cared about everything I did," she said in a tone he couldn't quite interpret. "They were very protective of me."

"I see."

He could guess that they wanted to protect her from the horrible memory of how her mother died, especially if there had been any truth to the rumors about Taylor's role in that death. If she really had started that fire, the guilt could be unbearable. He wanted to ask Taylor about that, but driving down the street wasn't the place for that conversation. They drove the remaining blocks in silence, with Taylor continuing to stare out the window and away from Des.

THEY PARKED on Virginia Street, the block north of Amelia and running parallel to it. The street looked different in the daylight, seedier than Taylor remembered it. Even so, she recognized this as the block where she had emerged from the trellis walk behind the guesthouse on her way to the Beachcomber last night. She would have liked to ask Des how he knew this back way, but if she started questioning him he might get back to questioning her also. She didn't want that. There were too many answers she didn't really have.

Why had Pearl and Netta been so adamant about keeping her away from this place? Why had she gone along with them? It had seemed natural that she should at the time. She recalled even feeling relieved, as if her aunts' opposition had saved Taylor from the burden of a ponderous decision, or maybe from the consequences of it. Why had all of that not bothered her more when it was happening? She never wanted to cause her aunts undue worry, but Taylor wasn't a pushover. She'd managed to live her own life despite their hovering. She hadn't put up a fuss over coming to Key West because she hadn't wanted to. But why was that?

Des held the door open, and Taylor stepped down out of the Jeep. She was happy to have a reason to stop tormenting herself. They walked directly to the opening in the greenery that marked the path behind the Key Westian. In the daylight, Taylor could see that the foliage wasn't as dense along the path as it had appeared to be in the dark. Gaps were visible now between the trees and bushes, even where they bordered the slatted trellis. Somebody could very possibly have watched her from there last night as she dashed through here to Virginia Street. Taylor shuddered at the thought. She must have moaned aloud, because Des turned and looked at her in a way she couldn't quite define.

"Are you okay?" he asked. "Maybe it's not such a good idea to be coming back here, after all."

"I'm fine, and I want to be here," she said emphatically.

Why was it that everywhere she went somebody was hovering over her and worrying about her? She wasn't the kind of person who wanted or needed that. In fact, she could barely stand it. Now, a virtual stranger was getting into the act.

Des pushed on the back door once, but it didn't budge. Taylor remembered the safety bar and that the door locked itself from inside. He didn't bother to try the door a second time, as if he might also have suddenly remembered the self-lock bar. Then again, maybe she was being overly suspicious. Still, she couldn't help wondering once again just how familiar Des might be with this guesthouse.

The Key Westian obviously wasn't one of the most prominent establishments in town, or in one of the most notable neighborhoods. Taylor had already come to that conclusion from her brief travels last night and this morning. Why would Des know anything at all about this particular guesthouse? Taylor had also concluded, from studying her map on the flight down here, that this was really a very small town. And maybe the locals all tended to know each other. Maybe Des and April had been even more closely acquainted than that. She had been an attractive woman. Taylor told herself she didn't feel a pang of something almost like jealousy at the thought of them together.

On second thought, if April Jane and Des had that kind of relationship, wouldn't he have been more emotionally upset by her death than he seemed to be? Taylor watched Des slide open the window nearest the back door of the guesthouse. If it bothered him to be breaking into a police-restricted area, he didn't show any signs of that concern. He was a cool customer all right. Maybe he wouldn't have betrayed signs of being upset over April, either. Or maybe he simply didn't care.

"Wait here," Des said as he prepared to hoist himself through the window opening. "I'll unlock the door."

Still cool as a cucumber. Taylor felt some of that chill herself. As she had told herself earlier this morning, she didn't really know anything about this man. In fact, that impassive facade of his made her wonder what he might be hiding. Yet, she was creeping through solitary back yards with him. She was even about to go inside a deserted building with him. She glanced around at what she could see of the neighboring yards beyond the high bamboo fence that blocked off the Key Westian property. This must be an outdoor lounging space for guests. There were two white-painted wrought-iron-and-glass tables with matching chairs clustered around them under the trees. The fence was probably to keep this area private. Taylor couldn't see a single soul in any direction. She and Des were definitely alone here. The back door opened, and he beckoned her to come inside. She didn't move. She wasn't sure what she should do.

"Come on," he said in a whisper loud enough for her to hear, "before somebody sees us out here."

Her sensible side, long conditioned toward caution by Aunt Pearl's training and example, told Taylor she shouldn't be alone in a vulnerable situation with a man she didn't know. Another side of her, which had grown steadily in influence since Pearl's death, had long since tired of being cautious. More than once in these past months, Taylor had suspected that her fledgling recklessness might get her into trouble someday. As she walked toward Des and the open door, it occurred to her that someday could be now.

# Chapter Five

Des held out his hand to Taylor who was still hesitating at the back door of the guesthouse. "Come on in," he said, more softly than before. "It will be all right."

He took her hand. Her palm met his as his fingers closed around her own. In a flash, a powerful sensation coursed through her. The heat of that sensation seemed to melt them into each other through every pore where her flesh touched his. She felt she couldn't break away, as if she were held to him by an irresistible force. She thought he might pull her to him and crush her mouth with his. Her heart raced.

Then, in the next instant, Taylor knew it was only a fantasy. In reality, he was holding her hand very gently and only trying to urge her into the building before somebody saw them here. She withdrew her hand from his and walked past him into the guesthouse. She wasn't certain that was the smart thing to do, but she had to move out of the spotlight of his gaze, glaring down at her and perhaps detecting what she had been thinking only a second ago. She turned toward the inside stairs without looking back at him and concentrated on being businesslike.

Taylor remembered last night when she had crept down these same stairs, feeling like a sixteen-year-old breaking curfew. Right now she felt more like a criminal than an adolescent on a spree. They weren't supposed to be here. Thinking of the reason for that brought a catch to her throat. There had been a murder here last night, only one floor and the length of a hallway from where she stood at this very moment at the top of the stairs. She fitted her key into the door of the room that had been hers last night but was now part of a crime-scene investigation. She couldn't imagine how anything connected with her might be relevant to a murder. Then Des pushed the door open, and suddenly she wasn't so sure.

Taylor gasped at the disarray. The bed had been completely stripped. Bedclothes lay around it in tumbled heaps on the floor, and the mattress was pulled askew, half on and half off the bed frame. The drawers of the dresser and bureau were wide open, their contents obviously rifled through. Taylor's clothes had been tossed out of the closet where she'd hung them up last night before going out. She stared from the bed to the dresser to the closet and back again, trying to make her brain register what had happened here.

For the first time, it occurred to Taylor that maybe she ought to be frightened. What if she had been here when the intruder came in? She might very well have gone to bed immediately after her arrival. She'd certainly had a long, exhausting day and should have been ready for sleep. She had been too keyed up for that and eager to get a look at Des Maxwell, too. She didn't like to think that an excess of adrenaline and some curiosity were all that had stood between her and ending up tumbled on this floor along with the bedding.

"Are you okay?"

When Taylor gasped in dismay, she had also taken a step backward directly into Des's path. He took her shoulders gently in his warm hands and turned her to face him.

"Are you all right?" he repeated, searching her face as if he might find an answer there.

*No, I'm not the least bit all right,* she longed to cry out. Instead, she only breathed a long sigh. This was all getting to be too much for her—yesterday, last night, now this morning—one shock after another. Des must have felt that anguish in her and been moved by it, because he put his arms around her and drew her to him in what began as a comforting embrace. She even thought she heard him making soft sounds in his throat to calm her. She couldn't be sure about that, because of the sudden rush of emotion that drowned out everything else she might be hearing or feeling.

Neither his embrace nor his soft words had what she assumed to be the intended effect. Taylor pressed closer to Des's broad body. She couldn't take her eyes off his lips, which were parted slightly and descending slowly toward hers. The moment was maddening. She longed to drag him to her, but she didn't move as the heat of desire burst forth and flooded through her.

At last, his mouth covered hers and she knew she had been imagining this kiss from the first moment she saw him. His lips were warm and insistent. He clasped her tightly against the hardness of his body. Her hands slipped up his arms to his shoulders and caressed the firm, full muscles that strained beneath his shirt. His tongue urged its way between her lips. For once in her life, Taylor didn't stop to think about how she would respond. She knew what she wanted, and it had nothing to do with the good sense and sound reason that had been drilled into her for as long as she could remember.

Taylor parted her lips to welcome him. She circled and caressed his tongue with her own, beyond thinking at the moment. She was being carried on a tide or a gust of prevailing wind into the very unfamiliar territory her aunt had warned against, beyond the boundaries of control. A small voice, probably Pearl's, told Taylor she should stop now, push him away and never let him touch her again. That voice of caution, which she had listened to and followed all of her life was little more than a whisper compared to the roar of passion rising inside her. Taylor knew as certainly as anything she had ever known that this unfamiliar territory was precisely what she wanted to explore.

When they finally moved apart, Des was the one who pulled away. "We can't do this now," he whispered as he held her at arm's length.

Taylor felt the sudden distance between them like a wave of icy water. With that cold blast came the shock of humiliation. What was she doing? She stepped backward out of his grasp.

"You need to check to see if anything is missing," Des said softly.

"What?" she asked, feeling suddenly as disordered as this room. Could he be talking about her pride and common sense? They had certainly deserted her for the few moments just past.

"You should check the room in case something was stolen," Des said. "Valuables. Jewelry, cash, that kind of thing." He sounded like his usual cool self again, as if their fiery kiss had never happened.

Taylor allowed herself only a second or two to reorient herself. "I had no jewelry or cash here to speak of. Nothing worth stealing, anyway."

That wasn't entirely true. She might be walking out of this room this morning minus something definitely worth accounting for, but it wasn't the kind of valuable he was talking about.

"Then they tore this place apart for nothing."

"Wait a minute." Taylor's mind was beginning to function again. She turned toward the bed. "I did have some papers."

The bed was still wedged tightly against the nightstand. Taylor walked over there, mildly surprised that she could move around without wobbling. A moment ago she wouldn't have been steady enough on her feet to cross the room on her own. She reached down between the bed and the nightstand. The portfolio was still there. She pulled it out and leafed through the contents.

"Everything is here," she said.

"Could that be what they were after?" Des asked. She noticed that he avoided looking directly into her eyes.

"These things wouldn't be of interest to anyone but me."

"Are you sure about that?"

Detective Santos had spoken from the doorway. He was dressed more casually than he had been last night, in an open-necked polo shirt and slacks with no jacket. However, Taylor didn't get the impression that he had also relaxed his vigilance.

"May I see that, please?" Santos walked into the room and held out his hand for the portfolio.

Taylor hesitated.

"You don't have to show him anything until he gets a search warrant," Des said, stepping between Taylor and the detective.

A moment ago, Taylor might have welcomed Des's protectiveness, the way she clung to remaining in his embrace. This situation was different. She touched Des's arm and moved him aside.

"A warrant won't be necessary," she said and handed Santos the portfolio.

He walked to the bed and sat down. He opened the portfolio and pulled out one piece of paper after another, checking each over then returning it to the case, until he came to the blue folder containing Netta's will. He spent more time on this item, studying the pages one by one, so slowly and carefully that Taylor began to feel like fidgeting from restlessness. Des, on the other hand, didn't appear to be the least bit impatient with the thoroughness of Santos's examination. Des was busy craning his neck to see the papers himself. Meanwhile, Taylor was growing impatient with both of these men who seemed so intent upon poking around in her private business.

"Is there something in particular you're looking for?" she asked.

Santos glanced up at her as if he might have registered the sharp edge in her tone. His dark eyes revealed nothing of what he might be thinking. He waited a long moment before answering.

"Actually, I may have found it." He folded the will slowly, carefully creasing the edges between his thumb and forefinger. He lifted the flap of the portfolio, as if to put the document inside. Instead, he tapped the folded paper on the corner of the flap as he continued to watch Taylor with the same enigmatic expression on his face.

"What have you found?" Taylor asked even more sharply than before.

"Most of these papers are about your aunt's house," he said.

"That's right."

"The same house that burned down twenty-some years ago."

"Not the same house," she said. "Another house built on the same spot."

Des had moved over next to her. She could feel some agitation in his manner, but he didn't speak.

"What do you remember about that fire?" Santos asked.

"Nothing," she said. "I wasn't there."

"You weren't?" Santos's interest had heightened enough to narrow his dark eyes into a stare lasered directly at her.

"No, I was not," Taylor snapped, no longer able to hide her impatience. "What does any of this have to do with April Jane Cooney's death? Isn't that what you're supposed to be investigating?"

"Why would *you* think your papers might have something to do with the murder?" Santos asked.

"I don't think any such thing."

"Wait just a damned minute here." Des stepped in front of Taylor once more. He put his hand behind him to keep her from pushing him aside again. "This has gone far enough, Santos. If you want to question Miss Bissett, you'll have to do it officially over at the station house with her lawyer present."

"I don't need a lawyer," Taylor began to protest until Des took hold of her arm and squeezed it.

The urgency of his grasp told her she should stop talking, even if she didn't want to. Reluctantly, she obeyed his signal. Common sense, so notably absent only minutes ago when she was locked in his embrace, now dictated that Des knew this territory and Detective Santos a lot better than she did. Maybe there was some justification for Des's urgency. She sighed her acquiescence, and he relaxed his grip on her arm.

Santos had watched this interchange. He might not have seen Des take her arm because that happened behind Des's back, out of the detective's line of vision. Still, she wouldn't be surprised if he guessed something like that had happened. He smiled. She wondered what else he might be guessing at about Des and her. Could he have been outside the door longer than she had assumed? Could he have heard the unmistakable sounds of their passionate kiss, or maybe even seen them through the crack at the doorjamb? Taylor did her best to suppress the urge to blush.

"I won't need Ms. Bissett for official questioning," Santos was saying. He slipped the will back inside the portfolio and closed the flap. "At least not today." He stood up and handed the portfolio to Taylor.

"Thank you," she said.

"Don't thank me." He was still smiling, still watching. "Thank your friend Mr. Maxwell. If he hadn't been here to give you your cues, you and I might still be comparing memories."

"I don't need anybody to give me cues." Taylor pulled her arm away from Des before he could give it another squeeze.

"Maybe you do. Maybe you don't," Santos said. "What you definitely need is to plan on staying in Key West till this investigation is completed."

"Why does she have to do that?" Des asked. "Is she a suspect?"

Taylor had been about to point out that she could ask her own questions without Des's help. His suggestion that she might be a police suspect froze the words in her throat.

"A suspect for what?" Santos had asked what Taylor wanted to know.

Des didn't answer.

"What could I possibly be suspected of?" Taylor turned Santos's question back at him.

"What have you got?" he responded.

"What is that supposed to mean?" Taylor could hardly believe she was speaking so disrespectfully to a police officer. That simply wasn't like her.

Santos walked past them to the doorway. He glanced over his shoulder, first at Des and then at Taylor. "Ask Elvis. Or was it Brando?" Santos said and walked out of the room.

Taylor made a move to go after him, but Des stopped her. "I want to ask him what he's talking about. What could Elvis Presley and Marlon Brando possibly have to do with me?" she asked, struggling against Des, who was holding her by the arms.

"I think he's talking about something one of them is supposed to have said."

Taylor stopped struggling. "What was that?"

"I can't remember who said it either, but the story goes that somebody asked one or the other of them what he was rebelling against and the answer was, 'What have you got?', meaning he was rebelling against everything."

"So Detective Santos was making a joke? I'm surprised to hear he has a sense of humor."

Des looked at the empty doorway for a moment then back into Taylor's eyes. "He doesn't," he said.

THE SIGN SAID Higgs Beach. The sand bore the indentations of heavy foot traffic, but the first sun worshippers of the day hadn't yet arrived. Des parked the Jeep just off the highway at the edge of the beach. The Atlantic ocean stretched clear across the horizon in front of them, silver-blue and sparkling with points of dancing light in the yellow-white morning sun. Any other day, Taylor would have pulled off her sandals and walked barefoot to the shore. She imagined how the sand would feel between her toes and wondered if it would still be cool to the touch or already warming in the tropical sun. She might have found that out for herself, but she was too troubled right now to move from where she sat.

Des seemed to sense that and didn't disturb her. He busied himself with opening the bakery box from the back seat. The two croissants he took out were large and puffy. The delicate crust flaked easily as he set each on a napkin atop the deep dashboard, one on her side of the vehicle, one on his side. The rich, buttery aroma came to her along with the scent of the sea. Some memory of her former hunger stirred in her, especially when Des unscrewed the top from the widemouthed Thermos he had pulled from beneath his seat and the smell of coffee overpowered both pastries and ocean.

"Café au lait?" he asked as he poured the pale, foamy liquid into a metal cup.

Taylor didn't speak. She only nodded a little and tried to smile as she took the cup from his hand.

"You really should try the croissants," he said. "They're delicious, and it must be a long time since you've eaten."

The solicitousness of his tone produced exactly the opposite effect in her than it probably should have. "If I want to eat, I will eat," she snapped. "I can take care of myself."

"I don't doubt that," Des said, only a little less solicitously. She could feel him studying her, even though she wasn't looking at him.

"I'm sorry," she said. "I know you're trying to be kind to me. I shouldn't jump all over you for it. I'm afraid I have a problem with people who think I need taking care of. It makes me feel suffocated." She turned to look at him. "Does that make any sense to you?"

"I suppose I can understand how somebody might feel that way. Being smothered by attention hasn't exactly been the experience of my life."

A cool distance had entered his tone. Taylor wondered what his experience of life might have been and if a man as carefully controlled as Des would be willing to talk about that experience much. Right now, however, she had a more pressing question to ask.

"What do you know about the Stormley fire?"

He watched her for a moment from behind his dark glasses. Then he sighed, deep and long, like letting out a breath he'd held for quite some time. "Just about everything," he said.

Taylor hadn't expected that. She pulled a chunk of feathery pastry from the croissant on the dashboard and put it in her mouth for something to do while she decided whether or not she really wanted to know "everything." The flavor spread over her tongue, as sensual as it was startling.

"You were right," she said. "This is delicious."

He had cocked his head quizzically to one side, as if he might know that she was avoiding something. "I'd tell you to try my coffee, if you weren't so touchy about being urged to eat."

Taylor could tell by his slow smile he meant that as a friendly tease rather than a taunt. "You made this?" she asked, lifting the cup.

"Every morning, sure as sunrise."

She tasted and was even more pleased than with the croissant. A hint of cinnamon and just strong enough.

"It's still hot," she said and was glad for the warmth as it began melting the constriction in her throat. She had been feeling the urge to cry ever since they left the Key Westian. Too much confusion, too little sleep were her best explanations for that feeling, and for something else . . .

"There's a special technique involved," he was saying. "You have to heat the milk to just the right temperature before pouring it together with the hot coffee into the cup." His voice was as warm and liquid as the process he was describing.

"I've seen that done," she said, wanting to let herself flow along with the spell of that voice, just as she had wanted to stay in his arms back at the guesthouse.

"Your Aunt Netta made coffee that way. She was the one who taught me."

Her aunt's name returned Taylor from her momentary reverie to the question she'd danced up to and then retreated from a few moments ago. Still, she was reluctant to abandon contemplation of being entranced by Des's voice.

"Tell me about the fire," she said, not because she wanted to, but because she had to.

"You don't remember any of it?"

Taylor hesitated. She knew that she was asking these things because of what she guessed Detective Santos was about to say this morning at the Key Westian. There was also what Jethro had told her last night about how old he remembered her to be when she was last in Key West as a child. She already suspected what they had both been getting at. For the flicker of an instant, she was gripped by the urge to jump out of the Jeep, run down the highway to the airport and fly back to her insulated life in the drafty rooms of northern New York. She waited for the instant to pass before she asked the most dangerous question of all.

"Should I remember?"

He didn't answer right away. She could feel the intensity of his gaze, but she couldn't actually see it. His dark glasses were in the way. She had to see his eyes when he spoke. That was suddenly very important to her. She fitted her coffee cup into the holder on the low hump between the car seats and reached with both hands to take off his glasses. She had eased them away from his face when he stopped her hands with his own.

"You were there," he said.

She had expected that was what he would say, but the reality of the words was no less a shock for being anticipated. He took his glasses from her grasp with one hand but kept hold of her with the other. She knew she was hanging on to him for dear life again, just as she had done earlier this morning, but as if to keep from slipping over the edge of something this time. She also knew somehow that he would hold her back from that precipice as long as she wanted to be held. Finally, she knew that the plunge was inevitable and might as well happen now. She pulled her hand from his, not abruptly but with resolve. She needed to hear what he had to say on her own, without the kind of shielding protection she had been blessed, or burdened, with all of her hovered-over life—at least as much of that life as she could recall.

"If I was there," she asked, "why don't I remember?"

The sun brought out golden lights in his green eyes. She could see the compassion there softening his usual cool gaze, just as he had softened toward her at the guesthouse. She could also see that he wanted to take her in his arms once more. She wondered why he didn't. Maybe he understood and respected her need to be strong right now. Whatever his reason, he kept his distance, leaning against the door on his side of the Jeep. She was grateful for that.

"Why don't I remember something as unforgettable as the fire that destroyed my home and killed my mother?"

"I don't know the answer to that for sure," he said. "But I think Winona Starling might."

Taylor was struck silent for a moment. What did Winona Starling have to do with this? In that moment of Taylor's surprise, Des tossed what was left of his coffee out of the window and turned the ignition key on the steering column. She didn't have to ask where they were going.

THE WHITE HOUSE on Elizabeth Street still looked as quiet and asleep as it had when Taylor left it less than two hours ago. Under other circumstances, she might have tiptoed to ner room and waited for her hostess to make the first move before confronting her with such gloomy subjects on a lovely morning. But Taylor had questions that pressed for answers, pressed her past courtesy to urgency. She went straight to the front door. When she found it unlocked, she went directly inside, and she didn't tiptoe.

The foyer and the rooms off it were in shadow from the shutters that shielded all windows from the heat of the sun. The only morning light came from the far end of the central hallway that ran from front veranda to back veranda. Taylor headed toward that light. She pushed through the wide screened door onto a deep porch that spanned the width of the house.

Canvas shade curtains of dark green-and-white stripes had been rolled down partway at each end of the portico for privacy. A soft breeze whispered through the opening between the bamboo batten at the bottom of the shade and the white balustrade that surrounded the veranda, except in the space where three wide steps led down to the luxuriant lawn and garden. The genteel grace of the scene was much at odds with Taylor's agitated state of mind.

"Good morning, my dear."

Winona Starling was seated at a round breakfast table covered by a cloth and china, all as immaculately white as the caftan she wore. Her hair was hidden, as it had been the night before. This morning she was wearing a wide-brimmed hat instead of a turban. The hat was white with a purple chiffon sash tied around it as a hatband and knotted in the back to trail down behind her. That sash was the only touch of color in the scene, other than the flowers in the white vase on the table and the red of Winona's lips.

"What is he doing here?" Winona asked in a none-too-genteel or graceful tone.

Taylor turned toward the direction of Winona's stare. Des had followed Taylor through the house and onto the veranda, but she hadn't noticed him doing that. She was too engrossed in the urgency of her mission to notice much of anything. The questions that had surfaced since her arrival here yesterday, along with all those never entirely formed, which had haunted her most of her life, suddenly demanded instant satisfaction. She felt as if she must not delay that satisfaction a moment longer. She also felt, with a certainty she couldn't explain, that when Des said Winona Starling might know the answers to at least some of Taylor's confusion, he was right.

"I don't want him here," Winona said. "He is not my friend, and only my friends are welcome in my house."

She said that in the tone of a pronouncement, as if nothing but compliance were possible. Taylor, if she thought about it for a moment, would have preferred Des to stay. He had become a kind of unexpected and unlikely ally. The same instinct that told her Winona held the key to at least part of the mystery of the past also told Taylor that Des could guide her through the thorny passages of that labyrinth. Despite her resolve to face on her own whatever life and the future might bring, she sensed that the murky recesses of times gone by could be much more perilous territory. She would have welcomed Des's company for this particular journey, but Winona's manner made it clear that was not a choice.

"Des, I need to speak with Mrs. Starling alone," Taylor said. "You had better go."

He didn't move. Standing there in his jeans and T-shirt, with his feet planted resolutely apart, he reminded Taylor of a tree rooted on this veranda, as solid as any northern New York oak.

"Please, Des," she said. "I would rather do this by myself."

That wasn't entirely true, but she understood that only her insistence was likely to dislodge this particular mighty oak.

"If you say so," he finally agreed, but not without adding, "I'll be at the Beachcomber if you need me."

Then he was gone. Taylor turned to face Winona and whatever she would reveal.

BAHAMA VILLAGE was west of Whitehead Street. The differences here from the rest of the island were subtle but always apparent and welcome to Des. He had spent a good deal of time in the Village as a boy, at the same house he was headed for now. The sidewalks were dusty and sunbaked. A nearby mural celebrated Caribbean life in bright, primary colors. Cocks crowed here throughout the day. A particularly handsome specimen emerged from under a bush to watch Des step down from the Jeep where he had parked near the corner of Thomas Street. The rooster's dark, beady eyes looked Des over as if from a great height. Then the bird turned with an unimpressed squawk and strutted away.

Violetta Ramone had been the housekeeper at Stormley when Desiree Bissett was alive. Violetta's house on the corner of Thomas and Olivia Streets had been Des's refuge on many occasions after Desiree died. He'd been looking for trouble in those years, anything on which to vent his anger. He was a rebel teen all the way, but it had only been a pose. He knew that now. He had to stay that angry on the outside so nobody would see the pain on the inside from the loss of the mother-protector Desiree had been for him. It wasn't a good idea to let anyone know you were hurting. That meant you were soft somewhere, ready to be picked off. Des saw life that way more than ever after Desiree was no longer around to urge such thinking out of his head. So, he stayed hard-shelled and in trouble. When that trouble got too far out of hand he would come here to Violetta's for spicy chicken and homey comfort.

The house was cottage-size, one story surrounded by a white picket fence and full, green shrubbery. There were sun shutters on the windows and a low sitting porch across the front. No matter how often the rest of the houses on the street might go in and out of disrepair, Violetta's was always freshly painted, white and shining in the sun. It was shining that way today, like a beacon beckoning Des to put into harbor and rest at anchor. He might have heeded that call and let down his guard for a while if it hadn't been for the reason he was here.

Violetta came to the door with her arms already open to greet him. "Destiny Child," she said, calling him the pet name she had used since he was a boy. "If you aren't a sight to make my old eyes young."

Des let her enfold him in her sturdy, brown arms that barely reached around his chest. She was so much shorter than he was that he had to crouch to return her embrace. They stood for a long moment hugging hard, a longer moment than was usual for Des. Violetta would be sure to notice that. She noticed everything.

"What's troubling you, *chéri?*" she asked with a hint of the patois of the islands and the delta. She had lived in both of those places before settling in the Keys.

"I need you to talk to somebody for me," he said.

"And what would you want me talking about?"

They had walked through the house into the kitchen with its screened porch and the exotic perfume of the aromatic vegetables and cayenne that were the staples of Violetta's cuisine.

"I'd want you talking about the past." He lifted the lid from the white-speckled porcelain kettle simmering on the stove, the same kettle he'd been peeking into since he was a kid. "What's cooking?" he asked, just as he always did, taking a sniff deep enough to make his eyes water from the potent spices.

Violetta took the lid from his hand and slapped it back on the kettle. "Never you mind what I'm cooking. What part of the past do you mean to have me talking about, and who exactly am I supposed to be talking it to?"

Des had expected her to react this way. Violetta's mind was as sharp as a witch doctor's bite, as she would put it. She'd no doubt guessed that he was referring to Desiree and Stormley. Violetta didn't like to talk much about either.

"I need you to tell the truth about Stormley and the Bissetts to somebody who needs very badly to hear it," he said.

*"Mon Dieu."* Violetta faced the shrine to the Virgin on the wall in the corner and crossed herself quickly with her right hand.

There was a shrine like this in every room of Violetta's house, even in the bathroom, and the candles were lit day and night. Alongside the statue of the Blessed Mother, various mass cards, votive candle holders and crucifixes, Violetta also kept symbols of another faith—darker, more secret—that she refused to speak about, even in whispers. Des knew vaguely what those ribbons and small bones were about, but he had learned better than to ask more.

"Nothing about that time can do anybody any good by being dug up, now or ever," Violetta said.

She shooed Des to a chair at the Formica-topped table by the window. Years ago, he had built rows of shelves across this window for her. Pots lined the shelves, each with its own fragrant herb. The bottom shelves were cooking herbs. The middle shelves were medicinal herbs. The very top shelf she wouldn't explain, and those plants

weren't as pleasant in fragrance. Des had picked up
enough of Violetta's superstitions over the years to keep
him from sniffing that top shelf very deeply.

"I don't like thinking about back then any more than
you do, Violetta," he said as she poured coffee into the
hand-painted crockery bowl in front of him. "But you're
wrong about one thing. There is somebody who could be
done a lot of good by knowing what really happened at
Stormley."

"Who might this body be?"

Violetta had turned almost belligerent. Her ample
bosom rose high as she pulled her shoulders back and
looked down her nose at him as if she were towering
yards instead of inches above where he sat. Des told
himself he'd better proceed cautiously. With Violetta,
belligerence could signal an approaching temper surge.
He didn't want that. Her health wasn't what it had been
in her younger years. The doctor had told her that too
much agitation was bad for her heart. In Des's experience, Violetta losing her temper was the ultimate in agitation. He took her plump, smooth arm and held it gently
so she wouldn't dart away. He looked up into her face
and hoped she would see the urgency as well as the af-
fection in his eyes.

"Taylor Bissett is here on the island," he said softly.

"Oh, no," Violetta gasped and sank into the chair next
to Des's. "Taylor child, *ma petite chérie*. Why did she not
stay away as she was told to do?"

The look of distress on Violetta's usually cheerful face
couldn't help but cause Des alarm. "Why is it so important for her to stay away?"

"Oh, Destiny Child. It is not good for her here. *Nothing* is good for her here."

Des's natural skepticism warred with the concern caused by something in her voice that suggested more than just superstition.

"Tell me what you mean by that, Violetta. I need to know. She needs to know."

"There is only trouble here for her. There is even trouble in your heart for her, *chéri.*"

Des was taken aback by that. Violetta was a woman of uncanny insights. Could she know somehow what he was feeling for Taylor? But why would that mean trouble?

"You resented that child, lovely as she was," Violetta went on. "She was what you would have given anything to be, the babe of sweet Desiree's bosom."

Des did remember thinking of Taylor as a pest, when he had bothered to think about her at all. "I don't resent her now."

"I am most pleased to hear that. I am not most pleased to hear that the special child has come back here. So much was done to keep her away all these years, while the caring ones were in this world."

"Are you talking about her aunts?" Des had been listening to Violetta long enough to be able to interpret some of her ways of saying things.

"Yes, Destiny Child. God gave the aunts that work to do in life, to protect the special child."

"Is there some particular reason you call her that? The special child?"

"Oh, yes, indeed." Violetta glanced once more toward the corner shrine. "She had the light on her, like her mother. She was touched by God."

Des sighed his disappointment. He had hoped Violetta would tell him something real and important. Instead, this was just mumbo jumbo. She was talking about Taylor having powers of some kind. He had always been tolerant of Violetta's superstitions. Right now, however, he was feeling more impatient than understanding.

"I will speak to her as you ask," Violetta said, though she didn't sound eager to do it. "You are right this time. Truth is what that child needs. I must tell that truth as best I can and pray for only good to come of it."

Violetta clutched the spot between her breasts where Des knew from years of acquaintance she had hung a small, snakeskin bag beneath her muumuu. He could only guess what was in that bag, but he knew she was entreating its power now, as supplement to the power of the cross on a chain suspended higher and more visibly at her throat. A shiver ran through him. What if there was something to Violetta's superstitions after all? What if Taylor really needed that much power to keep her safe from the danger she could be in? He took a gulp of Violetta's coffee. The chicory edge was strong and dark, like the taste of dread and the sense of unbidden spirits in the air.

## Chapter Six

Winona had put on her sunglasses as she stared across the porch at Des. She still had them on now that he was gone, and Taylor would have liked to ask her to get rid of them. It wouldn't be polite to reach over and take them off as Taylor had done with Des earlier. She wasn't in a particularly courteous mood right now. In fact, she was feeling downright grumpy. Still, she wasn't ready to be openly belligerent, at least not quite yet. All Taylor knew was that the questions about her past had been mounting for two days now till their combined bulk threatened to bury her in confusion. She suspected Des could be correct in his opinion that Winona had at least some of the answers. It wouldn't make sense to alienate this information source, especially since there appeared to be few others. Nonetheless, Taylor couldn't help wondering how people down here figured each other out. At least that seemed to be a problem out-of-doors, where they all hid behind black glasses, hat brims and even gobs of sunscreen, like players in a masquerade.

"What is it that you feel so compelled to speak with me about, my dear?" Winona asked.

"I want to find out more about my childhood here on Key West. I have reason to believe you can help me do that."

"What specifically do you want to know?" There was no visible change in Winona's facial expression or tone. Of course, her eyes were hidden.

"I grew up believing I left here as little more than a baby. Now, I'm told I was actually six or seven years old. Is that true?"

"Let us determine entirely what it is you want to know before dealing with individual questions. That way we can seek out the truth of all at once." Still no alteration in her calmly modulated tone and noncommittal half smile.

Taylor recalled that Winona was some kind of therapist by profession. She certainly acted like one, enigmatic to a fault.

"What I really need to find out is why I don't remember those missing years here. If I was living on this island till I was six or seven years old, I should have retained some of those memories. Isn't that true?"

"Memory is a curious thing and most fascinating. It is, in fact, a particular interest of mine, especially the subject of memory repression."

"Do you mean when a person deliberately blocks out something from their past?"

"I would not refer to such behavior as being deliberate. That might make an individual feel responsible for, even guilty about, something over which he or she has no control."

"Then who is responsible?"

Winona smiled a bit wider. Taylor wished she could feel the warmth that smile was obviously meant to convey. Unfortunately, she was too agitated to register reassurance just yet.

"Most often," Winona said, "no one is responsible. We are speaking about involuntary psychological behavior. It simply happens."

"Is that what happened to me?"

Winona hesitated before answering, "Perhaps."

"What did happen to me? Do you know?"

"Actually, you were under my care then. Let me go to my office and find my journal for that period." Winona rose with a rippling of white material, like curtains gently moved by a breeze. "Then we will be certain to have the facts correct, without depending on my memory which can, of course, be as faulty at times as anyone else's."

She smiled once again before gliding across the porch and into the house, leaving Taylor to think about how difficult it was to imagine someone with such grace being faulty at anything. Meanwhile, the porch and the soft sunshine were pleasant and should have been relaxing, but Taylor was in no mood to relax. The minutes of waiting felt more like hours. She tried to be patient. Patience with inactivity had never been one of her virtues, even when she wasn't worked up as she was now. Her restlessness had begun as a child in northern New York. She could remember being so unsettled by that restlessness she thought she might perish from it.

Aunt Pearl had kept Taylor close to home most of the time, and there never seemed to be enough going on there to occupy the mind of an active little girl. Keeping her mind occupied had always seemed essential to Taylor. She had learned to invent activities to fill her thoughts, no matter how busy and sometimes lacking in real substance those activities might be. She had spent the rest of her life that way. She doubted she could stand it for long, here in the tropics where everything was geared much too low for her usual pace. Yet, she wondered, why was that so? Why did she find it almost impossible to relax, even in this luxuriant place where relaxation was such a natural part of life? Why could she never simply sit and let her thoughts drift wherever they might? It occurred to her that the problem might be precisely this—where those thoughts might drift to and what she would find there.

The house door opened, and Winona stepped out onto the porch. Taylor was relieved. She didn't like the direction her thoughts were already taking, into a realm of questions with no apparent answers. She had enough of those to deal with. She was happy to turn her attention to the hardbound ledger Winona was carrying. The faded fabric of its gray-green cover suggested that it could definitely have dated from Taylor's childhood.

"I regret that I cannot let you read my notes directly," Winona said as she sat and placed the volume on the table in front of her. "I have the cases of several patients besides yourself recorded here from that period. I would not care to risk violating their privacy in any way. I expect you understand that caution on my part."

"Yes, of course. I don't think I would want you to show anybody else confidential information about me, either."

"Precisely."

Winona removed her dark glasses and smiled again. This time Taylor could feel the warmth of that smile. In fact, the longer she gazed into Winona's eyes, the more powerful was the impression that this woman truly cared. Taylor actually did begin to relax a little within the comfort of that reassurance. For the first time in two days, she dared to think that everything could turn out right.

The gentle ebb and flow of Winona's voice suggested that might be true, and it was a suggestion Taylor was more than willing to embrace.

"Some of the things I am going to tell you will not be easy to hear," Winona said.

Taylor felt her short-lived sense of well-being begin to slip away until Winona's gentle touch on her arm stemmed the flow of that departure.

"Have no fear, my child," Winona said. "We will travel this memory path together. I will be at your side every step of the way, to help and to explain whatever may require explanation. You are not alone. You may be assured of that."

Taylor hadn't been spoken to in such a kind, soothing tone since Aunt Pearl died. The thought brought a small sob to Taylor's throat. Until this moment, she hadn't realized how much she missed being spoken to that way. Winona must have heard the sob, or sensed it, because she moved her touch from Taylor's arm to her hand. She let her fingers entwine with those of this woman who seemed suddenly so much older and wiser. Winona was speaking softly now, murmured words of comfort and support. It occurred to Taylor that maybe she could relax here, after all, and learn to fill her thoughts with something besides restlessness, especially with such a wise, gentle woman to teach her how.

AN HOUR OR SO LATER, Taylor wandered out onto Elizabeth Street when Winona wasn't looking. She had told Taylor to take a nap, and that was what she'd meant to do. Then, she found herself walking down the street with the white sun beating on her from twelve o'clock high. Tourists buzzed by on mopeds, pink and white and black ones. Taylor thought she might rent one too, but it was only a whimsical notion to distract herself from what she didn't want to think about. She would have been a collision waiting to happen in any vehicle right now. Dazed as she was feeling, walking was about as much as she could manage.

She told herself she had no specific destination, but that was only true on a conscious level. Her deeper instincts knew exactly where she needed to be. Still, she was on the block of Duval Street between Eaton and Caroline Streets and almost to the Beachcomber before she recognized where she was headed. The bar was already open with customers on several of the stools. The bartender might have smiled or even made a joke about her urgency, but he must have seen the bewilderment in her eyes because he simply directed her to Des immediately.

Des was in the café adjacent to the bar, an outdoor-indoor restaurant, which he also owned. Taylor had been surprised to hear that. She wouldn't have guessed him to be the restaurateur type. The café was a charming place. The tables in the courtyard were small and not too close together. More than half were filled with chatting customers as the lunch hour moved toward its busiest time. The table settings were of island design, with plates and cups painted in bright colors and patterns. Lush tropical flowers were everywhere, on the tables, in wide window boxes along the front of the café building, nearly covering the tall bamboo fence that bordered the courtyard and shielded it from the noise of the street.

The courtyard area centered around a huge banyan tree. Strings of pin-lights were twined among the branches, unlit now at the brightest part of the day but ready to create a romantic atmosphere at dusk and after. That thought brought Des back to mind. Suddenly, Taylor not only sensed but knew why she had come here. She

had felt the warmth of his embrace earlier today. She
wanted to feel that now. She needed almost desperately
to be in his arms and pressed against the firm certainty of
his body. She longed to lose herself in the oblivion of the
desire he made her feel. Whatever consternation that desire might cause would be of minor concern compared to
what she was now feeling.

But would he feel the same way about seeing her? Did
he know the things Winona had talked about? She said
they were the subject of public gossip. He must know.
Why hadn't he mentioned them? Taylor knew the answer to that question. He would have been hesitant to
bring up something so terrible. He might be direct and
even abrupt sometimes, but he didn't seem to be cruel.
He would have been more careful about her feelings than
to confront her with such a horrifying truth. Or, was she
crediting him with compassion he didn't feel? Could he
possibly find compassion in his heart for her after what
she was supposed to have done? Could anyone be that
generous, especially under these circumstances? She
doubted that she could. She was telling herself that she'd
made a mistake coming here to look for Des and she
should leave, when he appeared through the open doorway of the cafe.

He spotted her immediately and smiled, quickening his
pace toward her. It was too late for her to reconsider. She
could run away, of course, but it seemed she had done a
great deal of that in her life without even realizing it. The
time had come to stop running and face the consequences of the past, newly arrived to haunt her present
and create heaven knows what havoc of her future. She
was standing near the connecting wall between the
courtyard and the saloon. That wall was crisscrossed by
blossoming vines of sweet fragrance, but she couldn't

really appreciate their beauty or their scent at the moment. She sank into a chair at an empty table and watched Des's inevitable approach.

"Just in time for lunch. May I tell you about our specials today?" he asked with a small bow.

She could see that the other tables were being attended by female employees in jeans and T-shirts with the Beachcomber logo on them. Des was playing at being a waiter for her amusement. As he looked more closely into her face, his tone suddenly changed to one of sincere concern.

"What's wrong?" he asked. "Has something happened?"

"Please, sit down," she said. "I have to talk to you."

Des lowered his tall, broad frame into a white café chair that looked instantly too small and too unmasculine for him. That super-virile impression was all but contradicted by the gentleness in his face as he looked at her. She felt that gentleness wash over her like a warm bath. She longed to sink beneath its soothing waters and never come to the surface again. There would be peace and comfort there. She was certain of it. He reached across the table and laid his hand over hers in a gesture so kind and caring it seemed, for a moment, so out of sync with his usual coolness that she could hardly believe it was happening. She could hardly believe any of this was happening. She concentrated on the way the sun picked out the blond among the dark hairs on his forearm and burnished it into strands of precious gold.

"What is it you want to talk about?" he asked.

Taylor thought about pulling her hand away so that this conversation might be as dispassionate as possible, but she didn't. Instead, she did what she needed to do.

She turned her hand over and twined her fingers tightly through his, as if her life depended on it. As well it might.

"You know, don't you?" she asked. "You've known all along."

"Known what?"

She felt his sudden tension. She could see it in the way the tendons grew even more defined along his muscled arm.

"About the past," she said. "About what happened at Stormley?"

"What happened at Stormley?"

His eyes had lost some of their gentleness, but he still made no attempt to let go of her hand. There was a war going on inside him. She could sense it. She could almost see it. It occurred to her that the kind thing for her to do would be to get up from this table and walk out of this place right now. If she did that, she would spare him whatever discomfort this conversation was bound to cause him. She started to pull her hand away, but he gripped it more firmly.

"What do you know about what happened at Stormley?" He rephrased his question less harshly than before.

"*I* don't *know* anything."

Taylor felt the tears rising behind her eyes. She stared into her lap for a moment and willed them not to fall. "I don't remember anything about the night of the fire. Until yesterday, I didn't even think I was on this island when it happened. Now, I discover that I was." She hesitated long enough to take a deep breath before plunging on. "I have also discovered that *I* may be the one who set that fire."

Des looked away from her for a moment, in the general direction of the banyan tree with its many trunks and twisted tangle of woody vines and branches, like the tangle her life had so recently become. In the absence of his gaze, Taylor noticed that she had such tight hold of his hand that her nails were digging into his flesh. She loosened her grasp, and that brought his attention back to her face.

"No one knows for sure who started that fire," he said. There was a strangled quality to his voice, as if he were struggling to keep his emotions out of it and not entirely succeeding. "Didn't Winona tell you that?"

"Yes, she said there was circumstantial evidence, but nothing conclusive." Taylor's own voice had softened. She could feel that Des was the one who needed comforting now. She was surprised that, considering her present state of torment, what she wanted more than anything was to provide that comfort for him.

"Then you should believe what Winona said. Nobody knows what happened that night. Nobody knows who started the fire."

"Do you believe that?"

"Who am I to question Winona? She's supposed to be some kind of all-knowing guru."

Des had grown more distant with each word. Taylor felt him withdrawing from her as surely as if he had turned and walked away. He was retreating into the safety of his customary aloofness. She could almost see the mantle of that coolness fall over him like a protective cloak against the pain of the memories she was stirring in him. Her heart ached to pull him back to her. She wished to know the magic words to make that happen, but they didn't come. She held his hand a second longer, then untwined her fingers from his. This time he made no attempt to hold on.

"What else did Winona tell you?" he asked.

Taylor thought for a moment about whether they might both be better off if she left here right now. She would certainly save them at least one painful conversation if she did. She could go to the airport, abandoning her luggage, and catch the next flight north. The fastest escape possible might be the best. Detective Santos had told her not to leave the island, but Detective Santos wasn't here now. She doubted he would be at the airport, either. She could get out of this place before anybody knew she was gone and worry about the consequences later.

Wasn't that what her aunts had done all those years ago? Didn't they whisk her off this island to the safety of the north country and let the past take care of itself? But look how that had turned out. The past hadn't taken care of itself, at least not permanently so. The past had returned, rearing its hideous head straight through the fabric of the present and making a gash that might never be mended. What had been so long and so carefully buried beneath layers of falsehood had come to the surface at last. No airplane could soar high enough or fly fast enough to carry Taylor away from that. She relinquished the fantasy of escape and settled back into her chair.

"Winona told me that my mother and I hadn't been getting along. I was angry with her a lot of the time and very rebellious. I was what they call a problem child."

Des didn't comment so she went on.

"Winona says I had begun to act out, as she put it. Tantrums, refusing to do what I was told, that kind of thing. It sounds to me like I was the brat of the world."

That was more flippant than Taylor meant it to be, but she'd felt she had to release a bit of tension or she might explode. Still, Des made no comment and showed no reaction. He sat there watching her, his posture almost casual, his expression as close to a blank canvas as a human face could be. Taylor pressed on, though she had a sense of her words bouncing off the wall of his facade before he could even hear them.

"The fire was apparently set with fuel oil, the kind I could easily have found in the caretaker's shed. According to Winona, the general opinion was that during one of my fits of temper I saturated the place in oil and set it on fire."

Taylor couldn't bring herself to repeat exactly what Winona had told her, that the oil had actually been spread around only in Desiree's room. That was too horrible a fact for Taylor to speak aloud. She feared that if she did, the earth would open up beneath her feet and she would drop into a chasm forever.

"Apparently, charges were never laid because of my age at the time," she said in conclusion, "and the fact that my aunts agreed to put me into therapy."

"Therapy with Winona."

"Yes. That's why she knows so much about what went on."

"Does she say you admitted to setting the fire?"

Taylor sighed. She wished against all probability that this conversation could be instantly over and the topic never raised again as long as she lived. "She says I claimed not to remember any of it."

"Did she tell you that you were locked in your room at the time of the fire? That you were almost killed yourself?"

Taylor nodded. She had asked about the details, and Winona had mentioned the locked room. It was surmised that Desiree might have shut Taylor in to punish her for some bad behavior or other and her fury over that had driven her to light the fire.

"Then how did you get out of your room to start the fire?"

"They think I crawled out the window and along the roof to my mother's room. Supposedly I had done that before."

"And where did the fuel oil come from?"

Taylor looked down at her lap again. The tears rushed up again, no longer so readily controlled. They trembled on her lashes, and one fell onto the back of her hand. "That's the worst thing of all," she said in a voice that was barely more than a whisper. "The suspicion was that I had hidden the oil in my room, that I might have been planning the fire for some time."

Taylor bit her lip so hard she tasted the sharp flavor of her own blood. She held her breath against the flood of grief and guilt welling inside her. She was vaguely aware of the hum of conversation from other parts of the courtyard. For the past several minutes she hadn't been aware of anything but the sound of her own voices, the one that was speaking and the ones in her head accusing and condemning her for what her childhood self had very probably done.

Suddenly, her arm was in a firm grasp and she was being eased up out of her chair. Her newly reawakened awareness detected a lull in the conversational hum as surrounding lunchers must have turned their attention in her direction. She didn't see them do that because she was staring up into Des's face.

"I'm going to take you somewhere more private," he said.

Taylor thought about asking where that private place might be. Ordinarily, she wasn't the kind of woman who would allow herself to be led off to some unknown destination without inquiring about details. This moment, however, was hardly ordinary. Somewhere in the course of saying the things she'd just forced herself to say she had used up the energy that would have allowed her even to ask a question. She followed without resistance as Des guided her among the tables toward the restaurant building.

THERE WAS A DOOR at the top of the stairs that led from the café to the space above the restaurant. That door opened onto a hallway with a gleaming, wide-planked floor. A carved wooden table of Caribbean design stood at the far end of the hall and held a matching carved lamp. Des opened a door halfway down the hallway and moved aside for Taylor to pass. She drew her breath in sharply at the sight that awaited her as she stepped across the threshhold. She was facing a wall of glass that looked out over the tops of buildings to the harbor with its mounded green islands and lolling white sails. She walked to the window and looked out.

"Let's go outside for a minute," said Des, who had come into the apartment and closed the door quietly behind them.

The glass wall was actually a sliding door that opened onto a wide terrace. A table near the railing had been set for two with the same bright china Taylor had noticed in the café. Taylor stood transfixed in the doorway, uncertain of what to do next. Had he been expecting company?

Des must have noticed her staring at the table. "I had hoped you might join me for lunch," he said. He took her elbow and gently steered her toward a cushioned wicker loveseat that faced the railing and the spectacular view.

"Whenever I need to get things in order I come out here," he said. "Just looking at the water can make the world right some times."

*That's a lot to expect of a view in this case,* Taylor thought. "It is very beautiful," she managed to say.

"Yes, it is." Des's voice had deepened. Taylor realized he was looking at her and not at the harbor. Suddenly, she felt ill at ease. "Could I see the rest of the place?" Before he could answer, she had turned back toward the sliding glass doors.

The apartment was lovely, tasteful while still being masculine. They walked from room to room as Taylor tried not to think about the way being alone with Des made her feel. It seemed that she should be concerning herself with things other than passion right now. Still, she knew that was the source of the warmth that bathed her in places that felt as if they had never known heat before, at least not the kind she experienced with him.

"This is my favorite room," he said.

They had come to another set of sliding doors. These were made of teak panels decorated in an Asian design of long, curving reeds that looked as if they might have been brush-painted by hand. Des slid the panels open to reveal yet another astonishing insight into his world. The floor of the room was tiled in terra-cotta of a deep red-brown color. The ceiling was mostly open in a tinted skylight that let in the sun but shielded its burning rays. Beneath the skylight was an octagonal hot tub filled with blue-green water.

Des bent down at poolside and tested the water with his fingers. "Just right," he said. "I keep it more tepid than hot. I relax better at that temperature." He looked over at her where she stood by the door, still marveling at the beauty of his world and what it told her about him. "You could use some relaxing. How about taking a soak with me?"

Taylor was so startled by the suggestion that she couldn't think what to say.

"I wouldn't expect you to go skinny-dipping. There's a suit here that will probably fit you."

The mention of skinny-dipping turned the warmth inside her even more molten, but what really bothered her was the offer of a suit. What was he doing with women's bathing apparel in his apartment?

He must have guessed what she was thinking because he added, "It belonged to my wife. She left it behind when she had the good sense to get me out of her life. It still has the price tag attached."

"I don't really think I'm up to water sports right now," Taylor said.

"That's exactly why you need it. You can float your troubles away, or some of them at least."

She was about to say that she suspected getting rid of what was upsetting her wouldn't be so simple, but he had already hurried out of the room, probably to get the bathing suit. She shrugged. What harm could it do to go along with his suggestion? She was feeling so numb from repeated shocks to her system that she could hardly think what was wrong or right to do next. Until she glued herself back together enough to make that decision, maybe Des had a point. Maybe she could actually float some of her troubles away. She was suddenly ready to try.

The shimmering turquoise maillot did indeed turn out to fit. It slid over Taylor's body like a second skin, clinging to every curve. The color brightened the pale blue of her eyes. She couldn't help noticing how good she looked in the dressing-room mirror.

"Come on in," Des called as she stood in the doorway to the hot-tub room.

She could feel his eyes on her body as she did her best to keep from staring at his. He was submerged to just above the waist and must have been sitting on an underwater bench along the side of the pool. His chest was broad and golden in the sun from the skylight. His shoulders were so muscular and his biceps so rounded they made her breath catch in her throat.

"Hurry up before I come out there and get you," he said. His voice was husky in a way it hadn't been before. She could tell that was because he liked what he saw of her in the formfitting suit.

Taylor eased herself into the warm water. The air in the pool room was cooled by a touch of air-conditioning, and the water felt just right, as Des had said it would. The silkiness of it lapped over her as he moved along the bench to her side. He reached up and pulled her down next to him. Then he put his hand at her waist and drew her close. The sleek wetness of his body molded itself to her own as he reached up and tangled his fingers in the heavy mass of her hair.

His mouth met hers in a kiss that was long and intense. When he finally lifted his lips from hers, Taylor felt faint and breathless for a moment. The warmth of the water, the dizzy events of the day, the spell of his kiss. She wondered if it might all be too much for her to take and remain conscious. She leaned against him for support. Suddenly, he had scooped his arms under her and was lifting her from the bench. He carried her up the few steps to the rim of the hot tub.

"I don't want to soak as much as I thought I did," he said, his voice huskier than ever.

He carried her to a wide lounge chair just out of the direct sun from the skylight. He enfolded her in a large, thick towel and laid her gently against the cushions. Taylor let herself succumb to it all—the warmth from the water, the softness of the towel, the strength of Des's arms. She wanted nothing more at this moment than to give up her will and all of the confused reality that went along with it for her just now. She watched Des lower himself, inch by inch, onto the lounge next to her. The sweet ache inside her spoke, with an intensity that could not be denied, of how much she wanted him there.

His hands found the opening amid the folds of the towel and touched her body. His fingers slid downward from her shoulder, pulling the damp suit with them as they moved. His lips were on her forehead, her eyelids, her mouth, her throat, moving in the same mesmerizing rhythm as his hands. He unwound the towel from her body as though he were unwrapping some new and wondrous gift, then moved away for a moment to look down at her. She lay naked next to him and suddenly remembered her moment of vision the first time she saw him, of her pale body next to his darker one, just as they were now.

"You are so very beautiful," Des said. He spoke in a whisper, but she could hear the depth of feeling there all the same.

Taylor had never felt such tender urgency. She responded by taking his face in her hands and pulling his mouth to hers. His body followed, rolling on top of hers, his arms enveloping her, pressing her close. The muscles of his back rippled beneath her fingers. His chest hair teased her nipples. He slid his hand between their bodies to capture her breast. When he circled her hard nipple with his thumb, a moan escaped her lips.

"Oh, Des. I want you so much."

She slid her hands down his golden body, over knots of muscle under firm skin. She could feel how warm he was, burning with the same rising passion that seethed through her own veins and made her throb with the fury of desire. She pulled his damp suit down over his narrow hips and strong, hard thighs. Her bold words and actions enflamed them both beyond all thought of tenderness. Tenderness wasn't what Taylor wanted now. She arched her hips to press against him, as if she might push herself through to the very core of him, under his skin among his nerves and sinews, until the two of them became a single being straining toward release.

He pulled himself, rather roughly, just free enough from her embrace to draw his mouth down her throat, past her shoulders, and over her breast, licking at her along the way. He sucked hard at her nipple, and she gripped the edge of the lounge's cushion, feeling that she had to hold onto something or be propelled away by the force of her own passion. She was completely given over to him now, abandoned to the momentum that carried her along like a leaf on a flood.

She reached for him with her free hand, eager to set him on fire with the same wild, pleasurable pain she was feeling, as his fingers slipped between her thighs and she pushed herself against him once more. She flattened her palm along his chest, stroking the tautness of his skin and feeling the wiry golden hairs between her fingers, then sliding her hand down his side, over the jut of his hipbone. She drank in each sensation that the feel of him sent burning through her, awakening a thirst that must have lain dormant inside her for years and now demanded to be quenched. She touched the hardness between his thighs, and he moaned. His head fell back from her breast. He was still for a moment, as if helpless, while she stroked and caressed him.

Then he rose slowly, deliberately, moving his body over hers, pushing her thighs apart and lowering himself between them. Never in her life had she been as ready as she was now to feel a man moving over her. She was equally ready to be carried further and further from the control and caution that had kept her passions imprisoned for so long. She wound her arms around him and held him to her as her body echoed the motion of his.

It was as if they were struggling together over an erupting landscape, their voices urgent in each other's ears as they described the delicious torment of the journey. Then they reached their destination at last. With an explosion of almost unbearable pleasure, relief was theirs. They drifted gradually back toward consciousness once more, tangled in towels and each other's arms.

## Chapter Seven

Des pulled the fluffy towel around them both, swaddling their bodies together in a cocoon of softness. Taylor nestled in his arms, and he felt toward her as he had never felt toward any woman before in his life. He wanted to protect her from all harm. Most of all, he wanted to believe such protection could be possible in this nearly impossible situation.

"It's never been like this for me before," she whispered against his chest.

Her words were halting, and they snagged his heart in a way that made his throat fill with emotion.

"It's wonderful."

"Yes, it is," Des said.

"If only there weren't so many other things that aren't so wonderful."

"Let's not think about that now. We'll pretend there's just you and me and this moment."

"I'm not sure I can do that."

Des didn't respond. Already he could feel the passion between them beginning to cool, as the moist heat of recent exertion cooled from his skin. He held her closer and told himself that he must find a way to keep that fire from going out altogether. The voice of his usual pessimism piped up uninvited to remind him how fragile even the brightest flame can be, ablaze one minute and gone to ash the next. Still, he had to try, and he knew what the first step must be. He would take her to talk with Violetta. There were things she knew that Winona did not. He also suspected that Violetta's way of telling them would be less clinical, though no less true.

The truth will set you free, Violetta would say. He wanted Taylor to be set free. He wanted that for himself, too, no matter how strongly Taylor's eyes and his own thoughts told him that freedom and happy endings might exist only for other stories than theirs.

DES HAD TOLD Taylor there was someone he wanted her to talk with. She, of course, recognized the name of Violetta Ramone. She had been written about often in Aunt Netta's letters, as both the Stormley cook and a valued friend. Taylor wasn't sure whether she had memories of her own of Violetta or if those remembered associations originated with others. Whichever the case might be, Taylor found herself both eager and anxious about meeting someone who had been so closely connected with her childhood past.

Meanwhile, Taylor was grateful for the driving time between the Beachcomber and Bahama Village. She needed to ease herself back into the real world following her afternoon of lovemaking with Des. Those hours had been a transition in themselves, a contrast with the repeated shocks to her system over the past twenty-four hours. As for those experiences, she'd already reminded herself that she'd suffered shocks in her life before this. She had the will to survive anything she put her mind to surviving. "We are only given the burden to bear that we are capable of bearing," Aunt Pearl would say. She her-

self would most likely have been shocked that Des Maxwell had turned out to be one of Taylor's keys to survival
of this difficult time.

The Jeep bumped along over the uneven pavement of
the Key West streets. Des had driven south on Whitehead for several blocks before turning west into a part of
town Taylor had never seen. Of course, she had been here
too short a time to see very much, at least on this visit.
The awareness of there having been other visits she would
have been old enough to remember—but did not remember—only added to the unreality of the last two
days. As she gazed out from the bouncing vehicle, the
colors appeared too bright, the scents seemed too sharp,
the breeze felt too warm not to have made a lasting impression.

Taylor felt as if she were driving through a fairy-tale
scene done in poster paints and crayons, all in primary
colors, no subtle tones. Pastels and muted shades were
not the stuff of this tropical fantasy place, or of what had
happened to her since she arrived in it. That was why she
was less than surprised when, after the Jeep pulled over
and the engine stilled, a rooster sprang down from its
perch on a nearby fence post and lighted on the hood.
Taylor stared through the windshield at its sleek plum-
age and beady black eyes and wondered if, after last night
and the news today, she would ever be surprised by anything again.

Des shoved the door open on his side. The rooster gave
a squawk in response, tossed its haughty head, and
hopped to the ground. Taylor watched him strut away
into a yard where a number of chickens were already
pecking the dirt. They paid the rooster no mind. His
posture might suggest he was master, but the hens didn't
appear to be impressed. Taylor would have been content

to stay where she was and watch the antics of the local poultry, but Des was holding the door he had just opened for her. She stepped down, feeling the warmth of his hand on her arm and smiling to herself how natural it seemed to have him touching her.

They walked side by side across the dusty road to a small, white house on the corner. Des tapped on the screen door and waited for a moment, but no one responded. "Violetta," he called out. "It's Destiny."

Taylor was aware of his given name. She had seen it written down on paper in Aunt Netta's will, but Taylor had never heard it spoken. The sound of it startled her a little, maybe because of the meaning of the word. She shouldn't have been surprised, of course. A man with a name like Destiny was about as probable as everything else about her experience of Key West.

"Violetta," he called again. "She must be out in the backyard," he said after waiting another moment with no reply.

Des opened the screen door and stepped inside. Taylor followed. She was barely across the threshold when she understood that something was very wrong in this small, white house on Olivia Street. She peered around Des, who had stopped, transfixed, just inside the door. The sight was even more unnerving than that of her own ransacked guest-house room had been that morning. The state of her room had suggested that someone was looking for something. This one had simply been trashed. Furniture was upturned, and glass objects had been broken, leaving shattered hulks and shards strewn over the floor. A three-cornered hutch had been torn from the wall in one corner. It lay on a rumpled throw rug along with ripped photographs and what looked like religious icons, some in pieces, some still intact. A votive candle, luckily not still burning, was on its side with a stream of hardened wax spilling out. Whoever had done this damage felt no qualms about sacrilege.

Taylor was so taken aback by the devastation that she didn't realize Des had hurried on to the next room. Then she heard him, and the sound froze her to the bone. He cried out, not with what she might recognize as fear or rage, but something even more chilling. The cry she heard came from deep in his soul and a place even more devastated than this ravaged room.

"Oh, no. Please, no," were the words she heard.

She ran toward him through the debris. The kitchen was even more of a mess than the first room had been. The remains of plants, plant pots and potting dirt were everywhere, along with broken crockery and various pieces of cookware. There could no longer be any doubt concerning the source of the spicy cooking aroma. Red broth, vegetables and chicken were spattered across the stove and wall and puddled on the floor. In the midst of that puddle lay the most shocking sight of all—a stocky woman with black hair streaked with gray and splashed with sauce, clutched at something between her breasts. Her eyes were wide and staring. Taylor could still see the terror there, even in death. Des knelt over the woman with his head bowed. Taylor knew that, if she could see his eyes, she would find heartbreak there.

TAYLOR WASN'T SURE how much time had passed before she followed Des across a screened porch and into Violetta's backyard. He had called the police, who arrived shortly afterward with sirens blaring. Then Des said he had to get out of there for a while. The yard was a welcome change from the chaos of the house. Bougainvillea covered the tall fence that hid the dusty street from view.

A wide, cushioned chair swing had been suspended by chains from a tree limb at the center of the grassy yard. Des took hold of one of the chains.

"I made this for her," he said.

His tone was too controlled to reveal whatever he might be feeling, but there were other indications of his inner turmoil. He always stood straight and tall, but never as stiffly as he was standing now. The set of his spine was so rigid he looked as though he might break if he tried to bend. A muscle worked in his left cheek very near the dimple Taylor found so winsome. She would have liked to stroke that ticking tension to relief, but something about the way he was holding his head told her he wouldn't care to be touched right now.

Des's face was turned from her. He stared out over the low roofs of Bahama Village. She sensed that he wasn't really here with her at all, that his spirit had followed his gaze off into the distance. He had left her and retreated into aloofness once again. When he finally did turn to look in her direction for a brief moment, his eyes told her she was correct in her judgment. The warm, passionate Des who had made such intense love to her only hours ago was nowhere to be seen in this fleeting green glance. He had secreted the vulnerable part of himself behind the barrier of coolness that was his usual refuge. She longed to take him by his broad shoulders and shake as hard as her strength would allow, until his heart was jarred back to life and he returned to nestle in her arms once more.

But the message in his eyes had been clear. *Keep away*, it said. She heard that message, however reluctantly, and heeded it. A message of her own, from herself to herself, was almost as plainly spoken—that this man had a history of withdrawal into deep and probably brooding solitude and that his past history would project into his future. He most likely could never be a full-time emotional presence for anyone, and that included her. He would pull back inside himself on a regular basis, and she would be left alone. She could already anticipate the heartache that would cause her. She wanted freedom and to be her own person, but she wasn't looking for emotional abandonment. She felt herself pull back as well, to much more neutral territory than the wide-open place their lovemaking had taken her. She was about to walk around the side path to the front of the house when Armand Santos emerged from the screened porch.

"I'm running into the two of you a lot lately," he said in his now-familiar sarcastic tone.

Des turned slowly to face Santos. The message in Des's eyes had become a warning. Despite her resolve to keep her distance, she couldn't help moving to stand next to him now. She would be his ally and a mediator if one was needed. She was on his side, and she wanted Santos to know it.

"Des has had a terrible shock," she said quietly but firmly. "Maybe you could question him later."

"This morning he spoke for you. Now you're speaking for him," Santos said. "Isn't that interesting."

"I can speak for myself," Des said in a voice so tight it barely sounded like his own.

"She said the same thing. Do you remember that, Ms. Bissett?" It was apparent that he didn't expect an answer. "Which is also interesting. Is there something going on between you two that I should know about?" He looked back and forth from Des to Taylor.

"Nothing that has anything to do with you," Des said.

"When it comes to murder, everything has to do with me," Santos said. He turned his attention to Taylor. "I'm afraid it won't be possible to postpone my questions. In fact, I'll be asking some of them right here and now.''

''What kind of questions?''

''What kind of questions do you think I'd be asking after two homicides in two days? You can bet your ass they won't be about the weather.''

Taylor was reminded of two rams butting heads. They did that, harder and harder, until one cracked the other's skull. She couldn't help hoping Des would be the one to end up intact from this particular butting match.

''In most cases, I would interrogate you separately,'' Santos was saying. ''But this isn't most cases. So, why don't the two of you sit down?''

He indicated the wide swing. Des ignored that suggestion and walked to the picnic table instead. Taylor hesitated a moment then followed Des and sat down beside him on one of the attached benches. Santos watched them as he flipped open his notepad. Taylor had no doubt he would write down every detail. ''The subjects were reluctant to cooperate,'' might be his way of describing their behavior. He took his time joining them at the table, and then he didn't sit. He put his right foot on the opposite bench and stood there. That meant they had to look up at him. Taylor supposed this was an interrogation tactic. It was also the only way a man of Santos's stature could ever manage to tower over Des Maxwell.

''Where were the two of you when Violetta Ramone was murdered?'' Santos asked. ''Let's begin with you, Des.''

''What time would that have been?''

Des had cringed slightly at the mention of how his friend had died. He was cold and impassive again almost instantly. Taylor was reminded once more of his talent for emotional distance.

"A couple of hours ago, more or less," Santos said.

Taylor's small gasp was barely audible, but Santos picked up on it.

"Maybe I should ask you that question first, Ms. Bissett," he said.

"Are you asking me?" She was surprised at how cool she could also sound as she stalled for time and kept herself from glancing over at Des as she longed to do.

"Yes, Ms. Bissett. I'm asking. Where were you two hours ago?"

Taylor took a deep breath. There was no way to avoid telling the truth, or whatever Santos would make of it. She was about to say the words that felt too private and personal to be spoken, when Des said them for her.

"We were together."

"Aha," Santos responded, again looking from one of them to the other. "Isn't that convenient. Wouldn't you say that was convenient, Ms. Bissett?"

"In what way?" she asked.

"In the way that makes the two of you each other's alibi."

"Are you saying that we're suspects?" Taylor asked. "If we need an alibi, we must be suspects."

"I seem to recall this same topic coming up last night at April Jane's murder scene," Santos said. "Except that we were only talking about you at that time, Ms. Bissett. My answer to your question is this. Just as everything even vaguely connected with a murder case is subject to investigation, anybody even vaguely connected with a murder victim is subject to suspicion. You and Mr. Maxwell were on the scene last night at the guesthouse. You're on the scene here today. That puts both of you on the suspect list." He flipped back a couple of pages in his notepad and perused whatever was written there. "Your personal histories put you near the top of that list."

"What personal history are you referring to?" Taylor had to ask, though she dreaded the answer.

"Well, Ms. Bissett—" Santos tapped the notepad against his raised thigh. "—in your case, there's the matter of possible matricide and a childhood pattern of psychological disturbance."

"Wait just a minute, Santos." Des pulled up in his seat and jutted his square chin toward the detective. "You've got no proof of any of that."

"I said *possible* matricide, and the psychological stuff's documented."

"Documented where?" Des snapped.

"Winona Starling was her therapist—" Santos began.

Des cut him off. "That information is privileged. You can't use it."

Taylor knew she should be saying these things for herself, but she wasn't able to talk at the moment. Santos kept using the term for killing one's mother. Taylor could barely stand to hear it spoken. The sound cut her like a sword to the heart.

"There are also eyewitness statements taken at the time of Mrs. Bissett's death," Santos said. "Including the words of that lady in there." He nodded toward the house.

"Violetta made a statement against Taylor?"

"She stated the facts, as she witnessed them, of Ms. Bissett's behavior as a child. She also attested to Ms. Bissett being under Starling's care for emotional problems."

"Detective Santos," Taylor said after clearing her throat to force her voice back into working order. "Were any charges ever brought against me in my mother's death?"

"No formal charges."

"Then it doesn't seem appropriate for you to be bringing up unsubstantiated allegations now."

"What I call appropriate, Ms. Bissett," Santos said, leaning forward to sneer more directly into her face, "is that I'm the one working these current cases, and I'm not the kind of bleeding heart who investigated your mother's death. They backed off then because you were just a kid and your family agreed to get your head shrunk, then get you out of here. I wouldn't have handled it that way. What is also appropriate, as well as significant, is that the arson death of your mother is still an open case. There's no statute of limitations on murder."

"You're bluffing," Des said, more belligerent than ever. "You could never get a judge to try that case after all these years and against a kid."

"Never say never."

Santos actually smiled after saying that. He gave every indication of enjoying what was going on, especially the fact that he was obviously irritating Des. Taylor wondered if this was also an interrogation tactic. Maybe Santos reasoned that Des would be easier pickings once his cool facade had been broken down some. And maybe Santos was using Taylor's predicament as the sledgehammer to do that breaking. She didn't want that to happen, and she knew how to prevent it. She forced herself to take charge, though she hardly felt capable of doing so.

"I refuse to have my mother's death or any possible charges against me discussed further without my attorney present." She knew enough about the law to understand that was her right.

Santos gave a derisive sniff. He obviously understood the same thing. "What about you, Mr. Maxwell?" he asked. "Do you have to have a mouthpiece to talk for you too?"

"I'll talk to you on my own," Des said. "Any time. Any place."

"As long as you don't talk to him about me," Taylor added. She didn't look at Des to see how he felt about her butting in. She suspected he wouldn't approve.

Santos, meanwhile, pretended to ignore her. "Speaking of past histories, I had a look at your rap sheet, Des. I'd forgotten just how big a bad boy you were."

"That was a long time ago," Des said.

"They say the child is father to the man."

"You're full of quotations lately, aren't you?"

Taylor guessed that Des was referring to Santos's quip about Brando that morning.

"Besides, Ms. Bissett wasn't the only name I found in the file on that fire all those years ago. You were also very prominently mentioned."

Taylor could hardly believe what she was hearing.

"I didn't have anything to do with the Stormley fire," Des said.

He was as cool as a cucumber again. Taylor wished she felt the same.

"There was a strong body of opinion to the contrary at the time," Santos said. "The way I understand it is that you were a nobody who wanted more than anything to be somebody. When you saved the kid from the fire, you got to be a hero."

Taylor stared at Des. Could she be the "kid" Santos was referring to? She must be. There hadn't been any other child at Stormley, as far as she knew. Had Des saved her life back then? Before she could blurt out those questions, which felt so impossible to contain, Santos was talking again, to Des still.

"Then there's the matter of your feelings toward the victim. According to several of the statements on file, you were obsessed with her. One person described you as insanely jealous of anybody who came anywhere near her. You were even jealous of the kid here." He gestured toward Taylor. "Allegedly, that is."

Those last words were so sarcastically uttered that Taylor surmised that Santos believed everything alleged against anybody had to be true or it wouldn't have been alleged in the first place. However, Taylor wasn't up to challenging him on that point at the moment. Her head was too full of other, more personally troubling things.

Des had been the one who saved her from the fire. Why hadn't he told her that? Maybe because it placed him at the scene and because of what Santos had just said. When she went to Des so tormented about her own possible guilt in the fire, why hadn't he told her he was also suspected? He'd supposedly been trying to comfort her. Wouldn't that revelation have been a comfort, at least as an indication that there were wild suspicions of everybody at the time? Did Des fail to mention any of that because he actually did have something to hide?

"This is all ancient history," Des said.

Whatever emotion he had exhibited before was no longer in evidence now. Taylor wondered how he could stay so steely calm under these circumstances. It occurred to her that he appeared not only cold, but also calculating—and not just to Santos.

"It was ancient history until Ms. Bissett here reappeared on the scene. She tried to tell me she wasn't even in the Keys at the time of the fire, but we all know that isn't so. Maybe that's got something to do with these psychological problems I'm not supposed to talk about till she gets her legal eagle here to hold her hand."

Taylor opened her mouth to protest the way the conversation was going. Then she realized she wanted to know what else Santos had to say. She closed her mouth and let him continue. He nodded his head as if he might have recognized her signal.

"But just suppose she should start stirring up those old ashes again. Maybe they're not as cold as everybody assumes. What if she should find out how serious a suspect *you* were back then, Maxwell? What if she should even try to dig up some evidence against you?"

"There isn't any evidence," Des stated flatly.

"So you say. But what if she came up with something? Maybe they tossed her room last night to find out if she'd come up with something, or why she's back here after all these years."

"I was at the Beachcomber last night," Des said. "I have witnesses to that."

"The bartender and waitress both say you were up in your office by yourself for at least an hour that they know of. There's a door to the street from that office. I know. I checked it out. You could have slipped out while nobody was looking, snuck into Ms. Bissett's room, met up with April Jane, done her in and been back at the bar in way under an hour."

Was that possible? Taylor's head was nearly spinning. Would he have had time to do all that while she was walking to Duval Street? She had taken a detour after her encounter with that bummy guy. She'd ducked into a card shop and pretended to browse until she was absolutely certain he had to be gone. Then, she had made her way cautiously down the street, watching her back all the while. Even before that unnerving encounter, she'd been

walking a lot more slowly than usual. She wasn't used to
the humidity in the air. She remembered slowing down so
she wouldn't get uncomfortable and dishevelled again,
the way she had been when she first arrived at the Key
Westian. How long would all of that have taken? Enough
for Des to have done what Santos was suggesting?

"That all sounds pretty flimsy to me," Des said in answer to Santos's suppositions. Taylor hoped it would ap-
ply to her thoughts as well.

"The money motive puts some starch in it. Wouldn't
you agree?" Santos asked, looking at both of them.
"You wouldn't want anything to get in the way of inher-
iting Netta Bissett's dough. Would you, Des?"

"Still sounds like a flimsy case to me," Des said.

"We just might be able to get a grand jury to indict."

"Grand juries always indict. I suppose you have another flimsy case that says I killed Violetta, too. How was
she killed, anyway?"

"You might say Mrs. Ramone was frightened to
death," Santos said. "We figure that whoever came in
here and ripped the place apart scared her so much she
had a heart attack. You knew about her bad heart, didn't
you, Des?"

"I knew."

"What's even more interesting is what Violetta knew,
like all about the old days at Stormley. About you and
Mrs. Bissett and how you had a key to the house and run
of the grounds. Violetta knew all about your bad-boy
times too. Maybe she knew more about you than was
healthy for her to know. How does that sound to you?"

The detective was supposed to be talking to Des, but
Santos looked at Taylor when he asked that last question. It occurred to her that this interrogation of Des had

been partly for her benefit. Santos wanted her to hear what he had to say about Des, past and present.

"I told you how it sounds to me," Des said. "It sounds flimsy."

Taylor wasn't sure she could agree.

FOR THE FIRST TIME EVER, Des wished he were a manipulative person. Maybe then he could think up some clever way to get Taylor to come with him to Stormley. Instead, he had to rely on his usual direct approach, which struck him as inadequate and clumsy under the circumstances.

"I'd be willing to bet money that just about the last thing you want right now is to go anywhere with me," he began.

They were standing in front of Violetta's house. Santos had decided to forego further questioning at the station house. He'd repeated his warning not to leave town, then told Des and Taylor they could go. Des would have preferred to stick around till the medical examiner and the forensics people were finished inside, but it was obvious that Santos didn't want any civilians here while the official investigation was going on. Des couldn't have brought himself to go back inside that house, anyway. Even out here on the front porch, the occasional whiff of Violetta's chicken sauce threatened Des's precarious control over his ravaged emotions. He hadn't felt this much like breaking down since Desiree had died. It would be a good idea to get out of here before that happened.

Meanwhile, Taylor was looking at him and listening, but she didn't say anything. She was still wearing the same outfit she'd put on when he picked her up at Starling's this morning. There was an orangy-red stain near the hem of one leg. Des didn't want to speculate whether it was tomato sauce or blood, but he couldn't help himself. Her hair was fluffed out wilder than he'd seen it before. He remembered that her hair had gotten wet in his hot tub. He had felt the dampness there when he ran his fingers through the silky softness of those waves after making love to her. The thought of her naked and beautiful beside him brought with it a stab of both desire and sorrow. After what Taylor had just heard from Santos, Des wondered if she would ever be that way with him again. Maybe they weren't meant to be together, after all. Ordinarily, he would have been able to shrug and move on with hardly a backward glance. He was honest enough with himself to admit that accepting the inevitable wouldn't be so easy this time. He was also realistic enough to realize he probably had no choice. Still, there was at least one more thing they had to do together.

"I want you to come to Stormley with me," he went on.

"All right," she said.

Des had been ready with a barrage of arguments against her expected refusal. He stood staring at her now with his mouth agape. He was totally unprepared for her easy acceptance of his suggestion.

"I think it's time for me to go back there," she said, "and I would rather not do it alone."

"And, since I'm almost the only person you know around here, you're stuck with my company."

"You know about the past, more than I do really. I don't have to explain things to you like I would with somebody else."

He was grateful that she hadn't mentioned what had recently been revealed about his own past or the explaining that made necessary. Maybe it was the fact that she hadn't yet pressed him for answers that made him start talking the minute they started driving.

"There's some truth in what Santos said about me," Des began. "Maybe even a lot of truth." He grabbed his sunglasses from the dashboard and put them on. He was shielding his vision from the brightness of the sun. He was also trying to shield himself from a sudden stinging behind his eyes.

"What truth is that?"

"I did want your mother all to myself. You see, I'd never had anybody of my own. I'd also never known anybody like her. I was jealous of anyone who had even so much as a piece of her."

"Were you jealous of me?"

"I guess probably I was, though you were at that kind of pesky little-kid age that a teenager doesn't pay much attention to. Most of the time I was hardly aware that you existed."

He could see out of the corner of his eye that she'd managed another sad smile. "I can imagine how that would be. I was only about half your age at the time."

"That's right. But when you did come around your mother, I probably wished you wouldn't."

"But you saved my life anyway."

Des hesitated, trying to decide how honest he wanted to be. "Not altogether willingly," he said, going for broke. "I meant to save your mother, but I heard you calling out and went for you first. After that, it was too late to go back. The fire was too bad by then. Nobody could have gotten to her. Nobody." Des heard in his own voice the desperate need to justify his actions. He also felt the stinging grow sharper behind his eyes.

"I'm sure you did all you could," Taylor said quietly. "I'm very grateful to you. It's long overdue for me to thank you. I'd like to thank you now."

He knew she was looking at him, but he couldn't look back. "You don't have to thank me."

"I want to."

"I just want you to know I didn't do it for the reasons Santos said," Des blurted out. He was gripping the steering wheel so hard that his fingers hurt. "I wasn't trying to be a hero. He's right about how messed-up I was, but I wasn't that far gone. I could never have done anything to hurt Desiree. I cared too much about her. She was the only person I'd cared that much about since my mother died."

"Were you sorry you saved me instead of her?"

The question hung in the air between them. Des glanced over at Taylor. The breeze created by driving along in the open Jeep had swept her hair across her face, so he couldn't make out her expression. Twenty-four years of self-recrimination filled his heart, threatening to overwhelm him.

"I'm sorry I couldn't save you both," he said over the hard knot in his throat.

He glanced over again and saw her nod. She didn't speak.

"That's when I started on that rap sheet Santos was talking about. Winona would probably say I was trying to get myself punished. All I know is that I didn't care about much of anything, least of all me. If it hadn't been for Violetta and your aunt, I probably would have flushed myself all the way down the tubes a long time ago."

"I see," was all Taylor said.

Des almost went on pleading his case, just to see if he could get her to say more. Then his common sense told him there wasn't much point in that. She'd either believe him or she wouldn't. And why should she? He was a no-account saloon keeper with a shady past and just about nobody to recommend him but a bunch of barflies. Why would a classy lady like Taylor want to take his side in the first place? He'd always wondered the same thing about her mother, too.

# Chapter Eight

They had driven nearly to the ocean. Taylor noticed that the houses were considerably larger here than they had been in the center of town. Architectural styles varied more also. The smaller structures in town had been mostly wood-framed and squarish with simple siding painted white. Here, in what Santos had called the Casa Marina section of Key West, there were mansions and ranch-styles, porticoes and balustrades—just about every house layout that could indicate a wealthy owner.

Taylor wondered what Stormley would be like, and if she would remember something when she saw it. She might have spent some time pondering Des's amazing revelations on the way here, amazing because such openness seemed so unlike him. But Taylor's growing anxiety over returning to her childhood home had pushed all other subjects from her mind.

When they did drive up in front of Stormley, it looked very different from anything she might have expected. The three-story Victorian with its tall, narrow windows would have fit more naturally into northern New York than here in this open, airy culture. Most surprising of all, it was built of brick. Taylor couldn't remember seeing a single brick house in her last two days of jaunting around the Key.

"Does this place spark any memories for you?" Des asked after he had stopped the Jeep in front of the wrought-iron gate and fence that bordered the Stormley grounds. "Your aunt had it rebuilt according to the original plans. Only the exterior brick is different. It used to be white wood."

Taylor strained her mind, forward across the deep lawn as well as backward in time. She had seen so many houses like this one back home. She was careful not to let those connections confuse her. Two parallel rows of trees hung with green fruit lined the walk that led from the street to the veranda, which was surrounded by a white wooden railing along the three sides of the house that she could see. A scent drifted over her, probably from those trees, and for an instant familiarity might have come wafting with it. The instant passed.

Taylor shook her head. "Nothing," she said in a resigned tone. "I don't remember anything." She sighed.

"Don't give up yet," Des said. He opened his car door and jumped out. "We've just started this memory-lane thing. Something may come back to you yet." They were walking up the path between the lime trees when he added, "Don't try to force it. This may take some time. I'll help you any way I can."

Taylor looked up at him, but he wasn't looking back. She had heard the tender concern in his voice, but he wasn't letting much of that show on his face. He might have confided in her some during their drive from Violetta's house, but he was hardly an open book still. Taylor sensed that there were many things kept private behind the practiced steadiness of his green-eyed gaze. The answers to her questions about him lay there. She wondered if he would ever be able to let his guard down enough to reveal those answers. Even more pointedly, she wondered why that guard was so high and so vigilant in the first place. What exactly did he have to hide? How would she feel about him if she ever found out?

Meanwhile, they were climbing the steps to the veranda. The scent of the lime trees was more powerful here. Taylor felt herself suddenly assailed by it, and all other sensations were lost in the effect. She was almost certain she had been in this place before. She halted on the top step and turned around. These thick-topped, thorny trees held a secret for her. She knew it. She couldn't decipher it quite yet. For the first time, she experienced a real hope that she would decode the secret some day. She was so excited by the prospect that she didn't think to be frightened by what that secret might be.

She could hardly wait for Des to unlock the front door. When the key resisted turning for a moment, she wanted to take it from him and force its compliance herself. When the door finally did open, she was assailed again by yet another aromatic memory, from the more recent rather than the distant past this time. This had been Aunt Netta's house, but it smelled almost the same as Aunt Pearl's. Once more, as had happened many times in Taylor's life, she was struck by how similar these sisters had actually been, despite their outward differences.

Des stepped aside and Taylor walked in. She had forgotten for a moment her original intent in being here. She was in the presence of her aunts. She almost expected one or both of them to come bustling into this foyer and greet her with a hug to their wrinkled cheeks. Another scent, purely from memory, mixed with the familiar smell of the house. It was the soft, faintly floral fragrance of the powder they had both worn. Taylor was filled with a longing to be with them again. They had hovered over her and made her feel imprisoned sometimes, but they had loved her, too. And she had most certainly loved them in return.

"Are you all right?" Des asked.

Taylor had almost forgotten he was here. "It's Netta," she said. "I can almost see her here, and my Aunt Pearl too."

"I know what you mean. All of these beautiful things make me think of her every time I see them." Des gestured toward what Netta would have called her sitting room. It was filled, some might have said over-filled, with obviously precious antiques—tall Ming vases, tables inlaid in abalone shell and mother-of-pearl, Tiffany lamps, and much more. "Back in the mid-1800s, merchant ships would run aground out on the reef. Anybody on the island with a boat would take off like a shot to claim the salvage. Fine china, fancy furniture, gold plate. It was all there for the taking, and the laws favored the finder. Netta told me all about how so many of the best houses here on Key West were very elegantly furnished out of those wrecks. She spent years buying up as much of that old booty as she could find. There's a lot of priceless stuff in these rooms."

Taylor had been watching him with growing curiosity as he spoke. "Did you ever go with her on those buying sprees?"

"Many times. She was always picking out something she couldn't possibly carry. She was such a tiny thing."

Tiny and susceptible to influence, Taylor was thinking. Along with his substantial money bequest, Des had been left a considerable number of these antique pieces in Netta's will. A detailed list had been attached. Taylor remembered marvelling at how much they were worth.

She had just been thinking about how similar her aunts were at heart. Yet, Pearl had been a very frugal woman. Had Netta been that way too? Could she have been manipulated into the extravagance that filled these rooms? Manipulated by someone who planned to benefit from that extravagance after her death? Taylor turned away from the sitting-room archway where she had been standing, as if she might turn away from such distressing thoughts as well.

"I'd like to look upstairs first," she said and walked toward the wide staircase that ascended from the center of the foyer.

"The rooms are laid out the same way they were in the old house," Des was saying as he kept pace with her onto the stairs. "But there are a lot of differences beyond that. The brick exterior walls, for example. They weren't here before. Netta thought they would be more fireproof. She was always a little afraid of the same thing happening again, a big blaze burning the place to the ground. She had the bricks shipped from the mainland. It cost her a fortune."

There he was, talking about money again. "My aunt could afford it," Taylor said. "She was a well-off woman from a well-off family. She could buy expensive things if she wanted them."

"Don't I know it. I saw her do that enough times."

"Did you ever try to discourage her from spending so much?"

"Why would I? It was her money. She could do what she wanted with it. I was just along for the ride."

And a lucrative trip it turned out to be, Taylor almost added. She was also itching to ask if he had ever encouraged her aunt to make any of her pricey purchases. That kind of question would be more antagonistic than Taylor wanted to appear right now. She intended to find out more about Des's relationship with Netta Bissett, and with her money. The information would be harder to come by if he was set even more on his characteristic guard than usual. Taylor had to be careful not to do that.

They had reached the second-floor landing. A balustrade stretched in either direction with closed doors at regular intervals along the corridor wall. Taylor turned left without even thinking about it. In fact, she had been so lost in troubling thoughts about Des that she didn't really take note of what she was doing. She had walked to the last door on that side of the corridor and had her hand on the knob before she realized how purposeful her choice of direction had actually been. She looked back toward the staircase. Des was still standing there with one hand resting on the balustrade. He was watching her with a curious expression on his face. Taylor turned back toward the closed door. She knew but at the same time didn't know what this room was and who it, or its previous version, had once belonged to. She both longed and feared to see what was inside. Her longing must have been stronger than her fear, because she turned the knob and pushed open the door.

It was a lovely room. Filmy window curtains framed the deepening colors of the late-afternoon sky as sunset approached. A canopied bed was the graceful centerpiece of the furnishings, along with a matching chaise longue. A vanity table with a three-sided mirror was faced by a small, cushioned chair. The colors were mauve and white with touches of gold trim. Double mirrored sliding doors probably led to a large closet. Soft carpets and a few pale-tinted paintings completed the decor of this tasteful, uncluttered room that was so much unlike the heavily furnished sitting room and foyer downstairs.

"Your aunt tried to make this as much like Desiree's room had been as possible," Des said. He had walked down the hall to Taylor's side and was looking over her shoulder through the doorway. "Netta did a good job. This is almost exactly as it was before the fire."

Taylor barely heard what he was saying. She was too overwhelmed by what she was feeling at the moment for there to be room in her heart or her mind for anything else. The feeling that so overwhelmed her now was disappointment.

"I don't remember any of it," she blurted out. "Not a single, blessed thing."

Des must have been more alert than Taylor and heard the catch that was more than slight in *her* words. He laid his hand gently on her shoulder. "Take it easy," he said softly. "Give yourself time."

Taylor pulled abruptly away from his touch and lunged forward into the room. "Time?" she said with anguish in her voice. "This isn't about time. This is about something else. Only I don't know what that something is."

She walked rapidly across the room to the bed. Then she turned and paced to the northern windows that looked out over the roof at the the back wall of the house. The rooms along the corridor to the right of the staircase would have windows opening onto this roof. That meant this would have to be the roof Winona talked about, where Taylor crawled across as a child to reach her mother's room. Taylor knew about that, but only from being told by someone else. She could find no memory, or even the traces of a memory, of any of that within herself. She turned and bolted across the room toward the opposite windows. She was vaguely aware of how irrationally she was behaving. She knew how unlike her this behavior was. No matter what happened, she never made emotional scenes. She couldn't recall ever having so much as a tantrum as a child, much less the petulant, agitated kind of behavior Winona and Detective Santos had talked about. But then, Taylor couldn't really recall her childhood at all, could she? At least not the one everyone was telling her she had actually experienced.

The windows on the south side of the room faced the Atlantic. There were two of these windows, wide and free of panes to let in as much light and, when opened, as much sea breeze as possible. These windows must have been specially designed. They were very unlike the tall, narrow ones in the rest of the house. Taylor swept the gauzy curtain aside and looked out at the ocean. She yearned to find comfort in the vast vista of the sea, maybe as her mother had once done, but there was no such solace here for Taylor. A wave of what was almost despair washed over her, and she thought she might be in danger of fainting. She reached out and pressed her palms flat against the window glass to support herself till the moment passed.

That was when it happened.

The ocean disappeared, and in its place were flames on the other side of the window. Taylor could even smell the smoke, seeping through the seams of the closed sash. She was no longer looking out of the house. She was looking into it and from the other side of the room. She could make out the bedposts through the flames and the canopy on fire. She could also see something on the floor. A figure in white crawled with laborious slowness toward the window where Taylor was standing now, her palms riveted to the glass as she strained to see through eyes streaming from smoke and tears. She saw another figure as well, a man or maybe a tall boy. His back was toward her, as he raised something into the air over the figure in white, still dragging itself across the floor.

"Mama! Mama!" Taylor cried out in a strangled voice. Her throat was beginning to burn from the smoke that she was imagining so vividly it was virtually real.

"Taylor!" Des had her by the shoulders and was trying to pull her away from the window. "What's happening to you?" he shouted as she resisted his efforts.

Des let go of her shoulders and reached forward to grasp her wrists. He yanked hard to free her palms from the glass, where they had cleaved so tightly they felt to Taylor as if they might be fusing to the pane.

Taylor screamed, and not just from the shock of being so abruptly and forcefully moved. She stared down at the palms of her hands and could hardly believe what she saw. They appeared to be normal, maybe a bit red from their pressure against the glass, but nothing more out of the ordinary than that—which was very much in contrast with the way they felt. From inside herself, the flesh of her palms was seared as if deeply burned by its contact with glass heated by a roaring fire.

Taylor's eyes were still streaming, and her throat was raw, though she could no longer smell the smoke. She didn't want to look back at the window, but she had no choice. When she did, the fiery scene was gone. The ocean stretched before her, shading from deep blue into purple into dark red all the way to the horizon and the southern aspect of Key West's renowned sunset. That was the view Taylor had been looking at only moments before. She screamed again, more a cry of agony this time. The pain in her hands was subsiding, but the pain in her heart was almost unbearable.

"Take your hands off her!"

The voice that shouted from the bedroom doorway was as familiar to Taylor as her own, but almost as disorienting as the vision beyond the window had been. Des's hold on her arms loosened enough for her to turn toward the sound and then break away entirely.

"Early!" she cried. "I'm so glad to see you."

She ran into her old friend's arms. She was so reassured by the sight of his familiar face that she almost forgot Des was there until she glanced up and saw him standing by the window. He was watching her through eyes that were, at the moment, as unreadable as they might have been behind the darkest glass.

*I REMEMBER THIS GUY,* Des thought. *How could I forget him?*

Early Rhinelander was tall and spare, especially in the face, where his boniness made him look like a skeleton. That was how Des as a boy had thought of him, anyway. He'd been prematurely smooth-scalped on the top of his head even back then and was still, maybe a bit more so. Otherwise, he didn't look to have aged much. He'd been what they call a conch, a native-born Key Wester. They tend to be like that, aging to a certain point and not much more after that, as if the bright sun or maybe the salt air had preserved them.

"What is going on here?" Early growled. "What have you done to Taylor?"

"I don't really know the answer to that. You'll have to ask her."

"You had your hands on her."

"Just like you do now."

Early set Taylor gently away from him. She still looked shaken. Des would have liked to go to her and take her in his arms, but it didn't take a genius to see she didn't want that.

"She was screaming," Early said. He had taken a menacing step toward Des, who could remember Early being menacing quite often in the old days. "Why was she screaming?"

"I told you to ask her. I don't know any more about what was going on than you do." That was true. Des had watched helplessly while Taylor went suddenly hysterical at the window. He hadn't a clue to why she did that.

"You're lying, Maxwell," Early said in the low, mean tone he'd always used with Des. "You were a liar back then, and you're a liar still."

Des had held his temper about as long as he could. "I was a kid back then. I'm not a kid anymore. I would advise you against treating me like one."

Des meant that as a challenge. Early took the bait immediately. "I can run you off this place just like I used to," he said. "Have no doubt about that."

"You only thought you ran me off. I let you push me around because it upset Desiree when I fought with you."

"Don't you mention her name, you no-good bum." Early took another menacing step. "You may have cleaned yourself up some. But, as far as I'm concerned, you're still a tramp kid from the lowlife side of town who's got no business hanging around where you don't belong."

Des took a menacing step of his own, closing the gap between them as they glared at each other. Des's fists were clenched at his sides, and he was ready to do damage.

"Stop it, both of you," Taylor cried out. She still had anguish in her voice. "Something happened to me. Des didn't have anything to do with it."

"What happened to you?" Des and Early asked in unison, setting aside their mutual animosity, if only for the moment.

"I'm not sure what it was exactly. I was looking out of the window. Then, all of a sudden, everything changed. There was a fire."

She looked down at her hands, turning them over to stare hard, first at the palms, then at the backs, then the palms again. She appeared to be searching for something. Des couldn't tell what it might be. All he could see was her torment, and his heart ached for her.

"There isn't any fire. That was all over a long time ago," he began, trying to be comforting.

"No! It isn't over!" she said. "It's still happening. The glass felt so hot to me it burned my hands. That's how real it was."

"What is this all about?" Early asked, stepping into the path where Taylor had moved toward Des.

"I think she saw something when she looked out the window." Des gestured toward the ocean side of the room. "Something like a hallucination, I think."

"A vision," Taylor corrected. "I call them visions."

"This has happened to you before?" Early asked. He sounded genuinely concerned.

"Yes, it has," Taylor said.

She looked at Des. The anguish he had heard in her voice was now in her eyes. She could have been pleading with him for comfort, entreating him to come to her. Then she looked away, as if to shut him out again. He wasn't sure which message he should heed, the invitation or the rejection. This was one of the reasons he kept women at arm's length as a rule. Too often he had trouble interpreting their messages. Unfortunately, he had let this woman get a lot closer than arm's length. Unfortunately, she was threatening to creep into his heart, and he couldn't seem to stop that from happening. Maybe he wasn't even trying to stop it.

"How long have you been having these...visions?" Early was asking. He took Taylor by the shoulders and forced her to look up at him. "Was this going on back home, too?"

"Yes," Taylor said, sounding close to despair.

Des wanted more than anything to take her out of there right this minute to some safe place where there was no need for her to be desperate ever again. But, what if there wasn't such a place for her? What if she was still as disturbed as they were saying she had been as a child?

"But I never saw the fire before," Taylor went on. "I smelled the smoke, and I may have heard the flames crackling. But this is the first time I've ever seen it."

"You need to talk to Winona right away," Early said. "It's a good thing she called me to come down here."

He had stepped toward Taylor to take her arm, but she wouldn't be moved. "Winona called you?"

Early nodded. "She told me what's been going on since you got here. She's very worried about you. I'm worried, too. The way you ran off like that from home without telling anybody. It's not like you. Then I find you down here, all worked up, like when you were a kid. You talked about seeing things sometimes back then, too, but I thought that was all over with years ago. What is it you think you saw just now anyway?"

Taylor shrugged and sighed. "I'm not really sure." She sounded more discouraged than ever. "There was the fire. I think it was inside this room. And somebody crawling toward the window. I seemed to think it was my mother but I couldn't see her face."

Taylor hesitated, her expression transfixed, her eyes staring at nothing, at least nothing in this room at this moment.

"That's enough for now," Early said. "This sounds like the mumbo jumbo I used to catch that cook planting in your head when you were too young to know better. It's just your imagination working overtime."

"I remember now!" Taylor exclaimed as if she hadn't heard a word he said. "There was a man in the room, too." She was suddenly very agitated.

"Taylor, you have to calm down," Early said. "You don't have to talk about this now."

For the first time in memory, Des agreed with Early about something. "Let's get out of here," he said.

"I'm taking her to Winona."

"I'm coming along."

"What for?" Early snarled. "You're the one who started this."

"I didn't start anything."

"You brought her here to Stormley, didn't you?"

Des stopped in midstride on his way to extricate Taylor from Early's grasp. The ring of truth and a stab of guilt came with Early's words. "Yes, I brought her here."

"I rest my case," Early said.

"I'm coming along to Winona's anyway."

"No, you're not."

Taylor spoke up. "Wait a minute. Wait just one damned minute." Her voice was trembling, but she had calmed herself considerably. "In the first place, nobody *brought* me to Stormley. I wanted to come. Secondly, Des can come to Winona's with us if he wants. And, finally, this is not about the two of you. It is about me and my mother."

Des wanted to say that anything involving Stormley and Desiree had to do with all of them, but he kept his mouth shut. He felt he had already talked more in this one day than he had in the past six months. He wasn't at all sure he should have done that. Talking had never been his specialty, except maybe with Desiree and Violetta, and look what had happened to them. The pain in his heart told him how much he didn't want that to happen again.

DES HAD COME ALONG to Elizabeth Street. They had all been there together—Des, Winona, Early, even Jethro. It didn't take long for Taylor to realize what a mistake that was. Early and Winona joined forces against Des. Jethro darted nervously among them, groping for some miraculous means to make them all get along. Meanwhile, Taylor couldn't help but feel a bit neglected. She was the one with the problem. She was also the one whose needs were being paid the least attention. When she finally slipped away upstairs, she wondered if any of them even noticed. She especially wondered if Des noticed. She had more questions and doubts where he was concerned than she cared to think about. Still, every time she looked at him her heart did a small jump in her chest and her breath caught for a moment. Unfortunately, when she made her escape from Winona's very grand parlor, Des had his face turned away in the direction of Early's challenging scowl.

Taylor sank onto the thick comforter in her cream-and-chintz room with a sigh. She told herself she was relieved to be alone at last. Nonetheless, she hadn't forgotten the dream she'd had when last in this bed, of Des's hands and body so intimate with hers. She particularly hadn't forgotten how the dream had come true that very afternoon. She recalled, with a twinge of what felt like regret, the warmth of the hot tub as its silken water washed over her. Then, later, on the wide lounge among the enveloping towels, how Des had opened her up to parts of herself never truly awakened before. Those had been perhaps the most wondrous moments of her life. Certainly, she had never known anything as intense as the wild, thundering tempest of their passion or the complete sweetness of the calm that followed the passing of the storm.

So, why the twinge of regret? Taylor knew the answer. She regretted the loss of that intensity and the sure knowledge she would not find it with anyone else. Even so, it had to be lost to her as irrevocably as if Des had been the figure she saw perishing in the fire reflected by Stormley's window. She could not trust him, and that meant she could not love him. She had good reason to believe he had used her family for his own ends—first her mother, then her aunt, now maybe herself as well. He had been little more than a street urchin when Desiree found him. Her death left him with nothing, or so it seemed. Then, Netta took him up. He came out much better off with her, with a generous chunk of her money and more than his share of her valuable possessions. Now he was making love to Taylor. Her natural suspicion had to be that he was after the whole ball of wax this time, the balance of the Bissett money to which she was the major heir.

Taylor wasn't the only one to suspect that, either. Winona, Early, even Detective Santos had broached the possibility, even the probability, of questionable motives for Des's long and complicated involvement with Taylor's family. He had certainly profited from the connection. She wondered what Violetta Ramone would have had to say about that. Of course, Des wouldn't have been taking Taylor to Bahama Village if he thought Violetta would tell incriminating tales about him. Or, could he have known there was no danger of that? Hadn't Santos said that Des was the last person to see Violetta alive—except for her murderer? Hadn't Santos been suggesting that Des could in fact have *been* the murderer? That thought allowed in the other that had skirted the edge of her consciousness for the past hour or two, that Des could also have been the figure poised to strike in her fiery vision.

"No," Taylor said loudly enough, she hoped, to dispel this ugliness from her head.

"Are you all right in there?" The muffled male voice came from the other side of her bedroom door.

Taylor sat bolt upright among the deep folds of the comforter. Her heart had taken off at a pounding clip. The terrible suspicions she had been entertaining faded in the bright, thrilling light of the thought that Des could be only the half width of this room distant from her right now. Who else could it be, after all? She didn't think that was Early's voice. She hurried to the door, hoping with that haste to leave her misgivings behind.

"Are you okay?" her visitor repeated as Taylor opened the door.

Her expectations plummeted. She could feel her heart sink with them, so much so she imagined he might notice. It was Jethro at her door.

"You aren't okay, are you?" he asked.

"I'm just tired," she said, after a moment to collect her wits enough to know she did not want to talk to Jethro right then. She hoped the mention of being tired would help her get rid of him.

"Sure, sure," he said, agitated as always. "I just wanted to give you something I thought might help you out."

He looked up and down the hallway as if to make certain he wasn't being observed. Then, he pulled a card from his pants pocket and thrust it toward her. For a fleeting instant, the furtiveness of his manner made Taylor think he might have some piece of important knowledge to impart to her, maybe something that would cast some light on her confusion and the maddening doubts that tormented her. She grabbed the card before his obviously unsettled condition might prompt him to think better of trying to help her and make him run away.

Taylor stared down at the card, unable at first to comprehend its meaning. Madame Leopold, it read. "Woman of Wisdom and Power. Seer. Sage." There was a graphic image of a crystal ball in one corner and an address in smaller print at the bottom. Taylor looked up at Jethro. If this was a clue to something, she hadn't a clue what that might be.

"My psychic," he said with a grin, as if that description should clear up the bewilderment her face must surely be revealing.

Taylor glanced down at the card again. She turned it over, but the reverse was blank. She looked up at Jethro.

"She'll bring you your luck," he said. "I figured you could use it."

Taylor sighed. "I see," she said. She really wasn't up to this kind of foolishness right now.

"Really," Jethro insisted. "I go to her every single morning of my life. I never miss. I go there and she gives me my luck for the day. I wouldn't go out of the house without it. She's got the power to do that. I swear it's true."

"I'm sure you do." Taylor could hardly believe she was being subjected to such babbling at this most difficult moment of her life.

If Jethro heard the sarcasm in her tone, he apparently didn't register its significance. "She can do the same thing for you. Just try her. You'll see. She'll get your luck back for you." He looked up and down the hall again, then lowered his voice almost to a whisper. "I'd like to see you get your luck back. I really would."

"Thanks, Jethro," she said wearily. "I'd like that, too."

She tried to return the card to him. "No, no," he said. "You have to keep that. I know it's just what you need."

"Okay, Jethro." Taylor began easing the door closed. "I'll keep it."

"You mark my words," he said through the narrowing opening. "It will be exactly what you need very soon. You'll see."

Taylor nodded. "Thanks again, Jethro," she managed. "Good night, now."

She shut and locked the door then leaned against it. Ordinarily, she would have laughed at the absurdity of what had just happened, in fact, at the absurdity of the entire, convoluted situation in which she found herself. Instead, she crumpled Madame Leopold's card in her fist and tried her hardest to hold back the tears.

# Chapter Nine

The next knock was not at the door. Taylor knew who it was for certain this time, no guesswork or wishful thinking. Only one person would climb the outside stairs to her balcony, like Romeo on a moonlit evening. She could imagine him saying good-night to everybody downstairs and pretending to leave. Maybe he had even driven away and then driven back or parked the car a block down the street where it wouldn't be seen by Mrs. Starling and her guests. Then he would have crept around the house and up to Taylor's balcony quietly enough not to be heard. Thank heaven, for his sake, that Winona had no guard dogs. Jethro might be said to perform that function for her, and he must not be on the prowl this late.

The knock came again, just as it had this morning, only softer now. Taylor lay very still. The lights were out in her room. He might assume she was sleeping. She didn't think he would want to make much more noise than this. She didn't think he would want Early and Winona or even Jethro to know that Des Maxwell was knocking on Taylor's window at nearly midnight. Meanwhile, the romance of that was not lost on her. The handsome lover comes questing for his lady in the wee hours. Taylor would have preferred to lose herself in that fantasy, but the practical side of her nature could not do that. Des was not Romeo, though he might be said to be her enemy, as Romeo and his family had been to Juliet. That love story had come to a bad end. Taylor understood that the same outcome was inevitable where she and Des were concerned.

The balcony door handle rattled. Apparently, Des wasn't about to give up easily. She heard him try both handles on the double doors. They must have been locked, because he had no luck. She thought she heard him mutter something disgruntled after his efforts failed. He would, of course, know that she was in here. She had left the parlor virtually unnoticed. Still, if Jethro had figured out where she went, Des would certainly have done the same. He might also have guessed that she wasn't really asleep, that she was in here listening to him and refusing to respond.

He will go away now, she thought.

What she had observed of Des told her he didn't put himself out very far to pursue much of anything. His well-developed defensive instincts would sense rejection and signal immediate retreat, back behind the blasé facade he had practiced to near-perfection. The prospect of that distance between them tugged at Taylor's heart. Her honest soul had to admit that losing him was not at all what she wanted. However, it was what had to be. Her earlier conclusion remained true. If she could not trust him, she could not love him. Being reminded of that tugged her heartstrings harder still, till the ache there was almost too bitter to bear.

All was quiet now. The windows along the balcony were closed and latched to maintain the climate-controlled temperature inside. He didn't rattle those windows as he had rattled the doors. He might have noticed the closed latches, or maybe he had simply lost interest and given up. Taylor rolled onto her side and curled up under the comforter, which didn't really provide her much comfort. She would have liked to cry. Tears can bring relief sometimes. Right now, however, she was afraid that if she started crying she might never stop.

From her nesting place, muffled by the comforter, she only half heard the sound on the roof. It was a shuffling noise that could have been the movement of a woods creature like a possum or the long branch of a tree. Except that Taylor would be very surprised if there were possums in Key West, and the trees around this house were mostly coconut palms that didn't have long branches. By the time those realizations took shape in her mind she had heard something else, also coming from the roof and definitely too loud to be a small animal.

She looked up. At first, what she saw struck fear to her bones. A shadow was moving above the stained-glass skylight, too close to be travelling clouds. Hinges squeaked and the skylight began to open. When it was opened wide, a figure slipped through, all but filling the space. Taylor gasped. Of course, she knew the identity of this intruder. She didn't need to be afraid as she would have been of a prowler or a cat burglar, but she did feel another type of fear. She scrambled backward to the headboard of the bed and pulled the comforter tight under her chin.

He eased himself down from the skylight opening, gripping the edge and dangling a few feet above the floor. He dropped into a crouch with far less noise than she would have thought possible for a man his size. He hesitated for a moment, probably to let his eyes adjust to the darkness. Then, she could feel rather than see him looking directly at her. She had hoped against hope to disappear among the bed covers so she wouldn't have to deal with the dilemma of this man whom she did not want here but also longed to be with. That dilemma was standing now, and walking toward her.

"What are you doing in my room?" she asked in a low whisper. She knew she must take charge of this situation right away or she would be lost.

"I had to see you."

He had reached the bed and was about to sit down next to her.

"I want you to get out of here," she said. That was only half a lie.

"I'm afraid I can't do that."

He did sit, very close. She inched away, but he grabbed her through the comforter before she could get very far.

"I had to be alone with you. I couldn't go home to my bed without you beside me."

His voice was deep and quivering with what she recognized as desire. Her own body responded instantly, as if the sound of him were vibrating deep inside her. She silently cursed this betrayal and struggled against it as he pulled her closer to him.

"This isn't right," she said. "I don't want you here."

"It is right, and you want me as much as I want to be here."

He swept the comforter aside. His eyes must have become as accustomed to the darkness as hers were by now. He would be able to see the hardness of her nipples jutting against the thin material of her sleep shirt, which his grip on her shoulders had stretched tight across her breasts. He slid one hand downward, as if to confirm what he saw. When his fingers touched her taut flesh, Taylor moaned despite herself. She couldn't help it. Her body, the betrayer still, was at war with her mind. Her mind was losing ground.

"See how much you want me here?" he rasped next to her ear in response to her moan. "You want me, and I want you. We can't deny that."

His face was in the hollow of her neck. His lips nuzzled, and his teeth nipped, and her reaction tore through her like wildfire. She pushed at him, but the battle within her made those efforts too feeble to be convincing even to herself. He covered her hand with his and moved them together down the front of his shirt. She sensed what he was doing and knew she should struggle all the harder to pull away. She didn't do that. Too much of her longed too powerfully to be exactly where he was leading her, and to touch what he was guiding her to touch.

When her fingers reached their goal, a shock ran through her. The mound of him was large and hard, constrained as it was by the tightness of his jeans. Her last impulse to resist melted in the heat of that touch. She did not need his hand to guide her any longer. She caressed the evidence of his desire for her in a manner that made her own desire equally undeniable.

Des groaned. "I love it when you touch me," he whispered.

She had touched him that afternoon, in the wildness of their lovemaking. Her touch was even more urgent now, fuelled as it was by a deep-down hunger like nothing she had ever experienced before this moment.

"I know you don't trust me," he said between ragged breaths. "The things you've heard aren't true. I want you to believe that."

"Later," she said somewhat harshly.

She shoved her fingers through his hair, surprised by how thick and silky it felt. His mouth was against the fullness of the top of her breast as he spoke. She pulled his head upward. His hand remained over her breast. When she covered his lips with hers, his hold there tightened, sending an excruciating flash of pleasure straight to her loins. She thrust her tongue between his lips, which opened eagerly to greet her.

With one arm, he pulled her closer to him, till his hand on her breast was crushed between their bodies. Still, he managed to move that hand downward. She was left to assuage the ache of her abandoned nipple by pressing herself hard to his chest and rubbing her breasts slowly, agonizingly back and forth against him. Meanwhile, his hand travelled across her belly to her hip then to the top of her thigh, where it paused to yank the hem of her shirt upward impatiently. She shifted her body to help him do that.

Her own hand was also moving, up from the hardness of him that felt as if it might rip through the denim at any moment, to his waistband, where she was glad to find that he wore no belt. She wanted to reach her destination with as little obstruction as possible. She slipped the metal top button through its hole more expertly than she would have thought she could, then touched the top of his zipper and found the tab. She took a firm hold and was about to pull downward when Des's fingers raked along her inner thigh to the lace hem of her panties and then over the silky material that covered her most private place.

Taylor's head snapped back. Her body arched in a movement she had not willed and could not possibly control. Her mouth pulled away from his in the convulsiveness of that movement, and a cry escaped her lips. His hand was caressing her as hers had so recently caressed him, but through much flimsier material. His fingers tantalized her, first gripping almost roughly, then teasing with strokes that probed but could not penetrate because of the silken barrier that shielded her wet and pulsating flesh as it had no wish to be shielded.

Taylor was debating, in near frenzy, whether to continue unzipping his jeans or to use her hand to force his own beneath her panties where she needed so badly for it to be. This dilemma was a delicious one. Everything about this moment was delicious and abandoned and purely thrilling. The last thing she wanted was an interruption. Unfortunately, that interruption came—in the form of a sharp rap and a voice at the door.

"Taylor, are you all right in there? Did I hear you call out?"

It was Early. He must have been walking down the hall and heard her cry. Taylor didn't answer. She and Des had both frozen in place. Her body continued to throb beneath his touch, but her mind had already begun to intervene. She remained still for another instant, arched and thrust against his fingers. Then she made a slight movement away. He must have caught the message of that signal. He slipped his hand over to the more neutral territory of her thigh.

In the meantime, Early must have been listening outside the door. When he heard nothing, he apparently was concerned because the next thing Taylor knew, there was the sound of metal entering the keyhole. She had locked the door after Jethro's visit. Did Early have a key? If so, why? But, there was no time to think about that now.

"Get under the comforter," she whispered to Des, just loudly enough for him to hear without the sound traveling to the door.

Des didn't answer. If he had any misgivings about cowering beneath her bed coverings, he didn't express them. He made haste to do as she said and pulled the comforter over him, then crouched behind her, curled compactly as was possible for a brawny man over six feet tall. Taylor raised herself on her elbow. She was on the side of the bed closest to the door, and the room was dark. They might be able to keep Des's presence a secret. Then again, they might not. She dreaded the thought of having to explain this to Early.

"Who's there?" she called, making her voice annoyed, which was not particularly difficult at the moment.

"It's me. Early. Are you all right?"

The key had halted its turning in the lock.

"I'm perfectly all right. I was sleeping," Taylor lied.

"I thought I heard you call out."

"You must have imagined it."

There was silence for a moment on the other side of the door. "Were you having a nightmare? I'm almost certain I heard you."

"Early," she said, fully as exasperated as she sounded. "I was not having a nightmare. I am trying to sleep. I wish you would let me do that."

Silence in the hallway again. Taylor could almost see Early standing there, one hand on the doorknob, the other on the key. He would be sorely tempted to barge in, taking more liberties with her life than he ought to, just as he and her aunts had always done, in what they referred to as Taylor's "best interests." She had no doubt that was their motivation. She no longer wanted or needed that intervention, no matter what the motive. Still, she could understand why Early might debate which course to take. The events of these past days had been devastating. He had good reason to be worried about her mental state. She was worried about that herself. All the same, she was prepared to go to the door and stop him from entering if he made one more move toward doing so. Fortunately, that was not necessary.

"All right," he said in a reluctant tone. "But you must talk to Winona in the morning. We're both very concerned about you."

"Good night, Early," she said, deliberately not agreeing to any plan that involved having herself taken care of in any way.

"Good night, Taylor."

She heard the key being pulled from the lock. There were a few further seconds of silence, during which Early was probably wrestling with himself about whether or not he was doing the right thing. Then she heard him walk away. She breathed a sigh of relief. She simply was not equal to more complications in her life at the moment. Early finding Des in her bed would definitely be a complication.

Meanwhile, she had been aware all along of Des beneath the comforter and close behind her. He reached out to encircle her waist now. She pushed him away.

"You have to leave," she whispered. She turned to look at him. His head had emerged from beneath the covers. The moon shining through the open skylight provided just enough light for her to see the question in his eyes. Before he could ask it, she repeated, "You really must go."

He stared at her for a moment, then sighed and nodded. He tossed the comforter aside and stood up, looking down at her without a word. He turned away and walked to the balcony door. She heard him fumbling with the lock. Then the door was open and he stepped through it. He closed the door behind him and was gone. She should have been grateful for how quietly he had left, so quietly that she didn't even hear his footsteps on the balcony. Instead, she was thinking about how cold the place beside her in bed had suddenly become and how she could still feel the memory of Des's touch upon her skin.

WHAT IN HELL was that character doing with a key to her room?

That question pounded in Des's brain as he chained his motorcycle to a parking meter outside his cafe. He'd tried to sleep after coming back here from Elizabeth Street last night, but it had been no use. He had paced and cursed and pounded things to keep from pounding some people he knew. At just about dawn, he'd taken the bike out along the shore highway and up U.S.1 past Stock Island toward the Upper Keys. He rode fast against the wind, but nothing could blow away what was in his head—the sound of Early Rhinelander about to let himself into Taylor's room.

What was that all about? What kind of relationship did she and Early really have? Was he in the habit of stopping by her room for warm-up sessions back there in the godforsaken frozen north where they came from?

Des couldn't stand the thought. Taylor seemed so straight-arrow to him. Still, Early had her key, and she didn't act surprised that he did. After all, their being lovers wasn't so hard to imagine. Lots of women dated older men. Some even preferred them. Taylor had talked about how tired she was of being hovered over, but maybe that wasn't really true. Maybe she liked having an older guy around because it made her feel safer, more secure than she would with somebody younger. She'd definitely had a life that might make her desire safety over other things.

But did it have to be with Early Rhinelander? He had been a thorn in Des's side ever since he was a kid. Maybe that was because he couldn't put anything over on Early. Des had conned a lot of people in those days, but never Early, and never Desiree. Des hadn't wanted to be anything but honest with her, and he couldn't get away with being less than honest with Early. Maybe that was what bugged Des about Rhinelander. Whatever the reason, it had been good riddance to that guy when he left the Keys. Now, he was back, and Des didn't like it. He especially didn't like Early being so familiar with Taylor. In fact, just the thought of that tormented Des. He reminded himself that this was another argument for not getting hooked on a woman. No involvements. No torment. That policy had worked very well for him—till *she* showed up.

Des was not at all in the mood for company. He didn't feel like talking to anybody right now. He'd come to the café because there would be nobody here at this hour. Even the cook didn't come in for a couple of hours yet. Des would make himself a pot of strong coffee, maybe scramble up some eggs with jalapeños. If he made them hot enough, they might just jolt him out of this funk he was in.

The man who stepped up to Des at that moment must have been standing in the closed doorway of the Beachcomber barroom. At first, Des thought the guy was after a handout. Des reached into the pocket of his jeans for some spare change. Then he recognized the man—or sort of recognized him—as somebody Des had seen here and there around the island from time to time, though not very often. He wasn't a panhandler, only one of the local bumper crop of eccentrics. Des wondered if he'd end up like this guy someday, tanned to brown leather, with a grizzled gray head, dressed like he couldn't remember the last time he gave a thought to what he put on.

"Mr. Maxwell," the man said, "I need to talk to you."

Des looked at him in a way that wasn't likely to encourage conversation.

"It won't take but a minute," the stranger went on. "Well, maybe that's not quite true. It could take some more than a minute. But not much more, mind you."

"Listen, buddy, this really isn't a good time. Let's make it later," Des said, pulling out the key to the padlock on the bamboo gate to the café courtyard.

"I don't think this should wait, sir." The guy sounded serious.

"What was your name again?" Des had heard it somewhere, but all he could remember right now was that it had been pretty unusual.

"They call me Lewt Walgreen." He hesitated. "That's what I told everybody was my name. But it isn't."

"Lots of people around here don't go by the name they were born with." Des felt a confession coming on from this guy, whatever his name was. Des was definitely not in the right frame of mind for that. "Look, pal," he said as he fitted the key into the padlock. "I have to get going now. Check me out later."

The man touched Des's arm as he was pulling the gate open. "My real name is Paul Lawrence Bissett," he said. "I'm Taylor's father."

Des had been about to yank his arm away from the man's grasp and tell him to get lost in terms he couldn't ignore. Instead, Des hesitated only a moment, then opened the gate and stepped inside. "Let's talk in here," he said and motioned for the man to follow into the courtyard.

Des let his companion walk ahead across the courtyard. Des needed a minute to think about what he'd just heard. Paul Bissett had run out on his family and never been heard from again. He'd deserted the navy, too. Everybody had assumed he was dead. Netta and Pearl could have officially declared him deceased years ago, but they could never bring themselves to do it. Des remembered Netta saying that part of the Bissett estate was still in her nephew's name. Des had always figured the guy couldn't be alive. Otherwise, he would have showed up some time over all these years to get the dough he had coming. There'd be a pile of it, too. Maybe that's what he was here for now, *if* he really was who he claimed to be.

"Have you got any proof you're Paul Bissett?" Des asked, taking the seat across from the one he'd indicated for his guest.

"Yes, I've got proof. It's back at my room, and my prints are on file with the navy."

"What are you doing here after all these years? Why'd you take off in the first place? You left your wife alone, never knowing what happened to you. Because of you, your kid grew up an orphan. Now you show up out of the blue. What are you after, anyway?"

Des was suddenly very angry. He locked his fists around the arms of his chair to get himself under control. He would rather have socked this guy in the nose. Maybe he'd do that yet. He'd been itching to sock somebody for several hours now. This guy just might end up as the target of the moment. There was no question he deserved a punch or two, after what he'd done to Taylor and Desiree.

"I know I did wrong." The guy looked ashamed all right, but that didn't cut much ice with Des. "I have no excuse, except that I was very young back then and in over my head."

"So, you left your family to fend for themselves."

"I knew they'd be well taken care of. My aunts would make certain they never wanted for anything financially."

"There's a lot more to taking care of somebody than making sure they have money." Everything this guy said made Des angrier. He understood that some of his anger at Early might be mixed in there, too. But he didn't care. "Look, whoever you are. I asked you why you're showing up now. Either give me an answer or get out of here, before I do something you'll be sorry for."

"I heard about what happened to Violetta. I had a feeling it could mean trouble. Then I heard Taylor was here on the island and she was staying at the place where that Cooney woman was killed. I couldn't help putting two and two together."

"And just what did that little piece of math tell you?" Des's patience had about run out.

"It told me that Taylor is in serious danger."

TAYLOR WOKE UP with one of her Aunt Pearl's sayings in her head. It went, "Sometimes, child, you don't know if you're afoot or on horseback." Taylor used to tease her aunt by calling her one-liners "Pearls of Wisdom" in a slightly sarcastic tone. She wasn't feeling sarcastic this morning. Pearl had been right. Taylor knew she didn't have her feet on the ground at the moment, but she also had no clue as to what breed of mount she might be riding. All she did know for sure was that the situation was close to a runaway and she had only a tentative hold on the reins.

She dragged herself upright and pulled her fingers through her tangled hair. What would today bring her way? She shuddered at the possibilities, and those were only the ones she could anticipate, not to mention the surprises. One thing she could count on. Early would be up here soon knocking on her door. He didn't get his name from being tardy. He sometimes seemed to arrive at Taylor's thoughts before she got there herself, and he would often be the first to understand their significance, too. She had depended on that quality in him when she needed it over the years. But she neither needed nor wanted it this morning. She scrambled into her clothes and tiptoed out of the house.

She had noticed a bicycle propped against the side of the garage where Jethro kept his red sports car. Taylor hadn't ridden a bike in years, but they say you never forget how. She was about to find out if that was true. She walked the bike to the corner in case her foray on two wheels turned out to be a noisy one. There was almost no traffic at this hour. Key West was really little more than a sleepy tropical village. Most residents wouldn't rouse themselves to their first cup of Caribbean coffee for another hour at least. Taylor was able to launch her wobbling vehicle into the street without much fear of collision.

She was wearing a short jumpsuit with the cuffs rolled above her knees so her legs would be free to pedal and there would be no long material to catch in the bike chain. Her canvas espadrilles had soles of sensible thickness and tied around the ankles. They wouldn't fall off as she pumped along. She had pulled her hair back with a band after brushing the unruly mass as tame as it would go. Locks escaped into springs of curl around her face, but her vision was kept clear so she could see to ride.

The morning breeze swept her cheeks, which had already brightened from these past few days of sun. The coolness was welcome on her bare arms. She felt alive as she pedaled briskly along, and was glad to feel that way. She was very aware of how much Des had to do with this vigorous life force coursing through her. His hands had done more than arouse her flesh with their burning touch. They had reached inside her to the barrier that a reserved north-country upbringing had erected between her self and her senses. They had torn that barrier down and allowed her capacity for passion to come rushing forth. If he had not come along, she might have remained caged forever. Even though she had arrived on this island ready to be set free, she had needed a guide to show her the way. Des had done that for her, and she couldn't help but be grateful.

She hadn't worked out exactly what she would do when she got to his place this morning. She would tell him what she was feeling and thinking, but she wasn't sure how to go about doing that. She would have to trust the words to come when she needed them. She was pedaling down Duval Street when it occurred to her that Des would most likely be sleeping at this hour, and she had no idea how to get inside the gates to the café that also led to his apartment. She hadn't noticed anything so conventional as a doorbell. Maybe she would have to find a pay phone and call him to wake him up. She wondered if his number was listed. It further occurred to her that, though they had connected very intimately with each other, she knew nothing of the details of his everyday life. She wasn't sure whether that made her feel intrigued or uneasy. She was glad to stop debating the point with herself when she arrived at the café and found the bamboo gate ajar.

Taylor leaned her bicycle against the fence across from a black-and-chrome motorcycle that was chained to a parking meter near the curb. She wondered if that motorcycle might belong to Des. It was a large and powerful model. A feeling of menace swept over her when she looked at it. She told herself to stop being so skittish and walked to the gate. She considered knocking, but that seemed inappropriate for a bamboo fence.

She pushed the gate open. Des was seated at a table at the far end of the courtyard near the restaurant building. He had his back to her. The sight of his broad shoulders and strong, muscled back made her heart leap in her chest. She was so happy to see him that at first she didn't notice the tension in those shoulders as he leaned toward the gray-haired man sitting opposite him. The man noticed Taylor before Des did.

The stranger wasn't wearing the usual Key West sunglasses, so Taylor could see his eyes. He was staring at her very intently, almost as if he knew her, but she was certain she had never seen him before. He also looked surprised to see her, maybe even shocked. That impression could be another example of skittishness on her part, but she didn't think so. Her instincts, fine-tuned by the incidents of the past few days, told her there was more going on here than might be obvious on the surface.

The man touched Des's arm and nodded in her direction. Des turned toward her for a very brief moment. He didn't speak. Instead, he glanced back at his companion. Once more, Taylor's instincts were on the alert. They told her that the glance between the two men had been a significant one, and not meant for her to see. The former exuberance she had felt at the beautiful morning and in anticipation of seeing Des was deflated in an instant. It was replaced by the morass of suspicions that she had been struggling to elude.

# Chapter Ten

"This is my friend Newt," Des said in answer to Taylor's inquiring glance at his companion.

A slightly nervous smile passed over the older man's face. "It's Lewt actually," he said. "Lewt Walgreen."

"You must not be very close friends, Des, if you don't remember the man's name." Taylor was itching to be much more direct with her suspicious questions, but she would bide her time for now.

"I'm more a friend of Violetta Ramone. An old friend of hers," said Lewt, or Newt or whatever his name might be. "I heard what happened to her and came to ask Destiny about it."

Taylor was surprised to hear him use Des's full name. Hadn't he said that nobody knew him as anything but Des, except some people who'd known him as a kid? Or had Winona been the one to mention that? Yet, if Walgreen had been around since Des's childhood, how could he possibly not remember the man's name?

"I haven't seen Lewt in many years," Des said, as if he might have guessed her question.

Taylor was too far into suspicion mode to be that easily satisfied. "I see," she said. "Well, are you going to invite me to sit?"

"Sure. Sit."

Des rose and pulled out a chair for her at the table. She could tell he wasn't happy to have her here. She had interrupted something. She was certain of that. She had walked in unexpectedly on something he didn't want her to know about or be a part of. Ordinarily, she would have taken the hint and politely excused herself. However, she wasn't feeling particularly polite at the moment. In fact, she was closer to downright belligerent than she could remember being in a very long time. She was tired of secrets. She had the definite sensation of being surrounded by lies. She intended to stick around here this morning until some truth came out.

"Why don't you make us some coffee, Des," she said. She had noticed the empty table in front of the two men and would have thought it contrary to Des's professional-host mentality to leave a guest so unattended. "Did Des offer you some coffee, Mr. Walgreen?"

"Well . . . no," Lewt managed.

"Des is known far and wide for his special brew. Isn't that true, Des? He even delivers it in person to visiting tourists on occasion. I cannot imagine why he would let you sit here so long without offering you a cup." Taylor kept her voice warm and sweet, even syrupy, as if she had no awareness at all of the uneasiness these two were so obviously exhibiting because of her presence.

"I arrived only a few moments before you," Lewt said. "Destiny hasn't had time to offer me much of anything. Except some kind understanding about Violetta, that is."

"Kind understanding," Taylor said, sweeter than ever. "That happens to be another one of the house specialties. Isn't that also right, Des?"

Under usual circumstances, Taylor would have expected a smooth "Of course" and a slow smile from the cool Mr. Maxwell. Instead, he pushed his chair back so fast he nearly tipped it over. He stood up just as hastily.

"I'll make us some coffee," he said.

He looked back and forth between Taylor and Walgreen. Taylor had the strong impression that Des didn't want to leave her alone with his friend. She could hardly wait to start poking around in Mr. Walgreen's head in search of the reason for Des's reluctance. As Des hurried toward the restaurant kitchen, Taylor had another strong impression—that the unflappable Des was flapping rather wildly all of a sudden. She would have bet money that Lewt was the key to that loss of composure. She also suspected that all of this had something to do with her.

As soon as Des was out of earshot, she turned to Mr. Walgreen and favored him with her most charming smile. "Do you live here on Key West?" she asked.

"Right now I do," he said. "I tend to move around quite a bit. For the moment, I've got a room over near the Kraals."

He continued to stare at her, even more intently now that she was at close range.

"May I be so rude as to ask whether you might have some vision problems?"

"I don't understand what you mean."

"You know. Do you perhaps not see very well?"

"I think I see just fine. Twenty-twenty, or almost so." He was obviously confused. "Why do you ask?"

"Because you've been staring at me as if you might be nearsighted and having trouble making out my features up this close." Taylor paused for a calculated moment. "Except that, as I recall, you stared at me the same way when I came in the gate back there." She motioned toward the far end of the courtyard. "Isn't that curious?"

She smiled winsomely once more. She was almost enjoying this little game. Still, she hadn't forgotten its real purpose—to gain information.

"It's just that you put me in mind of somebody I used to know," he said softly.

"And who might that be?"

Taylor was so intent upon sounding glib that she didn't immediately comprehend the implication of what he had said. He didn't answer her. He was gazing down at his hands on the table in front of him. His shoulders had slumped into a posture of what looked like dejection. It finally occurred to Taylor that if he was an old friend of Violetta's and probably knew Des when he was a boy, then maybe...

"Is it my mother that I remind you of?" she asked.

Again he didn't answer, but he looked up at her this time. There was sadness in his eyes and maybe even a mist of tears. He nodded. Suddenly, Taylor's plan to pump him for information about Des was less important than it had been a moment ago. She realized that there were other mysteries, even more pressing, to explore.

"Did you know her well?" Taylor asked.

"I wish I had known her better," he said, almost in a whisper.

"Tell me what she was like. Please."

He looked into Taylor's eyes for a long moment. She hoped he would see the need there as well as hear it in her words.

He cleared his throat, and when he spoke his voice was stronger. "She was wonderful."

"Des said that, too. I was hoping you could be more specific."

"She was very beautiful," he began, slowly at first. "She had the loveliest hands I have ever seen."

"Very gentle hands," Taylor said. "I think I remember that about her."

"What else do you remember about her?"

Taylor's thoughts had wandered off for a moment. Now she saw that he was looking at her very intently again, but somehow differently from before. He seemed more troubled now.

"I don't remember much at all, actually," she said, wondering why she felt compelled to tell this stranger something so personal and sensitive. "I've tried, but all I come up with are vague impressions, like of her hands just now."

"I'm surprised you don't remember her better than that. She wasn't the kind of person it's easy to forget. You were old enough, nearly seven, when she..." He paused, obviously hesitant to speak aloud of Desiree's death.

"You must have cared about her very much," Taylor said.

"Very much."

The mist in his eyes was brighter now. He brushed at what might have been a tear on his right cheek. On the back of his hand he had a tattoo of a rose with an elaborate design among its vines. He managed a smile. Taylor couldn't help thinking there was something familiar about that smile, but she couldn't quite put her finger on what it might be.

"You should do your best to find out whatever you can about Desiree," he said. "Maybe that will jog your memory."

"My mind has its own reasons for not wanting to remember. At least, that's what I've been told, and I guess it makes sense to me that could be true. I shouldn't try to force things to come back. If they do, they do. If they don't, they don't."

He chuckled. "You sound exactly like Pearl. I remember her saying just those words. 'If they do, they do. If they don't, they don't.'"

"You knew my Aunt Pearl, too?"

"I knew the whole family." The chuckle had faded. He looked sad again after a brief moment of almost light-heartedness. "Key West is a small town," he said. "Everybody knows everybody."

"But that was a long time ago. Pearl left here when I did, and she never came back."

"I was around before she left, for a while at least. She was also a very memorable woman, like your mother. You come from a family of memorable women."

Taylor didn't believe for an instant that was all there was to it. She would have liked to interrogate him more about his relationships with those memorable Bissett women, but Des had emerged from the restaurant door with a tray in his hands. He hurried toward them across the flagstone courtyard. Taylor was still determined to find out more from Mr. Walgreen, enough to be able to get in touch with him on her own and pick his brain clean if she could. Unfortunately, there was no opportunity for that. He barely tasted his coffee before abruptly excusing himself. He said he was late for another appointment. Once again, Taylor didn't believe he was telling the truth, at least not all of it.

Des walked Lewt to the gate. She would have liked to accompany them, but they were both up from the table and gone before she could collect her thoughts enough to follow. She thought better of running after them across the courtyard. She didn't want to appear that desperate for information. In her experience, she got what she was after most easily when she pretended not to care much about having it. So, when Des returned to the table she kept her questions casual. Still, he revealed very little other than that he really didn't know Lewt well and had no idea where he lived.

"Near something he called the Kraals," she said.

"That would be the Turtle Kraals."

"Where exactly is that?"

"The Kraals are down by the harbor, near Caroline and Grinnell."

"Didn't we drive down Caroline Street once? Isn't that one of those streets of beautiful houses?" Taylor asked, trying to sound casual as she angled for more details.

"Not near the Kraals. They may be on the same street, but they're very different parts of town."

"I see," Taylor said, filing all of that away for future reference.

They drank their coffee in silence after that. They didn't talk about the night before or the more distant past or any of what Taylor had originally come here to discuss. She had all but forgotten those concerns for the moment. She did make note that it was regular coffee they were drinking, which aroused her suspicions anew. She guessed that Des had been afraid to leave her alone with Lewt Walgreen long enough to make the more complicated café au lait. She also guessed it would be futile to ask Des to tell her why.

LATER, BACK at the Starling house on Elizabeth Street, Taylor would be the one answering questions. She wasn't in the mood for that. The day had grown more humid during her hour at the café. The pedal back to Winona's was neither breezy nor cool. The air had grown heavy and unpleasantly damp on Taylor's skin. Her frame of mind contributed to that unpleasantness. By the time she parked her bike against the Starling garage, she felt sticky and out of humor. She only stopped on the back veranda as a courtesy to her hostess, whom Taylor anticipated would be there having breakfast as she did each morning. Taylor had planned to say a brief hello, then go immediately upstairs to shower and change her perspiration-soaked clothes. Just about the last person she cared to see was the man seated across from Winona incongruously, for him at least, sipping tea.

"Ms. Bissett, how nice of you to join us at last," Detective Santos said in his customary arch tone.

Taylor suppressed a groan.

"The detective insisted on waiting for you," Winona said. "I suggested that he come back later, but he wouldn't hear of it." She wore her dark glasses. If her eyes had been visible, Taylor suspected she might see an apology there for not being able to call Santos off her trail.

"I don't suppose you would be willing to wait a little longer until I can change my clothes?" she asked Santos.

"Your supposition is correct."

He pushed back the chair next to him so she could sit. Taylor chose a seat on the other side of the table instead.

"Dr. Starling tells me you've been out for some morning exercise."

"That's right. I have."

"You look like it was quite a strain," he said, pointedly observing her flushed, damp cheeks and disheveled outfit. "Did you bike to any place in particular?"

"No place in particular."

"And if I knew your destination would I maybe find a dead body there?"

"No, you would not." Taylor felt her exasperation with this annoying man rise toward the boiling point. She was too out of sorts to be subjected to his snideness right now. "And, if you don't have any serious questions to ask me, then I am going upstairs to change, whether you want me to or not."

"I wouldn't suggest you do that."

"What would you suggest, Detective Santos? That I sit here calmly while you do your best to provoke me? Is that your plan?"

"Who said I was trying to provoke you, Ms. Bissett? I'm just doing my job."

His condescending tone was extremely irritating to Taylor. She was beginning to feel very jerked around, and not only by this detective character.

"Ask me a specific question, or I am going to leave, no matter what you suggest," she said. "And if you don't like that, you will probably like harassment charges even less."

Winona's eyebrows arched visibly above her sunglass frames. Taylor recognized that as a signal to back off, that she was over the top and in danger of getting herself in real trouble. She knew that was true. Santos was the police, after all. He could probably even arrest her as a material witness or whatever. She had been pushed too far already this morning to care.

"Specific question number one," Santos said. "Where were you on the afternoon Violetta Ramone was killed?"

"Are you sure she didn't just die of a heart attack?" Taylor asked.

"As I believe I may have said at the time, it might be accurate to say she was scared to death—deliberately."

"Isn't that rather difficult to prove?"

"Don't worry, Ms. Bissett. I will be able to prove what I need to prove when the time comes. Now, please, answer my question. Where were you that afternoon?"

Taylor hesitated, even though she knew Santos was aware of exactly where she had been. She was wondering why he was pressing the point now. She and Des had both admitted their whereabouts that afternoon. Maybe Santos was looking for specifics after all. Policeman or not, she certainly wasn't going to tell him that she and Des had been making love.

"I was with Mr. Maxwell," she said. "Didn't we tell you that at the time, when you questioned us at Violetta's house?"

"I'm just checking to see if your story might have changed."

"Why would my story change? It happens to be the truth."

"It also happens to be very convenient, since it makes you each other's alibi for the time of the death." Santos leaned back in his chair and smirked at her. "I'd call that convenient."

"I don't really care what you would call it." Taylor's voice was low and angry.

"You had better care, Ms. Bissett. As I see it, you are intimately involved in two suspicious deaths, one of which is definitely a homicide."

Taylor pushed her chair back so hard that the wrought-iron legs grated loudly against the veranda floor. She stood up so that she would be looking down at Santos and he would have to look up at her.

"If you have a specific charge to make," she said, and her voice was trembling, "then make it and put me under arrest. But if you do that, you had better have the kind of evidence it takes to make that charge stick. Otherwise, you'll be hearing from my attorneys about false arrest, along with the charge of harassment."

"Well, well, well," he said. "I really seem to have pushed your buttons this morning."

"My buttons are not your business, Detective, unless you have a formal charge to make. And, if you have, you had better make it now."

Taylor could feel herself about to explode. She imagined she must look that way, too. Her cheeks were so hot that they had to be bright red, and she guessed that her eyes must also be spitting sparks for everyone to see.

"One moment, please, both of you," Winona said in a very commanding tone. "I feel that I must intercede here before this situation gets even more out of hand."

"Go right ahead, Dr. Starling," Santos said. "Ms. Bissett could use a referee."

"And what about what you could use, Detective?" Taylor snapped.

"I must insist that the two of you let me speak for a moment," Winona said. "You will accomplish nothing by yelling at one another."

"Ms. Bissett is doing all of the yelling here. I have not raised my voice."

"You may not raise your voice," Taylor said, leaning across the table toward Santos, "but you don't hesitate to be nasty, do you?"

"Enough!" Winona was the one to raise her voice this time. "Taylor, sit down this instant. And, Detective Santos, please let me ask the questions."

Santos shrugged but didn't comment further. After a moment's reluctance, Taylor sat.

"Detective Santos gave me no indication of any intention to put you under arrest, Taylor," Winona went on in her usual modulated tone. She turned toward Santos. "Was I correct in that interpretation of your intentions from our conversation before Taylor arrived, Detective?"

"Absolutely correct."

"And have you altered those intentions?" Winona asked.

Santos waited a moment before replying, "Not at this particular time."

"Good." Winona turned back to Taylor. "Are you aware, my child, that you need not subject yourself to any further questioning without an attorney or other representative present on your behalf?"

"I am aware of that." Taylor hoped she wouldn't have to go to such lengths. Her threat of calling in an attorney had been more a bluff than anything else.

"Then I would suggest that this interview is at an end," Winona said, "or at least postponed until Taylor is feeling more equal to the challenge and is properly represented, as well."

"I have a number of other questions," Santos began.

"As I understand the law, Detective Santos," Winona cut in, "once a suspect has requested the presence of counsel, the interrogation must cease until that counsel has been arranged."

Taylor opened her mouth to protest. She didn't like being referred to as a suspect, and she wasn't sure she wanted legal counsel.

"Please, child," Winona said firmly. "Let me take the leadership role here. I am convinced that I can act in your best interests, perhaps even better than you can at this point in time."

Before Taylor could decide whether she agreed with that or not, Santos stood and stepped back from the table.

"Dr. Starling is one hundred percent on target about the law. You have the right to have a lawyer present and, if that's what you want, my hands are tied for now."

Taylor wasn't sure what she did want, other than to have Santos out of here. Winona's way did seem to be the fastest means of accomplishing that. Taylor sighed and nodded her agreement.

"Excellent," Winona said with a level of enthusiasm Taylor thought hardly justified. "Now, child, why don't you go upstairs while I see the detective out. I will join you shortly."

Taylor hesitated.

"I do not believe there is anything positive to be achieved by prolonging this meeting."

Taylor couldn't really argue with that. "All right," she said.

She turned from the table without so much as looking at Santos. She could sense that he, on the other hand, was watching her every move as she walked to the door. She hated to leave a situation where she suspected she would be the topic of conversation after she was gone. She opened the door and went inside anyway, comforted only by the fact that Winona remained behind as her champion.

A HALF HOUR LATER Winona came to Taylor's room as promised.

"Where were you bicycling off to so early this morning?" she asked, obviously trying to keep the subject off Detective Santos for the moment.

She was dressed in white from chin to toe as usual, in a long lounge dress such as fine ladies in old movies might wear in the morning. A silver chain hung from her neck, from which a deep purple polished stone in a silver-filigree framework was suspended almost to her waist.

"What kind of stone is that?" Taylor asked while deciding whether to follow Winona's lead in softening the conversation.

"They call it sodalite. It is purported to possess the power to balance the opposing sides of one's being. I shall get you one of your own, my dear. We could all use a bit of balancing on occasion."

Taylor was tempted to laugh out loud. "You won't hear any argument from me about that right now."

"I hope that we shall not argue about much of anything, my dear."

Winona had brought a tray with her and put it on the table next to the bed where Taylor was seated, propped against several pillows. She accepted the cup of tea Winona offered. The amber liquid smelled softly of lemon. Taylor took a sip. It tasted good, and the warmth of it was welcome.

"I went to see Des Maxwell," she said, having decided to answer Winona's earlier question.

"How nice it is that you two young people seem to have struck up a friendship." Winona had seated herself on the edge of the bed.

"I thought you didn't approve of Des."

"As you say, I do not approve of Mr. Maxwell, nor do I trust his intentions. He is far too circumspect a young man for my taste. When with him, which I must admit I am relieved is not often, I am fairly assailed by the impression of tales unspoken, perhaps even dark tales unspoken. That is the main reason I avoid his company. I tend to experience such impressions as an assault, which can be quite painful. My intuitions are so keen as to be vulnerable to such overwhelming influences.''

Taylor sighed. Her own intuitions might not be as sensitively pitched as Winona's, but Taylor had sensed the same thing about Des and his secrets.

"Drink your tea, my dear," Winona said. "It will soothe you."

Taylor did as requested. "This is delicious," she said politely.

"I am so glad you like it. I will prepare a packet for you to take with you when you return home."

Taylor hadn't thought about going home in what felt like so long that the concept seemed strange to her, as foreign and distant as home itself was from this island and what had happened to her here. Those experiences should have made her eager to shake the sand of Key West from her feet and fly north as soon as possible. Yet, something had a hold on her here, making her not at all certain whether she wanted to go or to stay.

"We were speaking of Mr. Maxwell," Winona was saying as she refilled Taylor's cup from the pot on the tray. "I may not enjoy his company myself, but I should not attempt to impose those sentiments upon you. You are a grown woman of considerable intelligence and most certainly capable of choosing your companions for yourself. I am deeply apologetic that I may not have behaved appropriately when you brought Mr. Maxwell here yesterday."

"You needn't apologize..." Taylor began. She was about to add that she had very big doubts about Des herself when Winona raised her hand to interrupt.

"Yes, my dear. It is most appropriate that I express my regrets to you. It has long been my conclusion from my communications with your departed aunts that they held you entirely too close to their bosoms for your own good and, I suspect, too close for your preference as well.''

"Pearl and Netta were more protective than I wanted them to be." Taylor couldn't help thinking that, at the moment, she might welcome some of that protectiveness against the trials and troubles of life.

"To be sure, they behaved thus toward you out of the most loving motives. I would not want my comments to be interpreted as criticism of those sweet ladies. They were totally devoted to you. It is nonetheless also true that a caged bird knows less contentment than would be the case were he allowed to fly free. Tranquillity and contentment are among the supreme imperatives in life. Would you not agree?''

"Yes, I would agree," Taylor said, nodding thanks for another replenishment of her teacup.

"You have, most unfortunately, found little tranquillity on our island, either in the past or the present.''

Taylor sighed. "That is also true." Winona's mention of the past brought something else to mind. "By the way, do you know a man named Lewt Walgreen?''

"I don't believe so.''

"Are you absolutely sure?''

Winona thought a moment then shook her head. "I expect I would remember such a distinctive name had I ever heard it. Why do you ask?''

"He was at the café with Des this morning. Walgreen said he knew my family well, especially my mother. I thought that, since you were close to them too, you might have run into him.''

"What does he look like?''

"Curly, silver hair. Deep tan. Probably in his late fifties. Rather eccentric in his dress.''

"That would describe a great many men in Key West, my dear. Was there any other distinguishing quality or detail you might have noted?"

"Yes, now that you mention it, there was. He had a tattoo on the back of his hand." Taylor thought a moment. "His right hand, I think."

"Another very common sight in the Keys, I regret to say."

There was a knock at Taylor's half-opened door. Early thrust his head inside. "Is this a no-boys-allowed gathering or can I join you?"

"Come in, Early," Taylor said.

"Did I miss anything while I was out?" he asked.

"We had a rather disquieting visit from that police detective," Winona said, glancing at Taylor. "But we will not speak further of that at the moment. We were just now discussing a gentleman Taylor met at Mr. Maxwell's establishment this morning. Though, perhaps from her description, I deduce that he is not as much a gentleman as one might hope for."

"What's his name?"

"What did you call him, my dear?"

"Lewt Walgreen was the name he gave me."

Early snorted his obvious disapproval. "I'll bet he's a Lewt all right, just like that bar-bum friend of his."

"Now, Early," Winona said in an admonishing tone. "I have just been speaking about how outside the bounds of appropriateness it is for you and me to berate Mr. Maxwell or in any way to criticize the choices of a young woman fully mature enough to make such decisions on her own."

"So you told me already." Early both looked and sounded skeptical.

"And you would do well to listen." Winona rose from the edge of the bed with a rustle of white silk. She took Taylor's cup from her hand and put it on the tray. "Now, if you will excuse us, I am going to encourage this lovely child to take a small nap. She is looking quite done in. Wouldn't you agree, Early?"

"I wouldn't doubt she's done in after going off wandering all over this island at the crack of dawn."

"Now, Early, that will be entirely enough of your grumbling," Winona said as she shooed him toward the door. "I can see that you are in need of more than a little instruction in the art of allowing the bird to fly free." She looked back at Taylor. "Wouldn't you agree, my dear?"

Taylor nodded. She couldn't help smiling at the sight of stubborn, hardheaded Early being whisked from the room by a delicate-looking woman in white silk. Taylor also couldn't help feeling quite tired. The bicycle ride had used muscles too long dormant, not to mention the wear and tear this still-young day had already exerted on her emotions. Winona's suggestion of a nap was growing more and more appealing.

Taylor leaned back into the pillows and surveyed the lovely room with its soft, soothing colors. She imagined Winona had meant it to reflect the kind of tranquillity she talked about before. Taylor's life had been sorely lacking that kind of peacefulness for what felt like a very long time now. When Winona returned to the bedside and began to stroke Taylor's forehead ever so gently, she found herself wishing she could be more like this serene woman someday.

## Chapter Eleven

Des waited as long as he could manage before going to the Starlings', which he knew probably wasn't as long as he should have. Taylor had made it very clear, when she left the café, that she wasn't interested in talking to him. She'd said she didn't trust him. He couldn't really blame her for feeling that way, especially after the stunt he'd pulled this morning. She had every right to know that this joker Walgreen claimed to be her long-lost father, Paul Bissett. Des had intended to make him prove it, but Taylor showed up before Des could find out enough to arrive at a determination one way or the other. Then he'd pulled that fool move of lying about the whole thing. At the time, he had figured she'd be upset by hearing Walgreen's story. If that story turned out to be untrue, she would have been upset for no reason. Des had thought he was protecting her by shielding her from possible unnecessary pain. Now, he knew he'd made a bad mistake. He had to unmake it if he could.

He parked the Jeep on the corner, several houses away from Winona Starling's. He'd gotten into the habit of doing that in the course of his secret visits to Taylor's room. He might have tried that same clandestine route up to the outside balcony now, but he saw Jethro lounging

on the front porch glider. There was no way Des could get
down the side path next to the house, up the outside stairs
to the second floor and across the balcony without Jethro
seeing or at least hearing him. Des also definitely could
not get away with a repeat of the skylight stunt he'd
pulled last night. He couldn't help smiling at the thought,
anyway. He'd never done anything that crazy just to get
to a woman. Maybe he should say he'd never had a
woman drive him crazy enough to try. Either that or he'd
been watching too many Indiana Jones movies for his
own good. Des walked up the steps to the Starlings' grand
veranda, thinking he could use a little Indiana in himself
right now for facing Winona and Early on their turf.

"How's it going, Des?" Jethro asked, darting up from
the porch swing so abruptly that he set the chain clank-
ing.

"Not bad, Jethro. How's it going with you?"

"Lucky as always, Des. I make it a point always to
have my luck with me."

"That's good," Des said as he moved to ring the
doorbell.

Jethro was always carrying on about his luck. Des had
never seen any particular sign of Jethro's supposed good
fortune, except that his mother supported him so he'd
never in his life had to work a regular job. Maybe that
was what Jethro thought of as lucky. There were a lot of
guys who would agree with him. Des didn't happen to be
one of them.

"I suppose you're here to see Taylor." Early was at the
screen door before Des could ring the bell.

"That's right. And I suppose you're here to stop me."

Early looked down his skinny nose, which was hard to
do since Des was the taller of the two of them. "If I had
my way, that's exactly what I would do," Early said.

"But Winona's gone soft on me and says I shouldn't interfere."

"That is precisely correct, Early." Winona appeared next to Early. She was all in white as always, just one of the many affectations of hers that Des couldn't stand. "The poor child has been sleeping," she said to Des, "but she may have awakened by now. Early, would you please do me the service of going upstairs to ascertain that for us?"

Des had to restrain himself from crying out his objections. He didn't want Rhinelander going up there with that key of his again. Instead, Des said, "Thank you," to Winona. He hadn't expected to get to Taylor this easily. He had to be careful not to screw up that surprise advantage.

"You may step inside out of the midday sun if you wish, Mr. Maxwell."

He was actually standing in the shade of the veranda with its cooling ceiling fans that kept the air moving and the bugs away. He would have preferred to wait for Taylor out here, but again he didn't want to upset this unaccustomed equilibrium between Winona and himself. He opened the door and entered the foyer. As he did so the age-old story of the spider and the fly came to mind. Winona didn't invite him into her parlor, however, though she did remain in the foyer with him while he waited. Des wondered how much of an effort that courtesy might be for her. Winona's unrelenting smile gave no indication of the answer.

Meanwhile, Des was growing more and more agitated the longer Early spent upstairs. "Maybe you should find out what's going on," he said finally, unable to maintain his cool demeanor another minute.

Just then, Early appeared at the stairway landing. "She's on her way," he said, looking pointedly only at Winona. Then, to add to Des's frustration, Early went back upstairs instead of coming down.

"Early's room is situated on the opposite hall from Taylor's," Winona said. "I expect that's where he's headed."

Winona appeared to have guessed what Des was thinking. He was beginning to wonder if there might be some truth to the rumors about her supposed remarkable powers of perception. He was also wondering what else she might be perceiving. Before he could venture a guess at that, Taylor appeared on the stair landing and began her descent toward them.

Des had never picked up a date for the prom or had a real wedding where the bride walks down the aisle toward her groom. His life hadn't been the kind that afforded such experiences. This moment made up for all of that. The window above the landing was made of stained glass in deep yellow and blue tints. The sunlight washed through those colors and down onto Taylor, making a shimmering halo of her hair. She had changed into a sleeveless top and a long, full skirt in pale peach. She was wearing sandals again. The flick of her coral toenails was just visible to Des every time she took a step forward.

It was a simple outfit, decorated only by the slender, gold watch-bracelet at her wrist. Still, Des felt his heart cease its drumming for an instant at the sight of her. She might have been Cinderella decked out for the ball, glass slippers and all, as far as he was concerned. She was by far the most beautiful woman he had ever seen. He knew that assessment must show clearly on his face and that Winona was watching him. He didn't care. If he'd thought Taylor would tolerate it, he would have rushed forward and swept her up in his arms. But he knew she wouldn't want that. He was lucky she had agreed to see him at all. He would have to content himself with this small piece of good fortune for now. In fact, after he told her what he had come here to say, this might be the last favor she would ever grant him.

He had no intention of telling her anything here in this house, even though Winona left them alone in the foyer once Taylor was down the stairs. She made no secret of the fact that she didn't feel like going for a ride with him right now. She had too many doubts about his intentions. She continued in that resolve until he mentioned that what he had to tell her had something to do with Lewt Walgreen. She agreed to go with Des then, but only for a very brief while. Des felt Jethro watching from the veranda swing as he and Taylor walked toward the corner.

"This had better be as important as you say," Taylor said once they were in the Jeep and off Elizabeth Street.

"It is," Des said.

"Then why don't you tell me and have it over with?"

"What I have to say is very likely to upset you. I don't want to do it while we're driving along a public street like this."

"You have been upsetting me from the first moment I met you," she said, "and that was in a very public place. What is so different now?"

"Believe me. This is different."

They were headed east toward Angela Street. Des didn't know why he'd come this way. He had driven pretty much aimlessly after leaving the Starling house. The cemetery was just ahead, a vast field of above-ground mausoleums very similar to the one in New Or-

leans. The bedrock of Key West, like the marshy delta of
Louisiana, didn't allow for much digging.

"Pull up over there," Taylor said, pointing to the side
of the road near the cemetery fence.

Des didn't care for her choice, or for the irony it im-
plied—that this could be the setting for the death of any
chance he might have of a relationship with her.

"Now, what is it you have to say about Lewt Walgreen that is going to upset me so much?" she asked
when the Jeep had come to a stop and Des had killed the
motor.

"I should have told you this right off when you met
him this morning, but I wanted to find out if there was
any truth to it first."

"Just tell me."

"I still don't know if it's true. He could be lying."

"I said, just tell me."

Her voice was low but very intense. Des knew there was
no way to avoid what had to be said. He looked across
the patched asphalt at the sleepy street facing the cemetery. No one was in sight. If she made a scene, there
would at least be no witnesses.

Des heaved a sigh. "Well, here it is then," he said.
"Lewt Walgreen claims that he isn't Lewt Walgreen at all.
He says he's your father, Paul Bissett."

If Des had expected hysterics, he could not have been
more wrong. Taylor turned her head slowly to stare at the
rows of mausoleums only yards away. The steely calm of
her profile made him wish she would rant and scream.

TEN MINUTES LATER, they were headed toward Land's
End and the Turtle Kraals. Taylor was not surprised to
find out that Des knew where Walgreen lived, after all.
By now, she wouldn't have been surprised to find out Des

had lied with every word he ever told her. She was that suspicious of him. She even doubted his motives for finally telling her the truth about Walgreen. Des probably figured she would find out on her own eventually, what with a police detective checking out everything about her, and Winona seeming to know so much about whatever happened on this island. Or maybe Des had another reason. All Taylor could be certain of was that he most likely wouldn't be thinking in a straight, honest line whatever his motives might be. She had come to the conclusion that he was so accustomed to subterfuge and secrets he probably couldn't recognize the difference between them and the real thing any longer.

Taylor didn't like thinking that way about him. His actions had brought her to it. Now, she would be foolish to ignore the evidence of her own senses. She was even beginning to take seriously the possibility that he could be involved in what Santos had referred to as the ''suspicious deaths'' of April Jane and Violetta. That might also explain why Des had been hanging around Taylor so much. She had wanted to believe he cared about her. She didn't believe that any longer. The more plausible scenario was that he wanted to keep an eye on her—and her family's money—while he nudged her toward the spotlight of guilt for those crimes every chance he got.

He could be doing something underhanded like that right now. Maybe he was driving her into a trap, instead of taking her to Lewt Walgreen's room as he said. She considered telling Des to drop her off. She could get a pink cab or perhaps call Jethro for a ride, though she didn't really want the Starlings to know what she was up to. Despite Winona's promises to let Taylor fly free, she could feel how concerned and troubled Winona was about what had been going on these past few days. She seemed intent upon preventing Taylor from getting upset about things. She had cared for Taylor as a child when she was much more fragile emotionally. Winona might not yet have recognized how much stronger Taylor the woman was than Taylor the child had been. She might not understand that Taylor was equal to investigating this man's claim to be her father, no matter how upsetting that claim might be.

And, of course, it *was* upsetting. She didn't want to think about it, really. She preferred to preoccupy herself with Des and Winona or whatever other distractions might be handy. Before long, she'd be pondering Jethro's trips to his fortune-teller or the variation in barometric pressure. Speaking of which, she had heard somebody remarking about a storm warning. Hurricane season was still months away, but she understood there could be tropical storms or even tornados this time of year. The day had turned gray while she was napping at Winona's. The atmosphere seemed anything but stormy, however. In fact, now that Taylor was paying more attention to her surroundings, she noticed how almost unnaturally still the air felt, like the steely calm she had imposed upon herself in preparation for whatever she might find out from Lewt Walgreen.

Des drove them along a road next to the harbor. A thicket of white and aluminum and even mahogany masts stood straight up from the marina cove in the breezeless afternoon. Gulls flapped their wings vigorously to stay aloft without the usual hearty up-and-down bay blasts to soar upon. There was a strange light all around, gray with a bit of sun trying to filter through. This was an eerie day, both outside of Taylor and within her, making her feel restless and out-of-sorts. She was relieved when Des pulled the Jeep up in front of a shallow, sandy yard and a plain-fronted building in bad need of a paint job. He had been right. This neighborhood wasn't much like the other end of Caroline Street. Apparently Mr. Walgreen, or whoever he might be, didn't live a very prosperous life.

It occurred to Taylor that this could explain Lewt's claim to be Paul Bissett. According to her understanding of the family estate, her father, if he really was alive, would be entitled to a small fortune. She imagined that a man who resided in a place like this might very well concoct whatever story he could to inherit a new and much improved lifestyle. Maybe Walgreen actually had known her family all those years ago. He could have heard about Netta's recent death and figured that, with both the aunts gone, he might be able to trick people into believing he was the long-lost heir. He could recount family stories he had heard, the way fake psychics recycle scraps of information to fool their customers. Taylor would be on the alert for that kind of trickery. As for the possibility he could have told Des the truth, Taylor was not about to let herself think much about that. Her north-country caution was on full alert. This was a gift horse she would most certainly look straight in the mouth, as well as one she might not truly want.

Walgreen's room was on the first floor, in the back. Taylor followed Des down a hallway to Walgreen's door. While Des knocked, she looked around. Through the window at the end of the hall she could see a rear porch facing other backyards of mostly sand and scrub grass. When Des's repeated knocking brought no answer, she walked to the window and pushed it open. She didn't hesitate a moment before climbing out onto the porch. Her pale-colored skirt might come out the worse for wear from the splintered, dusty windowsill, but she didn't care about that.

"What are you doing?" Des asked as she pulled herself through the opening.

"I'm following your example at the guesthouse," she said.

"What if somebody sees you?"

Taylor glanced around. As usual at this afternoon-siesta time of day, there wasn't a soul in sight. She imagined that the especially humid and heavy atmosphere, along with the storm warnings, had most Key Westers planted in front of their fans and air conditioners for the duration.

"If somebody sees me, they can call the police," she said, feeling fairly certain that wouldn't happen anyway. "I won't be a new face to them."

Taylor walked to the window she had hoped there would be from Walgreen's room onto this porch.

"I don't think you should do this," Des said in a lowered voice as he scanned the back lots and the windows of the adjacent buildings.

"I didn't ask what you think. This Walgreen person is making claims about my family. It's up to me to decide how far I should go to investigate those claims."

"I care about your family too, but—"

Taylor interrupted him sharply. "That may or may not be true. Nonetheless, they are *my* family, not yours."

She saw in his eyes the flash of hurt those words caused. She wished she didn't feel her own flash of remorse for saying them. Then his familiar impassive facade returned, wiping anything readable from his face.

"That's true," he said. "I'll be careful to keep it in mind from now on."

He stepped away from the window. It occurred to Taylor that he might take off and leave her there. A wave of anxiety trembled through her. She really didn't want to search a strange man's room alone. What if he showed up and discovered her doing that? What if he really was a con man desperate to get his hands on her family's money? Would he hurt her to do it?

"In for a penny, in for a pound," Taylor whispered just under her breath. Another of her aunt's Pearls of Wisdom had popped into Taylor's head in a moment of fear and indecision.

She pushed so resolutely at the window to Lewt Walgreen's room that it opened more rapidly than she had expected, nearly toppling her off-balance. That also made more noise than she had anticipated. She scanned the neighboring buildings, as Des had done a moment ago. She thought she might have seen a shadow of movement in the upper story of the next house, but when she looked again she saw nothing. She hoped she had only imagined something there. Whatever the case, she was committed to this course of action now. She hiked her long skirt up above her knees and climbed through the window opening, thinking that, if she had known she would be engaged in breaking and entering this afternoon, she would have dressed more appropriately for the occasion.

The room was what she might have expected in a building such as this one. It wasn't dirty, though the simple furnishings were on the well-worn side. It wasn't very personal either. This might be a place where somebody slept, but no one really *lived* here. It definitely wasn't what she would call a home. Again, a flash of unbidden compassion overtook her before she could guard against it. She had deliberately hardened her heart to Lewt Walgreen. Ever since Des made his revelation in the Jeep, she had surrounded any thought of the man who claimed to be her father with a barrier of what was as close to iciness as she could manage. She had done that to protect her feelings from the kind of damage that revelation might do, whether it turned out to be the truth or was proven to be a lie. The lonely look of this room had found a crack in that icy barrier.

Taylor didn't want that. She was going to do what she came here for, and she wasn't going to allow emotion to get in her way. It had been her intention to investigate. She was going to investigate. As if to prove her own resolve to herself, she pulled open the top drawer of the maple-veneered dresser that stood against the wall opposite the neatly made bed. She didn't expect to find anything. If this guy was the con man she suspected him to be, he would have hidden anything potentially incriminating in some clever, less obvious spot.

The dresser drawer she had opened was filled to about half its depth with carefully folded stacks of men's T-shirts, shorts and socks. Taylor was mildly surprised. She wouldn't have expected such a haphazardly dressed man to be quite so orderly. She gasped as a shock of connection took her by even greater surprise. Her Aunt Pearl had arranged her bureau drawers exactly like this, in carefully stacked rows, and never more than halfway full. Pearl disliked clutter and crowding in all things. It was one of the traits she did not hold in common with her sister. Pearl had even folded things the way the clothes were folded in this drawer, into thirds with the edges tucked underneath and out of sight.

Taylor swept the piles together, as if to banish their orderliness and the uncomfortable recognition it had made her feel. She told herself this was only a coincidence, that the way a person folded his laundry had no real significance whatsoever. That reassurance did nothing to quell her uneasiness, especially when she saw what her impulsive movement had uncovered at the bottom of the dresser drawer. A flat portfolio, not unlike the one she had carried to Key West from the north country, had been placed beneath the underwear and socks. She didn't kid herself that Lewt Walgreen had been trying to hide the portfolio when he put it here. This spot was neither clever nor unobtrusive.

She took the portfolio from the drawer and set it on top of the dresser. She hesitated for a moment before opening the flap, then reminded herself of her resolve to investigate, and reached inside the portfolio before she could reconsider further. The papers she pulled out were as neatly folded as Mr. Walgreen's laundry had been. They were also soft to the touch, like old documents can become. She unfolded the first piece of paper on the pile and sighed deeply as she read. It was a marriage license. To be specific, it was her parents' marriage license, dated when she knew their wedding to have been and stamped with the county seal that indicated it was issued in Key West. Taylor's parents had been married here.

Taylor picked up the pile of papers and walked unsteadily to the bed. She was so numb she could hardly feel her feet touching the floor. She sat down on the faded bedspread with Lewt Walgreen's documents in her lap and unfolded the next piece of paper. It was an identity certificate from the United States Navy, designating that First Lieutenant Paul Lawrence Bissett was to be stationed at Key West naval base. The date was several months earlier than that on the marriage license. Taylor smoothed the document open very gently on her lap. When a tear fell on the paper, she brushed it quickly away. She didn't want anything to damage these artifacts that were as much a part of her own life history as they were the history of the people who had given her that life.

Beneath the navy document she found a color photograph. The tints had faded some. The edges were soft and frayed as if from being frequently held or even fondled. She knew the woman's face as well as she knew her own, partly because it was so much like her own. This woman's hair was straighter than Taylor's and longer. She wore a white dress with a short hemline in the style of the early sixties. She had on a small, veiled hat—the kind that Jackie Kennedy made popular back then—and she was carrying a bouquet of yellow roses. This was Desiree Loyola Bissett on her wedding day. Though Taylor had never seen any other pictures of the event, she was certain she was correct in that identification.

The man next to Desiree in the photograph was wearing a white naval dress uniform. The brim of his hat shadowed his face, but Taylor knew that if she could see the image more clearly, it would be the same face she had found in Aunt Pearl's photo album—the one Taylor had discovered in the attic at home, probably hidden there to keep it from Taylor herself. The man in this photo was her father. He had his arm around her mother, and it was obvious from the way their bodies leaned into each other that they were in love.

Taylor brought the photograph closer to her face so she could see every detail. They were standing in front of a white, verandaed building. It could be the place they called Truman's Little White House, where the late president had spent so many holidays. That building was located on U.S. Navy property. Taylor seemed to remember hearing that her parents had been married there. Had Pearl or Netta told her that? Taylor didn't think so. They had always been careful to tell her almost nothing about her mother and father. Her aunts had kept that part of Taylor's past, like the old photo album, hidden away from her. Suddenly, Taylor wondered, as she really never had before, why she hadn't made more of an effort to delve into those hidden recesses. Even that time she came across the album, she had looked through it just once. Then she had put it back where she found it and never took it out again. She also hadn't told her aunt about the discovery. Pearl would have been upset, and Taylor didn't want that.

That was how Taylor knew it wasn't her aunts who told her about her parents' wedding. Pearl and Netta would have been too upset by the subject to speak of it. Any mention of Desiree or Paul sent even rigid, conservative Pearl into a tizzy. So, who *had* told Taylor these things? Certainly not Early. He was the one who had warned her against bringing up the past because it would cause her aunts pain. "Let the dead bury the dead," he had said, sounding like Aunt Pearl. Of course, there had been no actual proof that Taylor's father was not alive. Still, there had always been the assumption that he must not be. Taylor had grown up believing that assumption to be fact. Until this very moment, she had not challenged this belief, nor let herself think much about it, either. To readjust her thinking now would require a drastic shift in all of her perceptions about her life. There would be questions to be asked—of Early, of Winona, of anyone still living who could have known that Taylor might not actually be an orphan after all, but did not tell her so.

Suddenly, the numbness was gone, almost as quickly as it had settled over her. She stood up and smoothed the wrinkles from the bedspread where she had been sitting. She walked to the dresser and replaced the papers and the photograph precisely as she had found them inside the portfolio. She slipped the portfolio back into the bottom of the dresser drawer. She arranged the socks and T-shirts and shorts in exactly their original neat order atop the portfolio, refolding when necessary just as she had so often watched Aunt Pearl do. Taylor closed the dresser drawer and straightened the scarf that covered the dresser top. She went to the window, but she didn't climb back out the way she had come in. Instead, she lowered the window, then turned and walked to the door.

She was not surprised to find Des still standing in the hallway outside the room. She had sensed he would be there. She didn't stop to speak to him, however. She barely acknowledged his presence as she walked past him and down the length of the hallway to the front door of the rooming house. Once outside that door, she walked directly to Des's Jeep. The keys were in the ignition. Again, she had sensed they would be there. It didn't even occur to her to think what she would have done had the keys not been in the vehicle. She climbed into the car and turned the key. The engine rumbled to life. She pushed in the clutch and put the car in gear. She had driven four-wheelers many times. They were a favorite on tough north-country roads. She knew she would have no trouble driving this one. As she pulled out into the street, she heard Des call to her from the sidewalk in front of the rooming house. She paid him no attention at all.

DES STOOD at the edge of the road watching Taylor drive away in his car. He knew there was no sense in calling after her again, even though the top was off the Jeep and she might have heard him. She had ignored him inside the house when she swept past him as if he wasn't even there. He had reached out to take her arm, but she was already gone, walking rapidly to the door, pushing it open, stepping through without so much as a second of hesitation or a break in her stride. There was determination in her straight-ahead gaze and in the way she moved, holding herself tall and upright as if a string were attached to her shoulders pulling her into perfect alignment from head to toe. Determination, and something else he didn't have time just now to define more closely.

He had hurried down the hall and out the door after her. She was already in his Jeep on the driver's side when he reached the front stoop of Lewt's building. Des bounded down to the uneven sidewalk and called out her name. She didn't answer. She must have turned the ignition key while he was calling to her, because the next sound he heard after that of his own voice was the Jeep engine starting up. Des didn't usually leave the keys in his car this way. He wasn't that trusting. He must have been so rattled earlier that he forgot his usual rule. Taylor had that effect on him more often than he liked to admit. Now she was driving away in his car, leaving him stranded here on the tail end of Caroline Street. He was not happy about that. He was even a little angry.

But anger wasn't the emotion Des was feeling most keenly at the moment. What disturbed him more was that he had grown suddenly afraid—afraid for Taylor. There had been something not right about the way she looked just now. He recalled his impression of a string pulling her rigidly upright. That image carried itself one step farther, calling to mind a marionette suspended by its command strings. The way Taylor had walked down that hallway made him think of a puppet being manipulated from above, not by its own will but by that of the puppet master. Des had no idea what that image might mean. He wasn't even sure his impression had been accurate. He only knew, with the instinct a person sometimes has toward somebody they care very much about, that Taylor was in trouble and she needed him.

Des thought about running back inside Lewt's building and pounding on doors till he roused somebody who had a telephone, but that would take too long. Maybe he could find a parked car with the keys left in it as his had been. He didn't think that was likely. He was desperate enough to resort to hot-wiring if he had to. He was looking around for a promising hot-wire candidate when a white-and-blue Key West police car came around the corner from Grinell Street and glided to a stop in front of him. He knew the cop at the wheel as a frequent customer at the Beachcomber.

"Landon," Des said, using the last name everybody called the cop by. "A friend of mine just took off in my car. I need to follow her. I think something's wrong. Can you give me a lift?"

"Sorry, Des. I've got a report of a possible B and E at this address."

"Would that report be about a woman climbing in a rear window?"

Landon had his hand on the door and was about to exit his patrol car. He stopped and stared at Des with a look that had cop-type suspicion all over it. "What do you know about that, Des?"

"I know that woman was my friend. The one who just drove off in my car."

Landon slammed the door shut again. "Get in," he barked as he popped the patrol car into gear.

Des thought about protesting when the siren began to wail. He didn't want to scare Taylor. But he did want to catch up to her, and she had a head start. He felt that flash of fear for her again.

"Step on it," he said.

Landon gunned the police car across Caroline Street. There wasn't much traffic. "What's the story on this friend of yours?" he asked.

"I'm not sure," Des said. "I just have the feeling something is very wrong with her right now."

"How good a friend of yours is she?"

"I'm not sure about that, either."

"This better not be some kind of love chase you've got me going on, Des. I haven't time for games."

"Nothing like that," Des said though he was feeling there might be a game going on, at that, with him as the guy behind the eight ball. "Besides, don't forget about the B and E complaint," he added to make sure Landon wouldn't give up the pursuit.

Des's strategy worked. Landon floored the gas pedal and sent them barreling along even faster as cars pulled over to make way for the siren-screeching police car.

"There she is," Des cried, pointing straight ahead. "In the red Jeep."

They were at the westernmost end of Caroline Street. Taylor was several cars in front of them, leaving the intersection to turn left on Whitehead.

"Where in the hell is she going?" Des muttered.

"Damned if I know," Landon said. "She's your girlfriend."

Des might have said he wished that were true, but he was too caught up in his growing sense of urgency to say anything. They had passed the intervening cars and turned onto Whitehead just in time to see the Jeep two blocks ahead and turning again, to the right this time.

That would be Southard Street, Des thought. Where *is* she going?

She was past the Little White House and Truman Annex. She seemed to be on her way to Fort Zachary Tay-

lor State Park, the narrow spit of pale sand and
windblown pine trees that ran along the Atlantic shore on
the west side of the island. Des remembered Netta telling
the story of how Taylor had been named for that park
because her parents went there several times while they
were courting. Des had suspected that might have been
where Taylor was conceived. Netta would have found
that too indelicate to talk about, so he never asked her.
Now he regretted he hadn't pressed harder for the details
of that particular Bissett family legend. Maybe it had
something to do with what was going on with Taylor this
afternoon. That possibility seemed very remote. Des
knew he was grabbing at straws to make sense of her behavior. When she crashed the Jeep through the wooden
arm barrier by the gate house to the park, he wished more
desperately than ever for that explanation.

"What is this dame doing?" Landon shouted. "Is she
dangerous or what?"

He had reached to unsnap the holster holding his pis-
tol. Des took Landon's arm to stop him from drawing his
weapon. Des could feel the tension in that arm.

"She's not dangerous," he said. "She's just going
through a bad time in her life."

"Is she crazy?"

"No, no. Nothing like that," Des was quick to reply,
but he felt a twinge of doubt that knotted his stomach.

What if Santos had been right when he talked about
Taylor being emotionally disturbed as a kid? What if Violetta's portents were really true? Until this afternoon,
Des had been convinced that couldn't be possible. He'd
even stopped believing Taylor could have had anything
to do with setting the Stormley fire. Now he was unsure
again. Look at how Taylor acted yesterday in Desiree's
bedroom. Taylor admitted to having what she called

"visions." Normal people didn't see things that weren't there. At least, not any normal people Des had ever met.

What happened next would shake Des's faith in Taylor's sanity even further.

"She's headed for the water," Landon exclaimed.

He was right. Taylor had torn through the parking lot and out of it on the other side, jolting the Jeep over the barrier brake bump at the border of the lot. She maneuvered the Jeep among the trees, but her course was still fairly straight. She was driving toward the beach and, maybe, toward the ocean beyond.

"We have to stop her," Des shouted.

Landon didn't answer. His expression was grim. The sedan cruiser was no match for Des's tough four-wheeler. There was no chance they could catch up to Taylor, especially once they reached the sand beach where the police car would most likely bog down. Meanwhile, Taylor plunged on ahead of them. She was almost to the dune line now where the trees ended and a scrub-grass ledge dropped off into sand below. The Jeep flew over that lip of grass as Des had anticipated it would, all wheels clearing the ground for a moment before landing with an impact that must have jarred Taylor to the bone.

Landon was on his police radio now, calling in a request for backup. Help would be on the way in moments, but that help could not possibly arrive soon enough to save Taylor, who appeared to Des to be on a headlong dash to the sea. Des prayed for the Jeep engine to sputter out of commission when it hit the water, but he suspected it wouldn't do that, at least not until she was too far out for them to reach her in time. The frustration of that made Des feel entirely helpless. He knew the feeling well. He had relived it every time he dreamed or thought about Desiree and that fiery night twenty-four years ago.

"No!" Des screamed.

The scream tore from his throat. He thrust the car door open and jumped free, rolling onto a sharp angle of exposed tree root. He ignored the pain of the impact and was up and running in an instant, surging ahead of the police car, which had been forced to slow down by the deepening sand as they approached the tree line.

"Desiree," Des cried as he bounded down the dune sweep toward the beach floor. He wouldn't realize what name he had called until later.

Meanwhile, something was happening up ahead. Taylor's beeline course was faltering. She zigged and zagged to the left and right. Could she be losing consciousness? The thought made Des plunge on harder through the sand that dragged at his feet and made him flounder. She was almost to the water's edge when the Jeep veered suddenly and sharply to the right.

A scramble of boulders had been piled along the beach in that direction, jutting out to form a rocky point into the ocean. Taylor was headed toward those boulders, some of which were several feet in diameter. The beach was nearly deserted on this darkly clouded afternoon. What beachwalkers there were had scattered out of her path to watch from a safe distance as she barrelled along.

She hit the first boulders with a crashing impact. The Jeep mounted and jounced over that initial barrier, but its speed slowed considerably. Des caught up just as the boulders were accomplishing what he had prayed they would do and the Jeep was grinding to a stop. He tore open the door as the engine finally stalled out. All he could hear was his own gasping breath and the sound of Taylor's soft sobs as she slumped over the steering wheel.

## Chapter Twelve

Taylor wished she had an explanation, but she didn't. Unfortunately, Santos wouldn't accept that.

"Tell me again. Exactly what happened?" he asked her a third time.

"I won't tell it any differently from before. Don't you think that I want to understand it myself?"

Santos leaned back in his chair at the Key West Police Department office and contemplated her for a long moment. "I don't know what to think about you, Ms. Bissett," he said. "You have me almost stymied."

"Almost?"

"The one thing I'm certain of is that there's more to you than you let on." He rocked forward in his chair and tossed the notebook he had been holding onto his desk. "Maybe we need a psychiatric evaluation."

"Of me?"

"That's right."

Taylor would ordinarily have been outraged. Instead, she nodded her head wearily. "Maybe that wouldn't be a bad idea."

Santos looked surprised. "Why so agreeable all of a sudden?"

Taylor shrugged. "I'd like some answers. I think I might do just about anything to get them."

"Would you commit murder?"

Santos had leaned toward her across his desk and was staring into her eyes. She stared back. "Absolutely not," she said.

He settled back in his chair. Taylor expected some kind of sarcastic verbal jab at her expense. He was well over-due for one. Instead, he went on in a serious, even kindly tone.

"What is Des Maxwell's stake in this? He's out there acting like he's going to take the station apart brick by brick if I don't let him in on this questioning session."

"You'll have to ask him what stake he has himself. I can't answer for him."

"Is he only being protective?" Santos asked. "Or is there something more to it than that?"

"I told you. I don't know."

Taylor didn't mean to sound belligerent, but she couldn't help it. The subject of Des tended to make her lose some control. Besides, she was being completely truthful. She hadn't a clue what his intentions might be, why he did what he did or, as Santos put it, what stake Des had in all of this. She only knew that after she hit those boulders this afternoon, he came running up and yanked open the jammed Jeep door with what looked like all the physical force in him. She had lifted her head up from the steering wheel just in time to see that resolve along with something close to terror in his eyes. He picked her up out of the Jeep and carried her at almost a run to the tree line. There wasn't much probability of the Jeep exploding, but he said he wasn't taking any chances. Even then, he didn't put her down. He cradled her in his arms as if she were a treasure of infinite value to be preserved at any cost.

Taylor had longed to bury her face against his chest and sob her heart out while he held her close. At that moment, she hadn't cared who or what he might have been to her family or what his true intentions could be. She only cared about the strength of his arms and the solidity of his body as a bulwark to hide behind right then, or even now. Of course, she couldn't cry her heart out then any more than she could crawl into hiding now. She must keep herself strong without either of those sources of refuge.

"Were you trying to kill yourself?"

Santos's question brought Taylor back to the present. "It would seem that must have been my intention."

"Don't you know?"

"As I have already tried to tell you, I don't remember." Taylor knew how weak that sounded and was all the more indignant because of it.

"That's the part that has me stymied," Santos said. "I keep hearing that you weren't wrapped too tight mentally as a kid and that you aren't much better now, but I don't see it."

"What do you mean?"

"I mean that you strike me as being pretty much on top of things. In fact, sometimes you might even be wrapped too tight in the control department for your own good, if you see what I'm saying."

"I see what you're saying."

Santos plopped his feet down on the floor under his desk with a resolute thump. "Then tell me how you could drive your car hell-for-leather almost straight into the drink and not remember a thing about it?"

"I remember the Jeep hitting the beach hard and feeling like I was just coming out of a fog when it did. I can see myself turning the wheel away from the water, or trying to, but it's like I'm watching someone else do it. Then I managed to make one sharp right turn. That's why I hit the rocks instead of the water. I can't tell you any more because that's all I know."

"Why do you think you were headed for the water in the first place? Just make a guess if you're not sure."

Taylor thought for a moment. The detective wasn't going to be content until she gave him some kind of response. "Irresistible impulse?" she ventured. She'd read about that in some court-case article or other.

Santos nodded his head.

Here comes the sarcasm, Taylor thought.

"That might be closer to the truth than you think," he surprised her by saying.

Taylor nodded in return. She hesitated a moment before asking the scariest question of all. "What are the charges against me?"

"Could be Reckless Driving or Public Endangerment. I haven't decided yet."

"When are you going to make that decision?"

"Maybe tomorrow."

Taylor just barely kept herself from gasping. There was an even scarier question she hadn't anticipated. "Does that mean I have to spend the night in jail?"

Santos turned back toward his desk blotter, picked up his notebook and heaved a long sigh. "I'm going to let you go on your own recognizance for now."

"Thank you," Taylor said. She could not recall ever having said those two words more sincerely. "Does that mean I can go?"

Santos pursed his lips in thought for a moment, then nodded slowly. "Yeah, you can go now."

Taylor stood up from her chair. Her legs felt a little shaky. Santos stood up, too. He didn't look shaky at all. He did look as if he had something weighty and unresolved on his mind. He shoved his notebook into his pocket.

"Don't make me sorry for doing this," he said.

"I won't," Taylor replied. Then she hurried out of the room as fast as she could go, short of breaking into a dead run.

Des was speaking to the desk sergeant in the reception area. Actually, he was arguing with him. Taylor could hear it all the way across the room.

"I demand to see Taylor Bissett," Des was saying in a growl that would intimidate just about anyone, even an officer of the law who was wearing a gun. "If you bulls have violated her rights in any way, I'm going to make sure she sues every last one of you for every penny you're worth."

Taylor hurried toward Des. He spotted her when she was about halfway across the floor and rushed to her side.

"Are you all right?" he asked. "Are they pressing charges? What's going on?"

"I'm fine, and there are no formal charges yet. That could happen tomorrow. For now, Santos has released me on my own recognizance."

"Maybe you'd rather I let her go in your custody, Maxwell." Santos had followed Taylor out of his office. His customary sarcastic manner had come along with him. She wondered why he had let down that sharply barbed guard with her before, if only for a few minutes.

"Didn't Ms. Bissett tell you she is perfectly capable of taking care of herself?" Des asked.

Santos half smiled, half sneered. "I seem to remember hearing that from her."

"Good," Des said.

Taylor grabbed Des's arm and hustled him toward the door. She didn't want him aggravating Santos. Maybe that could get her locked up after all. She managed a goodbye smile at Santos and another thank-you before hurrying Des out of the station.

"Let's get away from this place as fast as we can," she said when they were in the parking lot.

The Key West Police were housed in a long, low white-stucco building with a balcony running the full length of the second story and palm trees all around. The place looked more like a resort hotel than an institutional structure. Des pulled Taylor aside between two parked patrol cars. She thought for a moment that he was going to take her in his arms. She wondered how she would react if he did. Instead, he leaned close and spoke to her in a muffled voice.

"They have Lewt in custody," he said.

"What?" His blunt statement was so unexpected that she had trouble taking it in.

"Lewt Walgreen. The guy who says he's your father. They've arrested him."

"For what?"

"I'm not sure. I think it might be something to do with his claim to be Paul Bissett. Maybe that old navy desertion."

"How do you know about this?"

"I overheard it when I was inside waiting for you. The cops don't know about his connection to you yet. They've got him pegged as a drifter who's been living under an assumed name in a rented room. Somebody apparently called in an anonymous tip on him.''

''I want to see him.''

Taylor started back toward the door to the station house, but Des caught up with her and took her arm. ''You can't go back in there,'' he said. ''Santos might see you and start asking questions you're not ready to answer.''

Taylor stopped trying to walk out of Des's grasp. He was making a valid point. ''But I need to talk to Walgreen,'' she said. That was also true, though she wasn't sure how wise it might be.

''Then let's go straight to the lockup. It's over this way.''

Taylor followed Des across the parking lot toward a separate section of the building, wondering how he'd come to know so much about the layout of the local jail.

THE GUARD LET Des and Taylor into the interview room together. Des had claimed to be a cousin of Walgreen's and that Taylor was a family friend. The Key West jail system was almost as easygoing as the rest of the island, so the sergeant in charge didn't question them further, especially when Walgreen said he'd accept the visit. Des would have tried to talk Taylor out of this if he thought there was any chance she'd listen. She'd been through enough already today. Short of talking her out of it, he'd at least had to insist on coming along. They sat down at the long, gray Formica table and waited.

Des could tell she didn't want to talk right now. He understood that. He'd lost every parent figure he ever had in his life—his mother, his father, Desiree, Uncle Murph, now even Violetta. He could imagine how shaken he would feel if one of them was suddenly restored to

him, especially under these circumstances. Des longed to
take Taylor in his arms and comfort her. He was about to
reach out, if only to take her hand for a moment, when
the door at the far end of the room opened and Lewt
Walgreen walked in. Tension drew Taylor's features taut.
Des decided it would be best not to touch her right now.

Lewt walked steadily toward them. He was wearing his
street clothes. They let prisoners do that while they were
still in the holding cells. His eyes were remarkably clear
and looked directly at Taylor. Des recognized the love in
Lewt's eyes. Des also recognized that Taylor probably
wasn't interested in receiving that love right now. Everything about her at the moment—the thin line of her
pale lips, the rigid posture of her spine—indicated resistance and, as might be expected, anger. Des hoped Lewt's
expectations weren't too high. Most of all, Des hoped
Taylor wouldn't be hurt anymore than was already her
heritage. The slimness of that probability urged him to
inch his chair closer to hers. Lewt sat down in the chair
opposite them on the other side of the table. The guards
had left them alone in the room. Lewt was obviously not
considered a high-risk criminal.

"Hello, Taylor," Lewt said.

Taylor didn't reply. She stared at Lewt. Her eyes were
shining, but she didn't cry.

"I know that you must be feeling very confused right
now," Lewt began.

"What am I supposed to call you, anyway?" Taylor
snapped.

"I don't expect you to call me your father, if that's
what you're asking," Lewt said softly.

"Good. You don't have the right to expect anything
from me."

"I know that."

Des had never in his life been in the presence of such terrible tension. Under other circumstances, he would have exited this emotional cauldron as fast as he could fly. He stayed now because he knew Taylor needed him to, and maybe because the time had come for him to stop flying away.

"Where were you? Where did you go? Where have you been?" Taylor cried out.

The anguish in her voice cut to Des's soul. He could no longer keep himself from reaching out to her. He put his hand on her arm. She didn't push it away.

"I shipped out," Lewt said. He looked as if he might want to hide his head in shame, but was forcing himself not to do that. He kept his face, and himself, vulnerable to her. "I went to sea on the first freighter I could find."

"You shipped out, all right." Taylor's arm muscle was tight beneath Des's consoling touch. "You left my mother. You left me. Why did you do that?"

Lewt sighed. "I was just a boy. I didn't know where I fit in, or what I was supposed to do. Pearl and Netta had come down here because they didn't trust Desiree. They thought she was after the family money. I knew she wasn't like that, but my aunts had been the only mothers I'd ever known. I was caught in the middle and too young to handle it." Lewt paused for a moment. "I have lived to regret what I did more times than I can count. I wasn't much of a husband. I wasn't much of a father. I wasn't much of a man."

"You won't get any argument from me about that." Taylor wasn't going to let him off the hook even a little bit.

"I didn't intend to stay away forever," Lewt said. "I know you may not believe that, but it's true. I needed some time to grow up. Your mother was way too much

woman for me. She knew it, and I knew it. I thought that
with some time and distance between us I might get myself together enough to make up for that difference. Then
I could come back.''

"But you never did come back, did you?" Taylor said.

"Yes, I did, but by then it was too late. The fire had
happened. Your mother was dead. Pearl had taken you
back north. Only Netta was left.''

"Why didn't you get in touch with her, or with Aunt
Pearl, or with me?" Taylor was calmer now, but Des
could still hear the edge of anguish in her voice.

"I'm not sure why I did or didn't do anything just
then," Lewt said. This time he did look down at his
hands, maybe to hide the sorrow Des had glimpsed in his
eyes. "I went a little crazy, I guess. Crazy with grief. One
of the things I'd realized while I was out at sea was how
very much I loved my wife and my little girl. I came back
here to beg Desiree's forgiveness—and yours, too. I was
ready to do anything to make it right for us again, so we
could be a family.''

"But you stayed away too long," Taylor said. She was
calmer still, now. Des could almost see her clamping the
lid down over the wrenching emotions she had to be
feeling. He recognized that behavior because he'd re-
sorted to it so many times himself.

"Too long," Lewt echoed. He wasn't anywhere near
as skillful as Taylor at hiding his torment. It trembled in
every syllable he spoke. "I had hoped for a second
chance, but I was too late.''

"Why didn't you come north after me?"

Lewt sighed again, even deeper this time. He'd been
staring at his hands for the last several moments. He
looked up now. His cheeks were wet with tears. Des's
heart was touched with such a sharp pang of poignancy

that he had to look away. He was aware of being witness to a tragedy created by one man's inability to face the tough emotional times of life. Des was also aware, all of a sudden, of his own tendency toward that same kind of emotional cowardice. He prayed it wouldn't turn out to be too late for him, like it had for this poor guy who was now obviously struggling to speak.

"Why didn't you come for me?" Taylor repeated.

"I heard that you were all messed up by what happened," Lewt managed. "I was so down on myself right then, I figured the last person you needed in your life was a loser like me."

Taylor stood up, pushing her chair back from the table. Des's hand was still on her arm, but she didn't seem to notice it there. "That continues to be true," she said. "The last person I need in my life is you."

IT WAS SUNSET by the time Des brought Taylor back to Elizabeth Street. It occurred to her that Key West was famous for these sunsets. Tourists flocked to watch them from the dock downtown and along the westward shore. She had heard they even celebrated the event with a toast or two. Yet, since she'd been here, she hadn't seen a single one of them in anything like its renowned glory. She was destined to miss tonight's as well, and she certainly wasn't about to do any celebrating.

Winona was a dear. She seemed to understand exactly what Taylor was feeling. Almost before she'd heard the details of Taylor's traumatic day, Winona had prescribed a tray in bed and immediate rest. Even Des agreed with that. Taylor obliged them both without question and went upstairs after the briefest goodbye to Des. She wanted to tell him how grateful she'd been to have him at her side during that grueling scene with her father. However, gratitude would have to wait until tomorrow. She was too emotionally drained right now to get even those words out.

She climbed the stairs slowly, consciously summoning the energy for each step. She was vaguely aware of Early moving toward the staircase to help her and Winona holding him back, telling him that Taylor needed to be alone right now. Taylor was grateful for that as well. She would have lots of thank-yous owing in the morning. For now, she had to get herself up these stairs and into her room. That was all she could manage this evening.

She did accomplish that feat and closed the door behind her with an exhalation of relief. The scent of herbs, flowers and fresh linens perfumed the air ever so lightly. Taylor felt as if she had found sanctuary here, where the soft, lovely colors were so much in contrast with the harsh realities of what had happened to her since she was last in this room. Winona had left a lamp lit on the white-and-gold antiqued table next to the bed. Its glow was muted and of a creamy tint. Taylor was so relieved to sit down on the bed in the circle of that gentle lamplight that she almost cried, but she knew she mustn't do that. If the tears began, they might never stop. She feared the bottomlessness of their well of grief.

She was almost glad to have such emotionally perilous thoughts interrupted by a knock at the door. She was so tired, she didn't get up to respond but called out from where she sat, "Come in."

She might have expected Winona with the supper tray she'd mentioned, or even Early hurrying up here the minute Winona's back was turned to make certain Taylor was all right. She didn't expect it to be Des, not by this inside door, at least. She also did not expect her visitor to be Jethro. He eased the door open and stuck his head cautiously inside.

"I have to talk to you for just a minute," he said in a voice that was even more nervous than usual.

Taylor pushed herself up from the bed, though she would have much preferred to stay there sinking deeper into the folds of the downy comforter. Unfortunately, it was more important that she get to the door before Jethro could actually step into the room. She absolutely was not equal to a conversation with him right now. Even more unfortunately, she didn't move fast enough to accomplish her goal. Jethro had slipped his tall, narrow body through the opening and shut the door behind him before she could make it across the floor.

"Do you have that card I gave you?" he asked in a stage whisper, as if he might think he would disturb her less if he didn't speak out loud.

"What card?" Taylor had no idea what he could be talking about, and she was indeed disturbed.

"The card I gave you the other night. The one with my psychic's name on it. Madame Leopold. I want to make sure you still have it. You really need it now, more than ever."

Taylor could hardly believe this was happening. Yes, she did remember the card incident. She hadn't wanted Jethro bothering her then, either.

"Do you have it? Did you keep the card I gave you?" he persisted.

"I'm not sure," Taylor said. "I may have it here somewhere."

"Don't you know? You have to know."

He took a step toward her, and she noticed how agitated he looked. His dark hair was in disarray, as if he hadn't combed it in a long time or had been raking his fingers through it. His movements were even more spastic and darting than usual. His eyes were keeping frenzied pace with those movements, flitting from one end of the room to the other, as if he had to keep a vigilant watch in all directions.

Taylor hadn't thought much about Jethro. The few days since she'd met him had been too full and frantic to allow time for thinking about anything beyond the trauma and drama of the moment. She had noticed in passing that Jethro was something of an odd duck. Now it occurred to her to wonder if he might be even more odd than she had realized. In the first place, he was a bit old to be still living with his mother. Though he drove a new sports car and wore expensive clothes, he didn't appear to work at anything other than the occasional errand for Winona. Could there be something wrong with him mentally? Was Winona actually his caretaker because he couldn't live in the adult world on his own? It would certainly be like her to take on that role. But, how much care did Jethro in fact need? In other words, was he dangerous?

Taylor resisted the impulse to step backward away from him, but she did speak to him in a firm voice. "You have to leave now, Jethro."

"I need to know if you have the card. It's really important. Nothing could be more important."

Taylor forced herself to stay calm. She didn't want to do anything to increase his already apparent overexcitement. "I think I might have it," she said. "I'll look in the morning."

"That's not good enough," he said, darting closer.

Taylor did take a step backward now. She didn't like that he was between her and the door.

"I'll find the card in the morning. I promise."

"I told you that wasn't good enough," he blurted. "I'll give you another one." He pulled a white business card from his pants pocket and thrust it at Taylor, just as he had done that other time.

She took it. "Thank you, Jethro. I appreciate this. Really, I do. But right now I need to get some sleep and—"

"You have no idea what you need," he snapped. "You need this, woman." He jabbed his long, skinny index finger at the card she was holding. "You need her to get your luck back for you as soon as she can. If you don't do that, I can't be responsible for what happens to you."

"Jethro, you don't have to be responsible for anything."

"You don't understand. I know everything about you. I've been watching you all your life. I know about you back then. I know about you ever since. I even know everything that happened to you today." He grabbed her shoulders. "You have to get your luck back."

He was gripping her shoulders tightly and shaking her. The time for trying to soothe him had passed.

"Jethro, take your hands off me," Taylor said in a strong voice much like the tone she had heard Winona use with him.

He stopped shaking her but kept his grip on her shoulders.

"Jethro, let go of me right now or I will call your mother and Early."

He jerked his hands away as if her skin had suddenly turned too hot to touch. He backed away toward the door. "Go to Madame Leopold. Get your luck back," he said one more time. "It won't be on my head if you don't."

With that he yanked the door open and scrambled out of the room, his eyes darting everywhere at once as if there might be phantoms after him. Taylor bolted for the door and flipped the lock closed. She pressed her ear against the crack and listened to him scurry down the hall. She kept listening for several minutes longer, but he didn't return. She had the feeling that threatening him with Winona had done the trick for now. Of course, Winona would have to be told what had happened. Jethro definitely had problems. Given what he'd just said, one of those problems might be an obsession with Taylor. She wasn't about to ignore the possibility that he could be dangerous. She even had to think about whether or not he could be connected somehow with the strange and terrible things that had been happening to her lately.

All of that would have to wait until tomorrow, no matter how crucial it might be. Taylor was completely used up for today. When her supper tray came, she managed only a bite or two of the tiny sandwiches Winona had prepared. Even the softly scented tea went untouched as Taylor collapsed into a very deep sleep.

## Chapter Thirteen

The next morning, Taylor didn't awaken to the usual multicolored dappling of sun through the stained-glass skylight. The sky was too dark and ominous for that. The storm that had held off the day before might very likely make an appearance today. The eerie still of yesterday's barometric low had passed. The tops of the palm trees on Elizabeth Street thrashed back and forth like restless sentinels. There was no rain yet, but Taylor expected it would come. Back home, rainy-day mornings always made her want to stay in bed. She hardly ever did so, of course. This morning the temptation was stronger than ever. She certainly had been through enough these past few days to justify a late start. Jethro would probably be relieved to have her stay in one place for a while.

Taylor sat straight up in bed. What had made her think of Jethro? And, why that particular thought?

Something had been nagging at her, maybe even while she was sleeping, about her conversation with Jethro last night. In his agitation, he had blurted out that he knew everywhere she had been and everything she had done, or something like that. Now, she put that together with other snippets of previously half-realized perception—

glimpses of a red sports car here and there out of the corner of her eye, Winona's seeming to second-guess so much about Taylor's doings since her arrival in the Keys. Conclusion: Jethro had been following her, maybe even reporting on her activities to his mother.

Taylor could hardly believe what she was thinking. Was she turning paranoid? Had the chaos of Key West sent her off onto the lunatic fringe? Or, had her instincts and intuition been ground to the sharpest of points by the friction of her experiences here? Jethro did talk as if he might be obsessed with her. Taylor strained to remember exactly what he had told her last night when she was too exhausted to pay full attention to him and more interested in getting him out of her room than in whatever he might be saying. It seemed to her that he had been running on about watching her all of her life. That sounded like obsession to her. He certainly came across as wacky enough to be capable of that sort of thing. But how could he have been doing what he claimed—watching her since she was a child—unless he had *very* long-distance vision?

Taylor all but leapt out of bed. She'd had enough of answerless questions. She would get to the bottom of these mysteries, and she'd do it today. First of all, however, she had to get Jethro off her trail. She might be new at the sleuth game, but she did know she had best do her sleuthing in secret. She also knew that she had to be clever. Jethro might be wacky, but he wasn't necessarily stupid. She paced back and forth for a few moments between the rumpled bed and the glass doors onto the balcony. Then the idea came. She hurried to the bedside table and opened the drawer. The card was still where she had tossed it last night.

Taylor dialed Madame Leopold. An answering machine responded. Taylor wasn't surprised by that at this early hour. When the message about Madame's powers of foretelling and so forth had ended, Taylor said, "Madame Leopold, I was referred to you by Jethro Starling. I have a proposition for you that could be both challenging and lucrative, if we can come to terms."

The receiver was picked up on the other end before Taylor could continue. The transaction that followed was relatively brief and very much to the point. When Jethro came to Madame Leopold for his morning appointment, only an hour or so from now, he would be told that his luck had mysteriously deserted him for today and that he must lie low, preferably closeted in his room, until tomorrow. Madame was certain he would be more than ready to take that advice when she was through with him, and Taylor was able to pay for that assurance with a major credit card.

Taylor was less definite about what she would do next. She didn't really have a plan. She suspected that a plan might be hard to come up with, at least in long-range terms. "Just do whatever comes next," she told herself. That sounded as though it could be one of Aunt Pearl's one-liners, but it wasn't. Pearl would never have said anything so open-ended. Maybe Taylor was starting to come up with some one-liners of her own. She almost smiled at that possibility as she went about getting dressed in an outfit she thought would be practical for nosing around—jeans, a T-shirt and sneakers. It occurred to her that the sneakers would also be good for a getaway in case she needed to make one. She was tying the laces extra tight, and hoping that precaution wouldn't prove necessary, when there was a quick rap on her bed-

room door and Winona came rushing in without waiting
for an answer.

"Something terrible has happened," she said.

She was gasping for breath in what Taylor recognized
as near panic. "Come over here and sit down." She led
the obviously distraught woman to the bed and eased her
onto the disarrayed comforter. "Take a few deep breaths
till you calm down," Taylor said, feeling as if she had
become the therapist for the moment and Winona, the
patient. Winona's hand trembled beneath Taylor's
soothing touch, but her advice was taken. After a half
dozen long, ragged inhalations the trembling had stilled
some. "Now tell me what has happened," Taylor said.

"The man who claims he is your father and may well
be. What did you say his name was?"

"Lewt Walgreen." Taylor wondered if she would need
to do some deep breathing herself after she heard what
Winona had to say. "He's in jail."

"He got out somehow. Just a while ago, when Early
was on his way to get the morning papers, he was attacked by this Walgreen. If Early hadn't fought back, he
would have been killed."

"What happened to Walgreen?" Taylor had to ask.

"He got away."

Winona crumpled into a heap of wrinkled white
dressing gown on Taylor's bed. It was then that Taylor
took note of Winona's appearance. First of all, her hair
wasn't covered. Taylor was surprised to see so much gray
among the tangled strands of jet black. Winona was also
not wearing her usual meticulous makeup. The morning
was still gray and dull through the skylight above them.
Nonetheless, Taylor could see Winona well enough to
note how much older she looked without camouflage.

This was without doubt not an image she allowed to be seen very often, if ever. Her agitation at the moment must be so extreme that she was for once mindless of appearances. For the first time, it occurred to Taylor to wonder what the relationship between Early and Winona might actually be.

"I must go to him," Winona said, darting up from the bed. "Will you come with me?"

Taylor was about to agree. Then she remembered her own priorities. "I'll stay here and keep watch over things on this end, in case anyone calls or whatever." She heard how lame that sounded and hoped Winona was too rattled to notice.

"Yes, you do that," she said absently as she hurried to the door where she turned, as if as an afterthought. "Jethro. I forgot about Jethro. He's off to visit that charlatan crystal-ball reader of his. When he comes back, tell him what has happened."

"I promise," Taylor said, knowing she might be lying. I'll tell him what I need him to know, she thought, adding another one-liner to her repertoire.

As Winona scurried out of the door, Taylor couldn't help but feel guilty. Early had been her loyal friend almost all of her life. Winona had shown Taylor nothing but tolerance and kindness during these past few trying days. Now she was deserting them both in their own trying moment. She told herself that Early was all right. Winona had said that, hadn't she? Taylor reassured herself that Early in particular would approve of what she was planning. "Do what has to be done," she had heard him say more than once. Early had some one-liners of his own.

IN ANOTHER PART of the island, Des walked along his terrace. The rising wind told him there was definitely a storm on the way. He felt that same escalating tempest in his life. He usually liked to think he had more control over the personal front than he did over the weather. He wasn't so sure about that today. He had already been out at dawn pacing the town pier, watching the seagulls rise and fall on the harbor gusts above and bob atop the swells of dark water below. Menace rode the air with the gulls. Des had always loved everything about storms—anticipating their arrival in the tension of the roiling sea, waiting out the blast as it threatened to rip the world up by its roots and toss it into oblivion.

But Des didn't like this storm. He dreaded its coming and the devastation he feared it could bring. The harbor would be empty this morning. The party catamarans and glass-bottom boats would stay lashed to the docks, their tourist cargo left behind to find other amusements until the barometer rose again. Even the old salt who rowed his skiff out every afternoon with his mongrel dog standing watch in the bow would stick to the wharf with his pipe and his grumbling. No one who had a lick of sense or savvy would risk the waters of the Keys today.

Des wished he could put into his own safe slip of harbor and keep his head down till the worst was over. He had resigned himself to the impossibility of that even before the phone rang with one of his police-department buddies on the line and a message Des knew could not be good.

TAYLOR HAD CREPT downstairs after Winona left. Jethro was still out. If the cook was around, she would stick to the kitchen and her own business as she always did. Winona's office door was generally shut and probably locked. Taylor hadn't thought far enough ahead to know what she would do about that. She supposed she would have to improvise. Luckily, Winona had dashed out in such disarray to be at Early's side that the door was left not only unlocked but ajar. Taylor slipped inside and closed it quietly behind her.

The consulting room was decorated in restful colors and lots of large cushions probably designed to make the patient feel protected and safe to speak freely. Taylor could almost remember this room and feeling that way here as a child. She didn't linger to press that memory further. What she wanted was not here among these sedate furnishings and shaded lamps. Winona would be most likely to keep the confidential records in her inner office. Taylor headed for that door.

Winona's office was so neat and well organized it was hard to imagine that anyone had ever worked here. Even the items on the polished dark cherry-wood desktop were lined up in perfect trim to one another. Taylor wasn't really surprised to find such a precise arrangement. She'd half expected it. Winona would be likely to want every detail in order. That would be particularly true of her files, or so Taylor hoped. Sure enough. Some poking around revealed a sliding panel in the wall above a carved credenza. Behind that slide she found the journals, all in the same gray-green linen hardbound volumes as the one Winona had read from that morning on the back veranda.

Taylor easily located the volume she was looking for in its proper chronological place. She sat down in the high-backed desk chair. The cushion was just the right firmness and very roomy, but Taylor found no comfort there—not after she located the first entry for her case as a child and began to read.

Her eyes hurried over the words. She gave small gasps of disbelief as she read along. Her hand shot to her mouth to hold back a sob. Her eyes welled with tears as she realized what had been done to her vulnerable child-self. She might have started over at the first entry to make absolutely certain she had seen those shocking words, but she didn't need to do that. Something deeper than memory told her she was not misinterpreting these pages. What Winona had written here, in the phrasing of one very proud of her accomplishments, had been the truth of Taylor's young life after her mother's death. Taylor didn't actually recall the details of the sessions described, but she recognized them as having happened to her all the same.

Taylor supposed the technique would be called mind control or conditioning—or maybe there was some more scientific term that amounted to the same thing. For a full year after the Stormley fire, when Taylor was six and then seven years old, she had undergone a series of treatments which Winona described here as "experimental." These methods had been designed to venture further and obliterate the years leading up to the fire as well as all recollection of the treatment period after it. She'd had plans to replace these eradicated memories with others of her own choosing, but Taylor had been taken away to the north before that more difficult phase of her bizarre therapy could be pursued far enough to take effect.

It was in reading Winona's notations regarding those intended replacement memories that Taylor experienced her greatest shock. She could hardly stand to take in the

meaning of the words, even though they brought with
them a kind of relief. She had closed the journal and was
stumbling, half-blinded by tears, toward the door when
it opened in front of her. Early and Winona stared at
Taylor, who had stopped stork-still on the handwoven
Chinese carpet, clutching the faded volume to her breast.
She stared back at them for a moment before the words
came tumbling forth.

"You tried to make me believe I had killed my own
mother. Burned her to death alive. You meant to plant
that in my mind. You didn't manage it, but that was what
you intended. Wasn't it?"

Winona showed no response to Taylor's words or to
the anguish in her voice. Taylor didn't care. She was saying the words for herself, to hear their incredible sound
and know they were real. In the echo of that reality, another awareness clicked into place.

"You did manage to make other people believe it,
didn't you?" she went on. "You took examples of my
natural childish exuberance and twisted them to appear
disturbed and unhealthy. You even got people to believe
I was sick enough to start that fire. How did you do that
without anybody knowing what you were up to?"

Winona's unpainted lips were very thin. She moved
them into a chilling smile. "Suggestion at its most effec-
tive requires great subtlety. Only a drop of venom may
taint the whole. What is gossip, after all, but manipula-
tion of the public mind? The challenge was elementary,
barely engaging for me at the time, though necessary."

Taylor felt a shudder run through her. She could hardly
stand to keep on talking to this woman, but there was
more that needed to be learned.

"Your mind-control treatment of me, why didn't it wear off after a while? How did you keep me from remembering the truth all these years?"

"You underestimate my talents, my dear. My initial suggestions were very strong. Also, the process was begun when your mind was young and most susceptible. Your Aunt Pearl had only to supplement those suggestions on a fairly regular basis with minor twilight-hypnosis techniques."

"My aunt was part of this deception?"

"Yes, of course. The long-term result would not have been possible without her cooperation."

Taylor gulped back tears.

"You need not fret, child. The doting aunties sincerely believed themselves to be protecting you from the horrible truth. They were truly convinced you had set the fire at Stormley. They thought you guilty of matricide. They would have done anything to spare you the burden of that knowledge. They were in a very suggestible frame of mind themselves at the time, thanks yet again to my powers of suggestion."

Winona's voice had not varied from its cool, even tone all during that hideous revelation.

"You really are a monster," Taylor breathed.

"Only narrow minds such as your own would see me that way, my dear. Those of true intellect would call me a genius, as they shall surely do one day when the results of my work can be published."

Taylor glanced down at the journal still clasped in her arms. "That's why you wrote it all down, isn't it? You want the world to know what you're capable of. You were even willing to make a written record of your crimes to accomplish that. When did you plan to have it all come out? After your death or before?''

"Unfortunately, practical considerations require the former."

"Okay. That's enough talk for now." Early thrust himself past Winona. "Whatever happens, you won't be around to see it," he said to Taylor.

He wrenched the journal from her grasp and seized her arm in an iron grip. Winona stepped aside as he pulled Taylor through the doorway. Winona followed them across the consulting room to the central hallway, then out of the back door onto the rear veranda. Taylor's feet skittered beneath her as Early's powerful physical strength carried her along, practically on tiptoe, over the lawn to the double garage beyond the garden. Winona moved, still cool and serene, in their wake. Taylor considered questioning Early about his motives for being involved in this, but she had already surmised the answer. He was as much Winona's minion as the aunts had been, though obviously not as innocently. There was the Bissett money and life-style, which had been so generously shared with him while Pearl was alive, and even more so through her bequest to him after her death.

Maybe Taylor should have been shocked to see the man she had thought to be her friend and ally unmasked as the worst kind of betrayer. Reading the pages of that journal seemed to have used up all the shock she had in her. At the moment, she was feeling mostly numb. She wasn't even particularly surprised when Early shoved the garage door aside to reveal a late-model dark sedan with black-tinted window glass.

DES VERY SELDOM BROKE the speed limit in town. There were too many people on the streets. He had to remind himself of that this morning as he steered the Jeep toward Winona Starling's. His friend Landon had called because he knew of Des's interest in Lewt Walgreen aka Paul Bissett. When Landon showed up this morning for his tour on the day shift, he found out that Walgreen/Bissett was no longer in custody. He had pulled the oldest scam in jail-house history and got away with it. He was so mild-mannered and cooperative that nobody pegged him as a runner. When he pretended he was sick, the guard believed him. On the way to see a doctor, Walgreen bolted and was gone. Now, the cops were after him, and not just for the jailbreak. He was accused of assault as well, against Early Rhinelander, of all people. Lewt went straight from the jail to Elizabeth Street and laid low there till Early came out. Then Lewt followed Early and attacked him. That's what the police report said, anyway.

As if that wasn't bad enough for Bissett, Santos was after him for questioning about the murders of April Jane and Violetta. The detective seemed to think Bissett could be the killer, and that he'd tried to do the same to Early. According to Landon, Santos's theory was that Bissett was after the family money. Before he could resurface to claim his inheritance, he had to cover his tracks where the Stormley fire was concerned. First he broke into Taylor's room at the guesthouse, either looking for any evidence she might have, or to kill her. April Jane surprised him in the act, and there was a struggle. April ended up dead.

As for Violetta, she'd seen a lot more at Stormley than she ever let on. Even Des had said that. Bissett could have known about her bad heart from the old days and certainly about her superstitious nature. He shows up at her house, like a zombie returned from the dead. In case that wasn't scary enough to do the trick, he threw in some violence. He tore up her house and terrorized her till she keeled over. Whoever did that had murdered her as surely as if he'd used a knife or a gun. Santos had a hunch Bissett was the culprit. Then he went after Early Rhinelander, because he was now just about the only one left from the Stormley fire days. Desiree, Pearl, Netta and Violetta were all dead. That left Early—and one other person. Des was on his way to Taylor before Landon had finished what he was saying.

He slammed on the brakes in front of the Starlings' and jumped out of the Jeep. He whipped the door shut so fast behind him that it didn't catch and bounced open again. Des didn't stop to shut it. He was already halfway to the veranda steps. He didn't stop to knock on the door, either. He barged straight into the house, fully expecting Winona to waylay him at any moment with a stern-faced order to vacate the premises. He called Taylor's name out loudly anyway, but there was no answer. After charging through the parlor and dining room and looking out onto the back veranda, he began to suspect that the house was empty. The door across the central hallway from the living room was locked. As Des recalled, that was Winona's office. He pounded on the door, but there was no answer there, either.

He was about to head upstairs when he heard Jethro's Corvette tear into the driveway outside and screech to a stop. Des met Jethro in the hallway. He was on his way from the back door to the stairs at a near run. His gawky body appeared even more awkward than usual at that pace, like loosely connected slats of bone trying to jangle themselves apart. Des grabbed Jethro's arm as he was about to barrel past.

"Where is everybody?" Des asked.

"I don't know. I've been out." Jethro tried to jerk himself out of Des's grip.

"Was Taylor here when you left?" Des asked. "Do you have any idea where she might have gone?"

"Don't talk to me about her." Jethro jerked all the harder. "She's the reason I'm in this fix. I'm sure of it."

"What fix is that?" Des kept a tight lock on Jethro's arm.

"You've got to let me go. I have to get to my room."

Des heard the desperation in Jethro's voice and saw it in his eyes. This loony-bird appeared to have flown clear around the bend. Maybe Des could take advantage of that. He had to do whatever he could to find Taylor and make sure she was safe.

"If you don't let me go to my room, my bad luck's going to catch up with me for sure," Jethro was saying. He was more frantic than ever.

"I'll let you go to your room when you tell me what I need to know."

"You don't understand," Jethro pleaded. "Madame Leopold says my good luck isn't with me today. I have to stay in my room till it comes back."

Des wanted to shout at Jethro to stop his raving, but he guessed that wouldn't be a smart move. He forced himself to stay calm. "Madame Leopold is right," he said. "You need to get to your room as fast as you can, and I'm going to let you do just that as soon as you tell me what you know about Taylor."

"She's what took my luck away. If we hadn't done what we did to her, none of this would have happened. Everything's gone wrong ever since." Jethro was obviously beside himself, bobbing wildly back and forth against the restraint of Des's hold on him. "We shouldn't have done it. We shouldn't have."

"What shouldn't you have done?" It took all of Des's strength to maintain control of himself. Otherwise, he might spook Jethro so far out there'd be no chance of communicating with him.

"We shouldn't have messed with her head like that. Look what it did to me. All those experiments and treatments—she used to try them out on me. Look how I ended up." A sob rattled in Jethro's throat. He went suddenly limp and slid to the floor. "Are you talking about your mother? Did Winona do these treatments on you?"

Jethro nodded. His shoulders shook with sobbing.

"And she did something like that to Taylor too?"

Jethro nodded again. He crawled toward the wall beneath the staircase with Des still gripping his arm.

"Do you think Taylor might be with Winona now?" Des asked.

Jethro mumbled something choked and unintelligible as he backed himself against the wall.

"What was that, Jethro?"

Des crouched down and leaned close. Jethro was racked with sobs now, but Des was able to make out, "And Early, too."

"Where would they have taken her?"

Jethro shook his head loosely from side to side, like a balloon on a stick. "I don't know," he sobbed.

"Where do you think they would take her?" Des was beginning to feel as desperate as Jethro looked and sounded. "Just make a guess for me and I'll let you go so you can get to your room. You'll be safe there. All you have to do is tell me where Winona and Early could have taken Taylor."

The mention of safety had stopped Jethro's bobbing for a moment, though he was still trembling violently. He seemed to be trying to think of an answer. It was a long, torturous moment before he spoke. "They'd take her back where it all started."

Des dropped Jethro's arm. "Stormley," Des said. He was down the corridor and out the front door before Jethro made it to the bottom of the stairs, crawling on his hands and knees toward the safety he'd been promised.

TAYLOR KNEW what kind of trouble she was in. The gun appearing in Winona's hand only added to her sense of peril. Still, she kept herself calm and alert to any opportunity for escape. Then she saw Early take two cans of gasoline out of the trunk of the sedan and carry them toward the tall brick house, and panic seized her. He was going to set Stormley on fire and repeat the history of twenty-four years ago, only Taylor would be the victim this time. They had even set her up to look like the kind of nut who would start such a fire herself. It all fit together now—the talk about how emotionally disturbed she'd supposedly been as a child, her own agitated behavior these past few days, especially yesterday.

"What did you have to do with my nearly driving myself into the ocean?" Taylor asked over the tight knot of terror in her throat.

She and Winona were standing just inside the front door of Stormley, waiting for Early to join them. He was on the path approaching the house, hurrying along as huge raindrops pelted him. Taylor could smell the sharp odor of gasoline overwhelming the softer scent of lime trees on the thrashing wind. Winona smiled her scarlet smile. She had applied makeup in the car's visor mirror on the way here from Elizabeth Street. Along with application of that cosmetic facade, her icy composure had returned, erasing all sign of her previous frenzy when she first heard Early had been injured.

"A simple matter of posthypnotic suggestion, my dear," she said. "You were, one might say, programmed to act should you at any time begin to suspect either Early or myself of anything at all incriminating. Really quite elementary for a practitioner of my talents."

"Do you consider murder elementary?"

"One does what is necessary," Winona said without so much as a flicker of disturbance to her facade. "Right now it is necessary for you to climb those stairs toward your destiny."

Winona indicated the staircase to the second floor. She held the smooth steel gun with such confidence that there could be little doubt she knew how to use it. The chill in her black-rimmed eyes gave every indication that she would. Taylor began to climb the stairs as she'd been told. With each step she forced her fear into further submission until she was calm and alert once more.

"Did you do the killings?" she asked, stopping to face Winona, who was on the step below Taylor.

"Of course not, my dear. Miss Cooney was what you might call an accident. Jethro was merely trying to search your room. The rest was due to her overzealousness."

"How did you even know I was here in Key West?"

Winona laughed briefly. "You do underestimate us. Early has been keeping very close tabs on you since your aunt passed on. He knew of your impromptu travel plans almost as soon as you had made them. He alerted us to expect you, and I had Jethro at the airport to follow you from the instant of your arrival."

"In the dark sedan?"

"Precisely. Now, we must move on, child."

Winona motioned with the gun for Taylor to resume climbing. Early had come through the door below. He set the gas cans down long enough to wipe the rain from his face and slick back what hair he had from his shining, wet scalp. Winona motioned again. Taylor had no choice but to continue climbing. She didn't speak again until they had reached the second-floor landing and were walking toward the door of what had once been her mother's bedroom. Taylor had kept herself thinking clearly every step of the way. As Winona had said, Taylor would do what was necessary. She was only waiting for the opportunity.

She paused in front of the door. "What about Violetta?" she asked.

"Early was in charge of that," Winona said. "He had followed you here immediately on the next flight. He knew of Violetta's unfortunate health problems. If that hadn't been sufficient to remove her, however, he was prepared to employ more direct measures."

"You seem to have thought of everything."

"I pride myself upon my thoroughness, my dear."

Winona reached for the doorknob. In that moment, Taylor recognized her opportunity. "Maybe you're not quite as thorough as you thought," she said, hoping to widen the opportunity even more.

Winona had turned the knob and pushed the door open. She hesitated only a second, but that was long enough for Taylor to act. She didn't grab the gun. Winona had it pointed directly at Taylor and might shoot her on impulse. Instead, Taylor reached down and grabbed a firm handful of the white fabric of Winona's usual diaphanous costume. Taylor yanked hard and Winona's feet went out from under her. The gun clattered across the hallway floor. Winona had dropped it when she fell. Taylor would have gone after it, but she heard Early coming. He was already on his way up the stairs in response to Winona's scream.

Taylor dashed into the bedroom and slammed the door behind her, turning the latch to lock herself in. She knew this was only a temporary reprieve. There could be no real safety for her in this room, any more than there had been for her mother. Early was already shaking the locked door as Taylor raised the window onto the roof and crawled out. She shut it again behind her to slow him down a bit more. She glanced back through the pane to see the door splinter and Early come blasting into the room over the toppling door. The image that flashed next across her vision was partly past, partly present. She saw once again the man standing above her mother on the floor. He was poised to strike, as he had been all those years ago. This time he looked up toward the window, probably in response to Taylor's childhood screams. She saw his face. It was Early Rhinelander.

Her past vision merged with the present. She saw the same murderous glint in Early's eyes that she'd seen back then, only he had a gun in his hand this time—pointed straight at her. Then something happened that had nothing to do with that past image. Someone else was in Desiree's room, striking Early on the arm, struggling with him for the gun in an attack so fierce it made up for the attacker's smaller stature. Lewt Walgreen wrestled his opponent to the floor and disarmed him. Except that he wasn't Lewt Walgreen now. He was Paul Bissett, come to the rescue of his family as he could not do all those years ago. Taylor's heart had a moment to leap with overwhelming joy before she smelled the smoke.

DES DIDN'T WANT to believe this could be happening again. He was running toward the flaming house the same way he had as a boy. He gulped in smoke that ravaged his lungs, but he kept on running. Winona had left the front door open as she fled with the gas can still in her hand. The storm wind gusted into the house and lashed the flames to even greater fury. Des looked up to the second-story windows. No flames there yet. He had no certain idea where Taylor might be, but he guessed that she was up there.

"Taylor," he cried. There was no doubt it was her name engraved on his heart this time.

He couldn't get to her from here. The flames were blocking the front door. He was headed around the side of the house when he heard her voice.

"Des, I'm up here," Taylor shouted from the roof. "I can get out the back way. Save the house if you can."

"What about Rhinelander?" Des shouted back. "Where is he?"

"My father's taken care of him."

Des hesitated. "I'm coming up there."

"No," Taylor shouted even louder. "I can get out on my own. Please, save Stormley."

Des hesitated only a moment more, long enough to remember how Netta, in fear of another devastating blaze, had planted giant fire extinguishers all over the house, including under the front veranda. Then, he did what Taylor asked, what he had not been able to do as a boy— he saved Stormley for both of them.

TWO WEEKS LATER, Taylor and Des stood arm in arm under the lime trees watching the workmen hurry in and out, putting the finishing touches on their repairs to the fairly minor damage that had been done to Stormley. Netta's final wishes would be fulfilled all the same. She had feared her sister would sell Stormley. That was why Netta had asked Des to do everything in his power to block a sale. She had even left him enough money to buy the place himself if he had to.

Paul Bissett was inside, where he had been every day since the fire, personally directing the job. His navy hearing was still pending, but it was anticipated that he would get off with probation, especially since Armand Santos would be testifying on his behalf. The charges of assault against Early Rhinelander would of course be dismissed, even though Paul had actually been guilty of that attack. He had done it to protect Taylor. He had broken out of jail for exactly that purpose after Early had inadvertently tipped him off about he and Winona's plans for Taylor. All of which would be taken into consideration by the judge, along with the fact that Early was the one in jail now.

An inquiry had already determined that Winona Starling and Early, who turned out to be her brother, had conspired to murder Desiree Bissett to keep her from going to the authorities with her suspicions about Winona's therapy practices. There was a possibility that they also had something to do with Netta Bissett's death, and Pearl's as well. Slow poisoning with Winona's herbal teas was suspected. The aunts had apparently been quarreling over Winona, whether she was actually a healer or something much more sinister, for the year before Pearl died. All of that was still under investigation. Meanwhile, Winona and Early were in jail, where they were certain to spend the rest of their lives. Jethro was in another kind of custody, getting some real therapy at last.

"Would you like to be married here?" Des asked, pulling Taylor even closer to him.

She looked up at him, marveling as she knew she always would at the way the brilliant Key West sun touched the gold in his tousled hair. She trusted him now as she had never trusted anyone in her life. So, she could love him as well. There would be no more nightmares as long as she slept in her true love's arms.

"Yes," was all she said.